Praise for the novels of
JUDITH KELMAN . . .

While Angels Sleep

"SWIFT, SUSPENSEFUL, AND HIGHLY ENTERTAIN-ING . . . quickens the pulse from first page to last!"
—**Dean Koontz**

"A FASCINATING THRILLER, with characters the reader cares about, and a genuinely surprising, suspenseful finish."
—**Barbara Michaels**

"A SUSPENSE-FILLED NOVEL that packs tension and fear in every page. It's both literary and macabre—produc-ing a story of gripping intensity."
—*Inside Books*

Hush Little Darlings

"JUDITH KELMAN FURTHER CONSOLIDATES HER PLACE among the best of the suspense writers publishing today . . . a finely wrought story of chilling suspense."
—**Thomas Chastain**

Where Shadows Fall

"FASCINATING . . . Marvelously grim wit."
—*Publishers Weekly*

WHERE SHADOWS FALL

JUDITH KELMAN

BERKLEY BOOKS, NEW YORK

WHERE SHADOWS FALL

A Berkley Book / published by arrangement with
the author

PRINTING HISTORY
Berkley edition / October 1987

ISBN: 0-425-10181-9

BERKLEY®
Berkley Books are published by The Berkley Publishing Group,
200 Madison Avenue, New York, New York 10016.
"BERKLEY" and the "B" design
are trademarks belonging to Berkley Publishing Corporation.

PRINTED IN THE UNITED STATES OF AMERICA

10 9 8 7 6 5 4

To the guys, the folks, Jerry and Ezra.
And to all the good hearts who made our sweetheart good
as new, especially Jeremy Ruskin.

Special thanks to Natalee Rosenstein, my editor.

WHERE SHADOWS FALL

-1-

I am waking from the nightmare. Not that I think it will ever be gone completely. I imagine it scattered about the edges of my life like beach sand, hiding in the crevices of my mind and memory until some innocent event sends swirling grains to lash at what is left of my world. But I never thought I would come this far. And I am grateful for that.

On the day it started, I was as far from a nightmare as anyone had a right to be. Ben was still asleep in the cavernous bed where we slept and fought and made love and created Nicholas and Allison. He was curled in a tight, infantile ball, his graying blond curls tousled like a little boy's; not snoring, he would claim, but breathing with gusto.

I got up and slipped out from my side of the bed, tucking the warmth back around his firm body. As I dressed in my drab gray drawstring sweats and my nautical-red windbreaker, I was glad I had allowed him to talk me into this rubber-soled madness. Running was a bore, true. But I enjoyed the self-righteous rush it gave me and the fascinating discoveries my body kept making about itself.

For my birthday the week before, Ben had given me a new pair of jogging shoes. Professional quality, he solemnly said. And a watch that reduced the world to kilometers and milliseconds and rewarded my exertions with blinking lights and an electronic, off-key rendition of "Yankee Doodle Dandy."

A warm rain had fallen during the night, and a cottony mist rose from the pavement. My breath came in visible puffs as I did my preliminary stretching and complaining and, having run out of ways to put it off any longer, found my stride.

My feet slapped against the damp cement and made comical slurping noises in the occasional hillock of soggy leaves. Mine were the only sounds of life as I passed the slumbering colonials and contemporaries on Valley View Road and turned left on Hillsdale.

This was our twentieth year in North Stamford. When Nicky was two months old, we fled New York City with its "no children" signs and the oversize British prams and nannies for this world of expansive lawns, cutthroat Little League, and deliberately casual executive trappings.

Ben and I both commuted to the city. He to his management consulting firm, I to the District Attorney's office where I had worked for the twelve years since graduating from Columbia Law. After a stint as the junior head of Homicide I was put in charge of the Sex Crimes division, where I was referred to, behind my back, as "Doctor No." But I didn't mind the jibes. Having colleagues make jokes at my expense meant I had arrived. After years of hard work and dedication I was finally worthy of jealous nastiness.

My department was doing well. We had made significant changes in rape prevention, prosecution, and victim support. Terrified young women, violated and bruised by the most demeaning, destructive, brutal of crimes, were no longer forced to recount their sexual histories in defense of their innocence. A woman was not automatically judged a harlot because she wore red lipstick and black stockings or had suspiciously large blue eyes. "No" was beginning to be accepted as a reasonable answer to a sexual request. And it was not considered mandatory, as it once was, for a woman to pay for her drinks or dinner with a foray on the nearest Posturepedic. Women in general were no longer seen, in forensic terms, as sirens who turned poor, unsuspecting males into raging beasts. Certain males, it seemed, were able to do excellent raging beast imitations without a bit of outside inspiration. We still had a considerable way to go, and I had hopes for the addition of countless programs and services, but attitudes were shifting, at long last, in favor of the victims.

My daily run took me out past the reservoir, over the dilapidated auto bridge, and into the foothills of New Canaan, a pristine community of Mayflower descendants and martini enthusiasts. The houses grew as I ran, as if they were superbly nourished and blessed with perfect genetic endowment like their owners.

Near the center of town was a high-school track where I did my obligatory three laps. I waved to the regulars: the jut-jawed old woman tugging her twin Yorkies on a pair of sequined leads; the craggy-faced kid with the body by Michelangelo; the policeman with his sweat-stained uniform jogging in stiff parody like a cartoon Keystone Cop. Pat was sprinting along the far turn.

"It's about time you showed up, Counselor," he called. "You oversleep or something?"

My watch said five forty-five. "Hardly. What is it with you? Don't you need any rest at all? I have to tell you, my friend, I find people with unlimited energy very, very depressing."

He jogged over and fell in beside me. "You're not going to find me depressing today, Counselor. Not when I have this kind of good news to deliver. It seems you're actually going to get that grant from People Resources. You really pulled it off. Not bad for an old broad."

"Old broad indeed." From somewhere I found a burst of speed and left him puffing behind. Pat, short for Paterson Scofield III, was a delightful child aged twenty-seven though he didn't look a day older than my son, Nick. He had worked for me at the D.A.'s office since graduating from Harvard Law four years ago. With all his impeccable credentials and aristocratic good looks, he was one of the world's few remaining idealists, eschewing high-paying jobs with the prominent Wall Street firms that were forever wooing him; seeking meaningful relationships; searching for soul and purpose. We had become close, unlikely friends.

I pretended to tie my sneakers and gave him time to catch up. I was ruled, as usual, by curiosity and a powerful craving for reassurance. "You really think we're going to get it? What did you hear? You know, I've been afraid to hope. If Hodges gets the funds, he promises a full service program: a mental-health staff, interim counseling, follow-ups, public education, research studies, the works. Sounds too good to be true."

"I happened to see my friend from the agency last night, and she happened to mention it's practically nailed. Especially if we win the Harper case. And that's practically a wrap before the jury is selected."

"You"—I sighed dramatically and for air—"happen to have a friend everywhere. I think you should consider running for president of the world."

"If only I had the time. But I work for this lady who's a real slave driver."

"You watch who you're calling a lady, buster," I quipped in my best Humphrey Bogart. "And what does 'practically nailed' mean?"

"Just some rubber stamping needs to be done, that's all. The agency is looking for crumbs to toss at the feminists. I know that's a lousy way to put it . . ."

"Who cares? All that matters is getting the program, not the motives behind the largesse. Hodges is a decent

D.A., but he can squeeze a nickel until he gets nickel juice. If we don't get the funds from an outside agency, that's that. I'm happy about it. Thrilled ... if you're sure. Though I hate to have anything hooked on the outcome of a case, even *The State of New York* versus *Hotlips Harry Harper*. There are always things that can go wrong.''

"I am sure. And you certainly don't have to worry about the case. It's waterproof, airtight, Sanforized, and sodium-free. When the jury hears your brilliant presentation, they'll tar and feather that guy. Go celebrate with a hot shower. You're going to be late for the train—again.''

He kicked out and away from me with ease. Pat was such a gem. For the millionth time I rummaged through every possible young female acquaintance for a suitable match. He was too good for everyone, it seemed. And for the millionth time I wished my daughter, Allison, were old enough for him. But then, my semi-adorable adolescent daughter with the rapier wit and the hair-trigger temper was not good enough for him, either. At least not yet.

I watched him exit through the cyclone fence and train his long, loping strides up South Avenue. Despite my warnings about suburban suffocation and the single person, he had sublet a small condominium within running distance of the train station. He was happy there. Pat was one of those infuriating individuals who made the best of any situation.

Buoyed by the good news, I jogged back out to the road. Most days I retraced my path along Elm Street and then took the gentle downgrade on Weed, which delivered me just a few blocks from home. Now I allowed a burst of euphoric energy to carry me past the turn toward the long route that was Ben's daily six-mile trek. Cool trickles of perspiration ran down my face and licked the sensitive crevice between my breasts. My heart bumped the happy cadence of a dance, and I smiled at the occasional headlights that glowered at me on their way to catch the 6:08 express.

The run was airy, effortless. I might have continued forever if the little jogger on my watch didn't remind me there was more to life than pure pleasure. With reluctance I turned toward home.

The house was dark, and I thought Ben must have overslept. Perfect, I thought. I could drag his warm hide out of bed and we could take a shower together. I could almost feel the firm warmth of his soapy body, the slippery press of his hardness against me. We could always take the 8:25. Or we could drive in.

As I opened the door I smiled at the image. I would tiptoe up to our room and wake him with a sweaty kiss. But there he was, sitting on the plump tweed sofa in the living room. Just sitting there, staring at nothing.

"What's wrong, Ben?" His face was so slack, empty. My heart started stabbing against my chest, and the trickles of perspiration turned to ice.

His eyes were frosty dull, his words echoes from a deep well. "They called from Nicky's school. He's . . . he's dead. He killed himself."

"What are you saying? What are you talking about?"

"They said . . . he was dead when they found him. They said he probably did it during the night. When his roommate went to look for Nicky this morning, he was gone. Mike, the roommate, got worried for some reason and called the campus police. They found Nicky . . . at the bottom of the gorge."

I squeezed his hand as hard as I could. "Stop it, Ben! Stop it! What are you saying?"

His head flapped from side to side. "I know. It's crazy. So hard to believe. So impossible."

"Stop it!" The scream bubbled up from a boiling blackness in my gut. "Stop it!" The room was blurred, the light dimmed to an eerie vanilla fog. The air so soupy thick, I couldn't put my hand through it. And Ben couldn't touch me. I was too far away.

"Sarah, you okay? Sar? I'm going to call Dr. Jasper. He'll give you something. You need it. We both do."

"Stop. . . ." The word fell through my lips and died on the air. No substance to it. "Nicky?"

"I know, baby." Ben was using up my air, leaning too close, suffocating me. "I know. Somehow we'll get through it."

"Nicky?" A tiny whisper. Maybe it was all a joke. A hideous game. I could see him peeking in the front door, smiling his mischievous smile. Nicky loved surprises. Always did. "Nick?"

"Somehow we'll manage, Sar. At least we have each other. And Allison. At least we have something left."

I tried to push him away, but my fingers had no bones. Everything was shrinking, falling away. A rush of sweet emptiness.

I could sleep forever, I thought. It was possible to let go and simply fall to oblivion. Why hadn't that occurred to me before? Sleep forever, why not? There was nothing else, nothing. Things were as terrible as they could possibly be.

Or so I thought at the time.

-2-

My mother and Aunt Lorraine stood beside me, forming a fleshy wedge of protection. The air was as warm and thin as weak broth, and a relentless stream of people kept pressing their condolences on me until I thought I would drown in words. "Nicky was a special favorite of mine, Sarah. I'm so sorry to hear."

"It's a tragedy. The worst," Lorraine said over and over, shaking her head and wiping the damp worms of hair back from my forehead. Her thick fingers smelled of sautéed onions and stale Shalimar. "How are you doing, Sarah? My poor sweet little girl."

"Do they know why?" a voice whispered.

"Shush," Mother hissed. "Not now." She turned to Lorraine and spoke in a tone of sisterly conspiracy. "That Martha Evantoff never had a brain in her head. Why should she change now, God forbid? You remember how she used to carry on at the club? I don't know how Lou put up with it."

"Lou was a saint," Lorraine said. "Martha never appreciated him. May he rest in peace."

Another face. "Sarah, darling. You remember Mrs. Pettrone, don't you? She used to live down the hall from us in Riverdale—in 3B. She had that nice little girl, Rebecca, you used to play with. How is Rebecca, Fran? Is she married? Any kids?"

I leaned against my mother, comforted by the sturdy softness of her body, the familiar scents of her powders and sprays. Let Mother do everything, Mother will take care of it. "So nice of you to come, Harold," she said. "Forgive Sarah. She's not herself."

Not herself, I thought. Not anyone. I was overwhelmed by the room's intensity. When I shifted my weight, the floor crackled underfoot like dry twigs and the air swirled with visible currents that left everything blurred and borderless. As I looked, Cousin Ruth seemed to spill over into Cousin Phyllis, and Ben's relatives from Philadelphia stuck together like a cluster of grapes. In the jumble of conversation I heard the odd melodies of normal life: giggles, greetings, people clinking together like cocktail glasses. How odd. Normal lives continued even as mine seeped away in pools of dark, sticky despair.

"You okay, darling? That's my girl." Mother patted my hand and mopped the perspiration from my forehead with a starched, embroidered hankie. "This is the hardest part, believe me. I remember when your father . . ."

"Such a tragedy. I was so sorry to hear . . ."

"So nice of you to come. Isn't that nice, Sarah? They drove all the way from New Jersey."

A tall young man with sour breath and acne scars leaned toward me and cleared his throat for attention. "Nicky was a real good friend of mine, Mrs. Spooner . . . from Stamford High. We played JV soccer together. And he sat next to me in biology."

"So nice of you to come. What a handsome boy. I bet you have the girls chasing after you. Isn't he handsome, Sarah? A girl would kill for those eyelashes."

Aunt Lorraine kept squinting at the tiny diamond watch stretched like a rubber band between the plump cushions of her hand and forearm. "When are they going to start?"

"Soon. You know they always leave a few minutes for latecomers," Mother said.

"Eleven means eleven. Anyone doesn't know that, it's too bad."

"Stop it, Lorraine. You're upsetting Sarah. You all right, darling? You need a Valium?"

Ben was in the middle of the room dispensing hugs and handshakes. So in control. So normal. Then all this was a play I was watching through a gauzy backstage curtain. None of it had anything to do with Ben. With me. With Nicky.

" . . . Sar, if there's anything we can do, just call. Anytime. Larry and I know just how you feel, poor darling. We went through it with Larry's uncle. He was in his early thirties, everything to live for. Terrible thing.''

A dour little man with sooty skin appeared in the doorway. He clasped his hands and drew an unexpected basso profundo from somewhere beneath his shapeless black mohair suit. "Ladies and gentlemen, we ask that all but the immediate family please take seats in the chapel at this time. . . .''

His godlike voice drew the crowd out through the corridor toward the chapel, which was filled with rows of stern wooden seats. Allison looked at me, her eyes full of angry questions. But I had nothing to tell her. The night before, I tried. We sat wrapped in a desperate, unsatisfying hug on her bed, dripping our failed mascara over her ancient collection of stuffed bears. "Why, Mom?" she kept chanting. "Why?" And I tried my hopeless best to salve her grief with verbal bandages. "I keep thinking it was all a crazy mistake, sweetie. You know how things can happen. Nicky was always such a joker, always fooling around." My words fell like dead rubber balls in the dark silence of the room. Useless. Her slim body still trembled and shook with grief. Moans of pain and betrayal tore from her throat. My comfort was nothing. I could not help her with this.

Only Ben seemed somehow intact. Even now he worked the room like a sales convention, presiding over the late arrivals. When the last of the stragglers went to the chapel, he threaded his arm through mine and took me over. "How are you holding up, Sar? Can you believe the crowd? Must be five, six hundred people. You don't really know who your friends are until . . ."

"We have to go in now." The voice was not mine. It was some tiny mouse voice peeking out from behind the thick folds of my nightmare. "I don't want to."

"That's okay, Sar. Let's go now. It's better to get it over with."

I drifted in the comforting currents of Ben's authority. My body had forgotten the simplest actions. Walking took conscious effort. With discreet, planned motions, I had to lift one gelatinous leg, place it in front of me, and fill it with enough substance to prevent collapse. I was aware of every breath. And every time my eyes blinked, the world disappeared and for a blessed instant I ceased to exist.

"I told him to keep it short and sweet," Ben was saying. "This is difficult enough without one of those three-handkerchief eulogies. Most of these guys are frustrated actors, you know. The last thing any of us needs is a tearjerker."

At the entrance to the chapel my feet refused to move. "Is Nicky in there, Ben? Is he?"

"Come on, Sarah. Not now."

"I can't . . . no, Ben!"

Arms were all around me, pulling and directing until I was settled in my place, so close that I could smell the fresh wood and see the twisted mask of my face reflected in the polished mahogany coffin. Someone had wrapped me in thick cotton batting so I could not feel the streaming tears, the tight grimace tugging at my mouth. The sobs came from outside of me, the sobs and animal cries and the desperate tearing at the world with my finger-nails. None of it had anything to do with me. I was tucked away where nothing could reach me, where the world's harsh edges were carefully rounded and padded, the poisons locked away. Nothing mattered. Nothing would ever matter again.

The man in the black robe was speaking in a low rumble, holding his splayed fingers over Nicky's coffin like an overbearing bird. There was a respectful hush as he droned on and on, pretending it all mattered to him, claiming some place in our private horror. ''. . . I did not have the privilege of knowing Nicholas Spooner person-ally, but speaking with his loved ones last night, I know this was a young man with a fine mind and a love of learning. Nicholas worked hard at all his endeavors on the field and in school. He enjoyed the respect of his peers and teachers. Nick was the kind of boy who never had a bad word to say about anyone. He was a devoted brother to Allison, an attentive, respectful grandson. At the time of his tragic passing he was attending one of our finest universities, planning to pursue a professional career. This was a boy with a bright, bright future. . . .''

The words, the meaningless lying gibberish, tickled me until I had to bite my tongue to keep from giggling. I kept expecting Nick to pop out of the somber wooden box, raise a hand for silence, and put Reverend Batman in his place: ''Now wait a minute here. I hate to interrupt a guy while he's making a perfect fool of himself, but

I'm afraid a lot of what you just said is a crock. You must be talking about some other Nick Spooner. . . ."

". . . and let us all say amen."

It was done. Chairs thundered against the wood floor. Relieved voices rose in rude chorus. Hands wove me through a maze of thick bodies and out to a waiting limousine. We would bury Nick now. Ben told me that again and again, as if he knew I could not understand.

Our house smelled of lemon wax and fresh coffee. Mother had dispatched a platoon of her oldest, dearest friends to render the place presentable for the payers of respects. Platters of bread, smoked fish, and miniature pastries lined the dining table. Liquor bottles stood in a row on the sideboard beside a silver ice bucket. Someone had found and polished my fifty-cup percolator, the one I hadn't used since Nicky's high-school graduation.

"Like a party," I said.

"Here, sweetheart, have a bite. You must keep up your strength." Mother's friend, Ethel, a bullet-bodied woman with hair the color and shape of a catcher's mitt, pressed a plate of food at me.

"No, please." The food made me dizzy. My head and stomach pulsed in strange discord.

"Leave her alone, Ethel. She'll eat later." My sister, Honey, a trim, tiny package of raw power, waved the woman away.

"Look, Honey. It's very important for Sarah to eat," Ethel said. "She needs her strength."

"Of course, you're right, Ethel. Far be it from me to question the healing powers of bagels and lox."

"Honey, that's enough," Mother said. "Ethel worked very hard."

"I know she did. That's why I think she ought to go rest herself and leave Sarah alone."

Angry pink patches rose on Ethel's sodden cheeks. "You used to be such a sweet girl, Honey. What happened to you?"

I took the heaping plastic plate and the foam cup full of steaming coffee. My mouth was coated with a bitter, chalky film, but I forced a few bites until Ethel was satisfied enough to resume her random bustling.

Honey shook her head. "Sorry, I tried."

"She means well. Everybody means well."

She squeezed my hand and rolled her heavy-lidded blue eyes toward the ceiling. "Dear Lord, deliver us from the good intentions of the terminally misguided."

I was holding on by a thread. "Please, Honey. Don't."

"Okay, Sar. I'll be good." Her mouth slumped, and sorrow clouded her expression. "Are you okay? Is there anything I can do to make it easier?"

"There's nothing." I wanted to cry, but the pain stuck beneath my neck, closing off the air. "I'll be fine."

"Sure you will. It's going to take some time, that's all. You'll see. Before you know it, you'll feel better and better. You'll look back on this time and not believe how far you've come."

She went on and on, draining me. "Not now, Honey. Please."

Catching her lower lip between her teeth, she hitched her slim shoulders in an apologetic shrug. "It's weird, Sar. I feel like I've landed in a foreign country where I don't know what to say or how to act."

"I know."

Somehow I managed to drift away and sit on one of the plaid armchairs in the living room. People were closing in on me again, the same ones from the funeral parlor and the cemetery. A ring of grave faces clucking their awkward sympathies. Would it ever end?

Pat was beside me. Dear Pat. As gentle and soothing as hot, homemade soup. "Whatever you need, Sarah. Just call. And don't worry about anything at the office. You're covered for as long as you need." I turned to answer, to thank him, but he had evaporated into the tense knot of people in the center of the room.

Mother's voice rose above the din in the kitchen. "So nice of you to come. Nicky was so fond of you. . . ."

Everyone was satisfied with my mumbled, meaningless responses. It seemed very little was expected. "There, there. Don't get up, Sarah. . . . Is there anything I can do?"

Allison was standing in the corner with a few of her friends. There were two girls I vaguely recognized—one a pert cheerleader type with little lemon-sized breasts and a bottom like twin Parkerhouse rolls, the other as round and pink as a prize sow. The boy was tall, blond,

and lanky, slumped against the wall so his body formed
a question mark. I wondered if he was the famous Wil-
liam "Coty" Wheeler, star of football field, French
class, and erotic fantasy. All three girls postured and
fawned, and the boy kept shifting his weight in response
like a rootless parakeet.

Ben pressed a glass of iced Scotch into my hand.
"You okay?"

Okay? Odd, impossible question. I looked into Ben's
eyes as if they might hold some answers. Green, intelligent eyes like Nicky's. The shock of thick, graying
curls. Where was the torment? The despair? His nor-
malcy was an affront. How could he be so complete
when I was reduced to slivers and mush?

"I'm just terrific, Ben. Why wouldn't I be? After all,
nothing happened. No big deal. Business as usual,
right?"

His face registered surprise. "Take it easy, Sar, will
you? Don't take it out on me."

"No, of course not." My voice was pinched as the
truth tightened around my throat. To Ben this was an
annoying inconvenience, a minor interruption in the normal flow of life. Nothing more. An icy horror overtook
me as I realized that I was alone in this. Ben was willing
to cast our son aside—gone and forgotten. Nicky's death
was my pain, my responsibility.

And I would have to make it right.

-3-

Dawn streamed through my bedroom window, nagging me to some purpose or action. I burrowed under the pillow in protest, trying to lose myself in the stale comfort of old sleep.

How long had it been? Hard to tell. Time was so elastic, sometimes stretching almost to oblivion, sometimes bunched in a thick, confusing mass. Bits of the past were thrown on me in no particular order: Nicky onstage in the sixth-grade citywide spelling bee; Ali and Nick playing at the water's edge that summer in Nantucket; my first date with Ben at NYU; Mother lecturing me as I left for the bus stop. "Don't slouch, Sarah. And point your feet straight. You look like a duck."

Everything ran together, and I had neither the strength nor the interest to do any sorting. Tiny Ali and Nick in the bathtub, splashing and wriggling their shiny bodies under a bubble blanket; Nicky covered with a terrifying splash of blood from a losing bout with a backyard boulder; Nicky as the ring bearer at Aunt Honey's third wedding, dancing on my feet in his little Lord Fauntleroy outfit. "When I grow up, I'm going to marry you, Mommy."

Drifting in and out of consciousness, I used tricks of breathing and position to stay as far from the harsh tug of reality as possible. I heard Allison's slammed comings and goings and Ben's halfhearted encouragement from the safe distance of my cottony cocoon.

Didn't I have the right to rest? I was so weary, so spent by the constant demands: "Eat, Sarah"; "Say hello to my old friend, Gail. We used to share a double desk at P.S. 197. Can you believe it's been that long?"; "Write a nice note to Mrs. Heptauer, Sarah. Here's her address. She made a donation to Cancer Care in Nick's name. Isn't that nice of her, Sarah? You remember Mrs. Heptauer. You used to sit for her boy, Arthur."

Layers of smothering, gluey people surrounded me for such a long time. First the police. The Mutt and Jeff of the Cromwell detective squad were dispatched to discuss Nicky's death. They called it investigating, though all they seemed to do was drink coffee and scrawl illegible things on scraps of paper.

"What kind of boy was Nicholas, Mrs. Spooner?"

"Is, you mean *is*." I tried to be patient with the police. But they kept asking me such inane questions. And they couldn't seem to remember my answers. "Was he despondent, Mrs. Spooner? Had he ever been treated for emotional illness? Suicides are, you know, a growing problem with our youngsters today."

Then there were the funeral people and the relatives and neighbors and friends, layers of them wrapped around me like stiff, antiseptic bandages, making it hard to think, to breathe. "Can't you ask them to leave? Mother? Ben? Please, I'm so tired."

"Yes, dear. I understand. Just be patient a little longer. You wouldn't want to hurt their feelings, would you, dear? Everyone means so well."

I was so grateful when they started to peel away. "Bye, Sarah, Ben. Bye, Allison. Hope to see you soon under happier conditions."

"Yes, Aunt Marsha." She still had that mentholated kiss I could remember from ancient family gatherings. Mother hadn't spoken to Marsha or her family for years. I had asked about their crime, but it was some affront too awful for anyone to remember.

One by one they left, in some unspoken order of guilt and distance. Finally Mother said her tentative, self-conscious good-bye. "You're sure you don't need anything?"

What could she possibly have in mind? Everything I needed was gone.

"I'll drop you off, Mother," Honey offered. I could tell my sister was anxious to get away from the stifling sorrow.

"Bye, sweetie. How about you come into town next week and we'll go for credit-card meltdown at Bloomie's and a million-dollar lunch?"

"I don't know, Honey."

"Come on, Sar. You've got to get on with life. Nicky wouldn't want you to be hanging around like this, looking like hell."

Looking like hell would be an improvement. My hair was flattened in the back, the rest a mass of curl and tangle. I had come to dislike the few coarse, gray strands wound into the fading blonde, and I intended to do something about them, but that was before all this, a different lifetime.

I couldn't remember when I'd last washed my hair or taken a shower. Not that I seemed to need either. My body had a musty, sweet odor I found somehow reassuring. I ran my tongue over the grainy surfaces of my teeth. My mouth was dank and sour, but I knew brushing wouldn't help. The foulness came from deep within me, a place I couldn't reach with anything but time.

The floor around the bed was littered with crumpled tissues and several cotton gowns I'd discarded during the night when I awoke saturated with the salty terror of a dream. The same dream over and over. Nicky reaching for me, screaming. His hand stretched in desperate struggle. My arm nearly torn away as I strained to help him. Reaching, grasping. Hot, metallic pain coursing through my body, searing my mind. Reaching until I was able to touch the surface of his struggle. But then, just as the first tingle of relief touched me, his fingers turned to cold, dead ash and fell away.

"Nicky!"

Was I a neat person? A slob? Miles of mental debris stretched between me and any recognizable form of myself. Where was Ben sleeping? Ben? His half of the bed was empty, cold and scentless.

I ran my hand absently over my body. How long had it been? I was thinner. Honey would approve of that: "What you want is the fattest wallet and the skinniest behind, sweetie."

Not that I gave much thought to either excess. My body was my most uncertain asset. At twelve, unruly bumps and embarrassing crevices had developed without my consent. From then on, people tended to talk directly to my breasts, as if they were the seat of my intelligence and my head was nothing but a superfluous knickknack.

Wealth was a simple matter of chance and attitude. Ben and I had little use for labels and symbols, a mentality Honey viewed with suspicion. My sister and I may have been crafted of the same genetic clay, baked in the same uterine kiln, but we were disparate species, doomed never to love each other except blindly.

The escape was not working this morning. My eyes refused to close. I stared at a plume of sunshine stuck like a sword in the bedroom carpet. Outside, a bird shrilled its hysterical refrain. A car honked, and I heard the delicate tread of Allison's sneakered feet on the flagstone walk. The door opened, unleashing a brief blast of rock music and adolescent enthusiasm. "Hey, Ali. What it is?" My child laughed. Somehow, for the minute, she was able to forget.

How long? I turned my pillow and sank into the fresh coolness. When had I last eaten? The thought of food made me queasy. I was disgusted by my body's ceaseless demands, the useless, endless monotony of my rhythms and urges. That was the trouble with people. One of the troubles. We were slaves to our physical needs. Higher human values came at the tail end of the list after eating, sleeping, excreting, lovemaking, breathing, achieving, and retaliation (not necessarily in that order). That was why there was so much pain and betrayal. Not that a reason made it all that much easier to bear.

Add examining to the list: the powerful urge to place life under a microscope, watch it squirm and wriggle, and make strong, erroneous statements about what one saw. I kept examining the broken fragments of my dreams as if there were some possibility of gluing them back together. What a ruinous waste of time.

"Sarah?" Ben stood at the door to the room, his look uncertain. "You up?"

"Yes, I guess so. What time is it?"

"Almost nine. June second, Year of our Lord nineteen hundred and eighty-seven. State of confusion. Planet Earth. Care to join the party?" He held a ceramic mug of steaming coffee toward me.

"Doesn't feel much like a party." I struggled to sit. My limbs had the force and consistency of farina. "How can it be, Ben? I still can't believe it, can't understand."

"It's hard, Sar. I know it is. But we have to get on with it. You can't hide under a rock for the rest of your life. Nicky wouldn't want that."

An electric current ran through my head. "How do you know what Nicky would want? You didn't know him. All you knew was Ben Spooner. All you knew was living your own life." A torrent of tears coursed from my eyes, as cool and soothing as rain in a drought.

Ben's words were tight. "Time to play the blame game? Sorry, Sarah. I'm not interested. If Nicky couldn't handle life, I'm sorry. Sorrier than you can imagine. But I'm not responsible. No one is responsible but Nick. It was his decision. His choice."

"That's not good enough. Not for me. A child doesn't just go and kill himself for no reason." The sobs bubbled up from my gut. When I tried to talk, my words bumped and jarred over the tension between us. "I don't understand, Ben. Why would he do such a thing? Why?"

He held me, and I felt my pain pouring over onto him. He cried for the first time; a few small pulses of grief escaped the iron control. "We have to go to the school, Ben. We have to find out what happened."

He drew away from me and wiped his face. "It's over, Sarah. Leave it alone."

"How can you say that? I have to know why. I can't just pretend Nicky disappeared. I can't."

He stood, wiped his eyes, and walked to the dresser. "I guess you're ready for this, Sarah. I guess you have to know."

Angry fists pummeled my chest. "What?"

Ben pulled open the top drawer of his armoire and felt under the socks. "Nick left a note. The police found it when they searched his room."

"Why didn't you tell me?" The remnants of the fog cleared, replaced by cold steel. "How could you keep it from me?"

He held a thin sheet of typing paper. Thin as air. "You were in no shape to see anything. The doctor said it would take time, warned me not to push you."

"Let me see it. Now." I was shaking so hard, the words danced around the page. The paper rustled like dried leaves.

"Read it to me, Ben. I can't."

"It says, 'Please forgive me. I can't go on. Life is too disappointing. All too much and not enough. Yours, Nicholas.' "

My insides turned to ice. "That's all? How can that be all? What does it mean?"

Ben shrugged. "It was all he had to say, I guess. Look, Sar. I showed it to that psychiatrist, Bardwin, who came down for the funeral from the university. He knew Nicky. Anyway, he told me their suicide rate has reached epidemic proportions. This year alone, there have been eleven deaths. For some reason these kids imagine killing themselves will solve everything. Dr. Bardwin told me that kids, even kids as old as Nick, don't realize they won't be around to enjoy all the attention and grief. On some level they don't realize suicide is for keeps."

"Read it again, Ben."

"Come on, Sar. It doesn't help anything. Enough looking back."

"Read it."

His sigh was filled with disgust. " 'Please forgive me. I can't go on. Life is too disappointing. All too much and not enough. Yours, Nicholas.' "

I felt myself rising like a wave. "I have to go to the school, Ben. I have to know why. I have to find out what happened." Weightless, I got up and started putting things in order.

"Get hold of yourself, Sar. You're not being rational."

Stepping into the shower, I felt the blades of hot water begin to slice through my grief. At last I had a reason to go on. "Pack a few things, Ben. We're going to Cromwell."

"What?" He pressed his face against the bubbled glass of the shower. "I can't hear you."

"We're going to Cromwell," I shouted. "We're going to find out what happened to Nicky."

I dried myself and wrapped a towel around my body, and another around my head à la Carmen Miranda. If we rushed, we could make the noon flight.

Stepping out of the steamy bathroom, I felt alive again, full of purpose and energy. Ben was leaning back on the bed, sipping my tepid coffee, his eyes glazed with distance. "Come on, Ben. We have to hurry."

He shook his head. "No more, Sarah. It's time to get back to living. You can't go on with this. I've been speaking to Pat Scofield and he's been covering for you at the office. You can't expect him to keep at it forever. And what about Ali? She's a good kid, but you can't go on forgetting she exists. You'll lose her too."

"You don't understand, Ben. We have to go. Nicky didn't just kill himself out of the blue. None of it makes sense. I can't spend the rest of my life wondering. I have to find out what was going on. It'll be better for Ali too. She wants answers as much as I do. You should hear her, Ben. She thinks some part of this was her fault, that things might have turned out differently if she and Nicky were closer or got along better. She'll be glad to know we're going. I know it."

"No, Sarah. You're not thinking clearly. And you're not accepting real life. Nicky is dead. You can't bring him back by killing everything else."

I looked at this man whom I had spent my adulthood loving. Could this be the man whose body was as familiar as my own? Whose thoughts came to me unbidden? Ben sat there like a stranger on the other side of an impassable sea. "I'm going, Ben. I have no choice."

His green eyes were floating in tiny pools of sorrow. "You can go with Nicky if you have to, Sarah. I can't stop you. But Allison and I have to keep living."

I didn't believe what I was hearing, but there was no time to argue. Ben would come to his senses and follow me soon enough. "Call Mom for me, will you? Tell her to come help you with things and keep an eye on Ali. Tell her I'll call in a day or two."

"It's no good, Sar. Don't you see?"

I threw a few things in a bag. "I'll be at the Elms. Or if I can't get a room there, I'll try that little motel on Route 23. Either way I'll call. Give Ali a hug and kiss for me, Ben. Tell her I love her."

Zipping my suitcase, I felt his hand settle on my back. "Please don't go, Sarah. Please."

I turned and stared into his face, so like Nicky's face that it hurt my eyes. "I have to, Ben. There is no other way. Don't you see?"

He drew his lips in a tight, angry seam. "I guess we all have to do what we have to do."

"Please, Ben. Not now. Don't be mad at me now. There's no time." If I missed the noon flight, I would have to wait for the five o'clock. That one connected through Albany and sat in the center of nowhere for over an hour. In that time I could be starting to find the answers I so desperately needed.

"I'm late for work," Ben said. Without looking at me again, he straightened his tie in the mirror and combed his hair. I felt a familiar tug of attraction. In another life we would have met halfway to the mirror and fit the matching parts of our bodies together in a fleshy jigsaw. He would have pressed his silken lips against the electric part of my neck and started a familiar chain of sweet events.

Another life.

I held myself in stiff control and filled my head with images of Nicky. First things first. Until I had my answers, there was no going back. "Please, Ben," I said in a whisper, "try to understand."

He strode out of the room. I heard his footsteps on the stairs; firm, deliberate. The front door opened and slammed shut. How could he live without knowing the truth about Nick's death? The questions and the doubt hung over me in a suffocating cloud. I knew my son. He was full of life and ambition and mischief. Closing my eyes, I filled my mind with his chiseled features, the dime-slot dimples, the devilish smile. I could smell the scent of him—clean sweat and summer air. I could feel his long, lean arms wrapped around my soul in the gift of a child's hug.

How could Ben let it go? Until I found the true end of Nicky's life, mine could not begin again. Maybe it never would. But I had to try whatever the cost.

I heard Ben's firm footsteps on the walk and the sliding clatter of the garage door. His car sputtered in protest and came alive. There was a fading hum as he backed out of the driveway and disappeared down the street.

Nicky's death was not the end of it. Things were shifting, changing, falling out of ordinary sense and control.

Breath held, I listened until Ben's car was out of my hearing, listened until I gave up the hope that he would change his mind and come back. Then I snapped the clasps on my suitcase and called a cab.

-4-

There was a single available seat on the 12:03 Enterprise Express to Cromwell on Apache Air out of Westchester County Airport. As I slipped in and fastened my seat belt I viewed the lone vacancy as a sign. My mission was being overseen by some cooperative force.

Small comfort.

My seatmate was an off-season Santa—a round, pink, ageless man with a swollen midsection and lips like link sausages. "Aldo Diamond," he said.

Aldo Diamond to you, too, I was tempted to reply. "Sarah Spooner."

"You have business in Cromwell?"

Interesting how some people crawled headfirst into your circulatory system, lodged in your personal affairs like a clot. "Sort of." I wished I had brought something to read. Without a magazine I had nowhere to escape from Curious Aldo. I looked straight ahead, pretending to focus on the flight attendant, a skinny blonde with a Kewpie-doll face and a plastic grin, who was demonstrating how cute it was possible to look in an oxygen mask.

We took off in an abrupt surge of power. I was pressed against the seat as the earth played tug-of-war with the atmosphere.

"Drink?" Mr. Diamond persisted. "Sucking candy?"

"No thank you."

He shifted his bulk and dug into his back pocket. The plane listed slightly, I thought, in response. "My card."

Of all professions I never would have guessed my seatmate was a forensic graphologist. Most of the handwriting experts I had encountered in court were slight, nervous women with the sort of eyes that left burn marks on your skin. I was a borderline skeptic. According to true believers, a person's penmanship yielded volumes of information about emotional stability, ambition, creativity, sexuality, you name it. Larue Marrick, the woman whose work most often graced Part Five of our Criminal Court, claimed she could look at a page of writing and tell you everything about the defendant from the quality of his relationship with his mother to whether he preferred his chocolate bittersweet or milk.

"Interesting," I muttered under my breath.

"More than interesting. Informative, definitive. After years of attack by legions of the misinformed, graphoanalysis is finally being recognized as a critical tool in service and industry."

"Yes, I know."

"Did you know that graphologists are being employed in personnel, in marketing, in public relations, in politics, in the arts ... ?"

"Yes, I knew that."

"And in forensics we have risen to the status of recognized expert. In the past year alone, I have testified in seventeen criminal proceedings and participated in eight other major investigations. Did you know that a writing sample is a routine part of the booking procedures in many jurisdictions?"

"Yes. Yes, I know." I pretended to be engrossed by the view and hoped he would fill his mouth with something other than more useless chatter.

The flight was choppy. We bucked over hard pockets of air, placed like stepping-stones in the gleaming pond of the spring sky. My stomach lurched in protest, and I concentrated on breathing measured amounts of pressured air. The tides of nausea kept me busy. And Diamond filled the brief moments of relief with his relentless monologue.

"Cromwell is the armpit of America, you know. Wouldn't catch me there without a hefty per diem. And expenses, of course. Wanted to put me up at the university hotel. You know the type. Run by students so even the roaches are smart-aleck know-it-alls. Wouldn't catch me dead in a place like that. So I told those university big shots: You want the best, you pay for the best. Can't do good work when I'm not comfortable. Simple as that."

We were nearing Cromwell. I recognized the black ribbons of water below as Lake Romaca. Stuffed squares of suburban towns yielded to rolling green farmland and the gentle swells of the first foothills of the Algonquin range. Cromwell lay between two modest mountains like an infant nestled in a firm maternal bosom. My breath caught at the sight of the university clock tower, a somber Cyclops winking in the distance.

Mr. Diamond pointed one of his porky fingers toward the window. "Only thing that town ever had going was the university, you know. That's why they're so fired up about all the suicides. It keeps up and no one will go to that place on a bet, top school or no. My sister's boy, Martin, was accepted at Cromwell, but he's going to U. Mass instead. 'Sure, Cromwell's got more prestige, but why take chances?' she said. Boy can get a fine education at U. Mass and come home in one piece, she figures. Can't blame her. You see all those black holes? Look like rips in the land?"

"The gorges, you mean." Nicky, Ben, and I had walked the flimsy footbridge over one during freshman orientation. The height was dizzying, a tightrope walk over oblivion, a small, safe flirtation with danger I would never forget.

"Yeah. 'Cromwell is gorges,' they say on the bumper sticker. But there's more to it. Much more than an interesting view. One of the old stories claims that Cromwell was built over sacred land, old Indian burial grounds. Story goes that Old Isaiah Cromwell filched the property from the chief of some small, obscure tribe used to be in these parts, I forget the name—Shmohawk, Arapashmo, something like that. Anyway, according to this particular legend, Cromwell was cursed right from the beginning. First it was fires. For the first twenty or so years, nearly every building in the place burned down at one time or other. Administration building went five or six times. Poof.

"Then, with all kinds of strict building codes and no-smoking rules and all that, they managed to get the fire thing under control. Now it's just an occasional dorm room gets barbecued. Kids can be mighty careless, you know."

My interest was piqued. I swallowed back a swell of nausea and looked at the rotund Mr. Diamond. "I don't see what that has to do with the suicides."

"Nothing directly. I'm told the fires stopped and everything was under control for a decade or two. University started to grow like topsy then, big donations from a few real prominent families. Cromwell always had its angels, you know. Angels and devils."

"The Humes . . ."

"Yeah, Humes. And the Warrintons. None bigger than the Parrish family, though. Built half the place."

"Funny. I don't think I ever heard the name."

"Wouldn't have," Diamond said, dismissing me. "Parrish didn't put their name on buildings or anything. Most of the donations were anonymous. Power was what they wanted. And position. Been a Parrish or two on the board since the Dark Ages. Only they're not ordinary trustees. They're anonymous, for one. Not even the other board members know which is a Parrish descendant. And all sorts of extra voting power is built in so that whatever the Parrishes want, goes. Never go by the name Parrish, either. Old family tradition that the kids take the parents' Christian names as surnames—so Randall Parrish's boy was Samuel Randall and his boy was Josiah Samuel, like that. Crazy bunch, the Parrishes.''

"I suppose.''

"Anyway,'' Diamond said, inflating himself until his face reddened and his middle threatened to explode, then releasing the air in a warm stream of relief, "Cromwell has had its fair number of sugar daddies over the years. Built the supercomputer labs, the finest science and engineering facilities, brought in Nobel laureates, you name it. That's what makes a university, you know.''

"I know.'' The seat-belt sign flashed on, and I sighed with gratitude, sighting the haven of land at the end of this sea of words.

"Anyway, where was I? Oh, yeah. The fire thing got cleared up, and next thing you know, it's an outbreak of typhoid fever. Hit the place like a brick. That was back in 1903. Rumor had it the real Typhoid Mary, this Irishwoman named Mary Mallon, was hired by the university as chief cook. Made a mean beef stew, I'm told, and terrific apple strudel. Light, flaky, tons of butter, just a hint of cinnamon and a dash of nutmeg. Mmmm, makes the old mouth water. Anyway, it took years for the health

authorities to track old Mary down and figure out she
was the one spreading the fever.'' Diamond shook his
head. ''Then they put her away in some sanatorium
where she could only infect the caretakers and the other
patients. They knew a lot more about good cooking in
those days than they did about contagion. You ever have
real old-fashioned bread pudding? The kind with heavy
cream and just a speck of vanilla? Or blueberry buckle?
Now that was cooking. Mmmm.'' Diamond's face settled in a drape of perfect contentment.

He took a few minutes to emerge from his trance.
Then he looked at me as if trying to find his place in a
book. ''Anyway, soon as Mary showed up, kids, professors, even visitors started dropping like flies. Lost hun-
dreds of people in the space of a few months. Had to
close the place down, total quarantine.

''Then, just as the school is getting back on its feet,
living down the typhoid thing''—he snapped his fat fingers, ''the Spanish flu epidemic of 1914 rolled over
Cromwell like a tidal wave. Killed off a third of the
town's population. University was hit especially hard.
Whole place was one big funeral parlor. Then they got
ten, fifteen years of peace and the Depression comes.
Cromwell had all its holdings in the market. Good-bye,
holdings. Had to start from square one. Rotten luck.''

''Plenty of people had that bit of rotten luck,'' I said.
''Cromwell hardly has a corner on the market.''

''True. But no one would accuse them of having a
shortage, either. Took years to get their finances back in

order, and next thing—the massacre. You hear about it?''

"Massacre?"

"You didn't hear? I'm not surprised. Not a bit. Money is the best gag, you know. Stuff enough in someone's mouth and you don't hear a peep. Yup, that was something else how they kept that one quiet. Few little bits in the local paper talked about some radical group playing Bomb the Establishment, but it was nothing like that.''

I sifted through the ash of my memory. In my office, major cases were always being tossed about and dissected. Funny that I hadn't heard of any so-called massacre at Cromwell. "What happened?"

A bell pinged, and the safety signs flashed atop the bulkhead. Diamond shrugged and stretched the ends of the seat belt to their limits and snapped them around the whalelike swell of his belly. "Gotta give up the pasta. That's my downfall: linguini, ravioli, fusilli, you ever have those? Curly ringlets of noodles like Shirley Temple curls. The sauce gets all soaked up inside real squishy-like so you get a good coating with every mouthful. You take a plate of those with a big hunk of Italian bread. And real butter, none of that awful margarine, tastes like salted motor oil.''

"The massacre?"

"Oh, yeah. Never caught the fellow who did it. Had suspects and all, but nothing panned out. No one's sure exactly what happened, but it seems someone on campus went poco loco and planted five or six bombs in the cafeterias. No warning, nothing. All of them were set for the same time, six sharp, just when the most kids were standing on line to get their chow. Pitiful. Blew up over a dozen kids. Died on the spot. More injuries than you can imagine—everything from cuts to amputations. Pitiful.''

''When was that? The massacre?''

''Ten, twelve years ago. Had the whole Cromwell police force on it for almost a year. Perkins County lent a few of their top men. And the state. But they just couldn't get to the bottom of it. Still a mystery.''

The cute blond stewardess was inspecting laps and collecting used plastic cups. Diamond followed her with his rheumy eyes, his leer comical. Over the intercom the captain's voice crackled some instructions I could not decipher.

''Some cases are like that.''

''Sure. Perpetrator may have blown up with the rest of them. That's probably what happened. But . . .'' Diamond lapsed into a welcome silence.

I might have passed the remaining seconds of the flight in peace, but my curiosity crept out from behind my good judgment. ''I still don't see the connection to the gorges. Or the suicides.''

''That's the latest. For the past few years the suicide rate has been going up like crazy. Used to have two, maybe three a year, tops. Pretty average for a school this size, but even those few gave Cromwell a bad rap. Then, in '82 or '83, it started climbing. Four the first year. Then six. This year there's been eleven already. Plus a bunch of failed attempts, overdoses, that sort of thing.'' Diamond clucked his chunky tongue. "No knowing where it'll end."

The cabin was thick with extraneous words. "And the gorges?"

He held up a hand. "Yeah, sure. I was getting to that. Legend has it that the land used to be all in one piece. The story goes that the chief of the Shmohigans, or whatever they were called, lost the place to Old Isaiah Cromwell. Cromwell supposedly got old Chief Slosh-feathers drunk and talked him into some sucker bet. Next thing, bye-bye, land. . . .

"After the tribe cleared out, seems the ancestors buried in the sacred ground got pissed off and started ripping the place up. Story claims that's how the gorges got there."

"Welcome to fantasyland."

Diamond blew his bulb nose on a kite-size hankie. "I know what you mean, but the wise guys like to pull out old maps of the place. Not a gorge in sight."

"Primitive maps. Big deal," I said. I enjoyed a good story as well as the next person, but this one was rapidly turning into a little kids' campfire ghost tale.

"Probably just that. Geologists have studied the gorges and figure there was some succession of mild earthquakes. Too slight to be picked up by the tracking equipment in those days, but enough to cause Cromwell to split along several preexisting faults. There's some logical explanation, sure. But . . ."

"But what?" Diamond's sudden reticence made me want to pull on his tongue.

"But the gorges have claimed a lot of lives. Most of the suicides were nosedives into the gorge. Story goes that the angry ancestral spirits demand sacrifice. Human sacrifice."

"Foolish superstition," I said in dismissal. Silly old tale. The kind that grew like crabgrass in the fertile soil of student imagination. Stone statues that came alive when a virgin passed at midnight. Crazed professors who drank student blood to improve their mental abilities. I had heard plenty at NYU, even though the urban site provided little in the way of fabulist inspiration. My particular favorite was the one about the Philosophy of Religion professor who bad-mouthed God one too many times and woke up one fine morning without a tongue.

Diamond sniffed. "Wouldn't surprise me if it was, but, well, there's something about Cromwell. Of course, the old Indian bit is only one explanation. There's a whole pile of stories that try to account for the sorry history of Cromwell University. I'm about halfway through this old book, *A Concise History of Cromwell*." He pulled a dog-eared tome with rumpled, yellowed pages from his inside jacket pocket. "Concise, hah. Has more pages than *War and Peace*. And nearly as many turns and characters. But I'm determined to get through it. Had a hard enough time getting hold of a copy. It was put together by some professor thirty-five, forty years ago, but the university went to great lengths to keep it under wraps. Not a reassuring little volume, I'll tell you that. But you can't really get a handle on a place without looking at its past. Especially a strange place like Cromwell.''

My throat tightened. "I've been there several times." I didn't want to mention Nicky. No point in baring my wounds to this flap-tongued stranger. "I never saw anything you'd call strange."

Diamond pulled a pack of gum from his pocket, held a stick toward me for my refusal, and wadded several pieces into his mouth. "Good to chew during the landing. Helps the ears," he said, garbling his words.

"Actually it's nothing you can see. Nothing you can put a finger on. It's more a feeling. When you've been in the crime game as long as me, your nose starts to itch when you get close to funny business." He scratched his radish nose for emphasis. "See? I think that's why there have been so many rumors and stories."

I didn't care to mention that I, too, was a player in the "crime game." We were descending. The cabin pressure took a noticeable dip, and my ears were squeezed by invisible hands. Swallowing, I felt a pop of relief, followed by a sinking sense of finality.

The plane circled in and hovered for a nervous instant over the runway before bumping down. My relief was interrupted by the angry roar of the engines. We taxied in to the single gate and slowed to a dull stop.

Around us there was a flurry of impatient activity. Overhead racks opened to reveal rumpled trench coats, serious brown paper files, and overnight cases. Passengers clogged the aisles, jockeying for position.

Diamond and I waited in our seats, bearing the warm, sticky rush of unprocessed Cromwell air. He was in no hurry to force his bulk into the mad stream of human energy. And my earlier burst of noble purpose had fallen away, leaving nothing to shield me from my sick stomach and the dull pounding behind my eyes.

Where would I begin? And what was I going to learn? Was there really anything to be gained by this search through Nicky's last gasp of hopelessness? I had no answers. Only a dry ache of emptiness that love and pleasure used to fill and a terrible need to struggle against my own sense of futility.

Most of the passengers had deplaned. Finally Mr. Diamond hauled his massive bulk from the seat beside me and stooped to collect his things. Sweat in the shape of a huge moth plastered his once white shirt against the broad canvas of his back. I stood waiting for him to clear the way, watched while he retrieved a motley collection of small cases from beneath the seat. He exuded an air of garlic and self-importance.

Diamond led the way. I followed him past the smiling flight attendants and down the movable metal stair. The midday sun poked me in the eye as we crossed the blank stretch of airfield and entered Cromwell's answer to the Port Authority Bus Terminal. The sign above the en-

trance declared Cromwell THE CITY OF THE FUTURE,
which was, I thought, some clear comment about the
present.

I spent an interminable time at the baggage claim. My
luggage hid from the commotion, emerging as I had,
only after the initial crush was safely over. By the time
I got to the taxi stand, the street was deserted.

With Nicky gone, I was struck by the full extent of
Cromwell's seediness for the first time. Beyond the air
terminal, a single thin strand of broken pavement connected the airport to the center of town. There, urban
renewal was a refrain in light comedy. Dilapidated mom-
and-pop shops and walk-up tenements were replaced
with regularity by soon-to-be dilapidated stores and ten-
ements-in-training. All the town's hope and dignity was
vested in the university. Blood transfused into the outlying community somehow found its way back to the
veins of intellect at the top of the hill.

When Nicky was a student, I saw Cromwell as a
bounty of fresh minds and fit bodies. Typical college
town dotted with cheap movie houses, pizzerias, trendy
boutiques, and high-minded bookshops. Typical uni-
versityville that took its name, fame, and meager fortune
from the ivied halls of academia. In an odd, egocentric
way I thought the town was attractive with Nicky at its
center. But the future was as loud and triumphant as a
Sousa march then. You could breathe in the scent of it
and feel alive and hopeful.

No more.

The blast of a horn brought me back. Aldo Diamond was pressed behind the leather wheel of a Lincoln Continental painted the color of a rare sirloin. "Want a ride? Not a bad set of wheels they rented for me, don't you think?"

Nothing of promise was happening at the taxi stand. Another ride with Diamond was only slightly more appealing than the eight-mile walk to the Elms. "I guess. Thanks."

The seats were done in ivory mock snakeskin. Diamond rested his melon head against the plump headrest and grinned in satisfaction. "I like to be treated right, Sarah Spooner. You know what I mean?"

"Who doesn't? I'm going to the Elms, you know it?"

He pulled away from the curb, bashing the turn signal with his elbow. "Know it? Almost came to blows with the owners the last time. Rip-off, that place. Charge a fortune and give you a lumpy little bit of a mattress and these tiny little bath towels couldn't dry a bird. The Barrington Arms. That's where I'm staying. Real class operation. That's where all the big shots stay. The visiting dignitaries. It's my kind of place. Out-of-the-way. Private. Got me a suite. No way I can handle a teeny little room in this god-awful town. If I'm gonna do all they want, I could be here quite a while. Poor me, huh?"

"What exactly is it they want you to do, Mr. Diamond?" I regretted the words even as they sneaked through my leaky lips.

"Well . . . it's not for publication or anything, but the university is on an all-out campaign to stop these suicides. I'm one of several consultants they've hired to figure out what's going on and what to do about it. My part's to go through all the admissions applications, check the writing, and pick out the kids who seem to have some screws loose. Then the shrinks can move in with the rubber suits and butterfly nets before any more of them have a chance to buy the farm."

"How poetic," I muttered. The words stung. Eleven deaths this year alone. If only steps had been taken sooner. Maybe Nicky could have been saved. Stopped.

"Nothing pretty about suicide," Diamond said gravely. "Never could figure it. Goes against the basic grain. You know, survival first. Suicide is the last thing a person would want to do. Heh heh, the last thing. Get it?"

"Yes, I get it."

Diamond sighed as if he found his humor as tiresome as I did. "Anyhow, I see plenty of writing samples where you just know the person would as soon cash in his chips as keep playing. Sad." He shook his head. "Especially when it's a kid."

My purse was a brick in my lap. Nicky's note was folded inside. I could almost taste the words as they danced and teased my tortured mind. I wondered what Diamond would see in the neat, printed hand. Secrets, I thought. Truths I was not ready to face. "Could you . . . can you tell anything about what made a person do such a thing?''

''Depends,'' Diamond said. ''I could certainly tell which boards were warped, you know what I mean? For instance, I worked on a case in South Philly. The Dance Bandit, they called the guy. You hear of it?''

''Yes, I think so.''

''Interesting case. Seems this character would go to a disco, wow them with his footwork, and while everyone was into clapping and making a big deal, he'd pick every pocket and purse in the place. He was driving the police nuts. Couldn't get a handle on the guy. Then he made his mistake. They always do, you know.''

''Yes, I know.'' I feared I would hear the relentless Diamond drone in my sleep.

''In this particular disco a cute little thing asked our bandit for his autograph. And he wrote a little note to her. He used a phony name, of course. But the police got hold of the autograph and called me in. I was able to tell he was prone to bad headaches. Shows up in the midline pattern in extreme cases. You know, where the letters would hit the line on a sheet of legal paper. Anyway, the cops checked the pain clinics, and sure enough, they found a migraine case who was known to be a terrific dancer. *Voilà.*'' Diamond snapped his fingers.

''So you might be able to tell something from just . . . say, a few sentences?''

''All it takes is a few words, Sarah Spooner. A few words and we can get the picture. Simple as that.''

Slipping my hand into my purse, I felt the crisp edge of the note. If I gave it to Diamond, he might be able to tell me what was tormenting Nicky. Would that be the answer? Would that end it? A tremor ran from my fingers to the center of my fear.

"But you know, Sarah Spooner, it's not enough to know why. Suicide is a minute, a single, desperate act. But it represents a whole series of events and decisions. You can't just say a person had this marble missing or this straw over the limit. You have to take the life apart, bit by bit, and see what went wrong. Otherwise you can't hope to prevent the next one and the next from going off the deep end. Takes time, patience, to figure out why one person ticks and another overwinds."

I withdrew my trembling fingers and closed the latch on my purse. Too much was at stake for pat answers and slick solutions. Having Diamond do a quick analysis of the note would not lay the matter to its final rest. "I guess you're right."

Diamond turned to face me. His smile was taut and self-satisfied. "That's one thing about me. When I'm right, I'm right."

My thoughts drifted past this large, foolish puff of a person. This town, this place, was so full of Nicky. I could see his familiar grin, the glint of a private joke in his eye. I half expected him to appear at the side of the deserted road and hoist a hopeful thumb.

Promise me you won't hitchhike, Nicky. Promise. It's too dangerous, baby. I want you safe. . . .

Safe.

A familiar flame of sorrow burned my throat, and I turned so Diamond could not see the pain in my face. Why, Nicky? How could it be? How could you do such a terrible thing to yourself?

And to me.

-5-

Diamond skirted the center of town and drove along the old state road toward the Elms. Fast-food stands and peeling billboards pocked the landscape. We passed the skeletal remains of a dozen dead farms: rolling acres given to crops of tangled weeds and litter; broken barns faded to the color of dried blood; silos rusted and tipped as if bowing to some dubious progress. The carcass of an ancient tractor marked the entrance to an abandoned Grange Hall.

According to the official university account, at one time Cromwell was known for its rich farmlands, a vital organ of northern grain and dairy production. For nearly two hundred years the town flourished on a bounty of fresh milk and yellow corn. Farmers ran the local politics and made certain that the schools, in what was then the town of Serenity Falls, taught the agrarian essentials.

Prosperity continued until the great drought of 1871, followed by a devastating weevil infestation. Then came a potato virus that all but obliterated the Eastern white spud. Isaiah Cromwell, a young independent banker at the time, made his fortune harvesting overdue farm loans and defaulted mortgages, by which, it is often said, he was terribly saddened (though business was business). Isaiah and the generations of Cromwells he spawned were known for their ability to turn adversity, especially the adversity of others, to advantage.

Over the next decade Isaiah took title to much of Serenity Falls, appointed himself mayor and chief selectman, took control of the municipal services, and ran the town like yet another arm of the family business, which by that time consisted of three more banks, a primitive chain of convenience stores, nearly every inn and boarding lodge in Serenity Falls (by then known as Cromwell), and several independent schools.

Then, having collected his fill of prime property—which the government paid him handsomely to ignore—and commercial enterprises, Isaiah turned his sights to the jeweled crown of land at the top of the hill overlooking the town. I don't know whether Cromwell acquired the university's property, as Diamond claimed, by bilking a hapless Indian chief. Nicky's freshman handbook said the property was given as a grant by the state after Isaiah Cromwell promised to devote the fledgling university's intellectual energies to developing a disease-resistant strain of baking potato. There was no mention of cheating or an alcoholic Indian chief with a penchant for gambling. But then, I suppose that would not make for good handbook copy.

Whatever its beginnings, the venture was a success. In the hundred and three years since its founding, Cromwell University had developed into one of the finest comprehensive institutions of higher learning in the country. The school was the undisputed leader in civil engineering, fine arts, political science, classical ballet, black and Asian studies, computer science, ice hockey, extemporaneous debating, nuclear medicine. And now, suicides.

Looking up and over my left shoulder, I could see the sun glinting off the cropped peak of the clock tower. The carillons soberly chimed the quarter hour. My memory filled in the green quadrangle of the main campus—a great, grassy expanse flanked by ivied stone buildings that housed the English, history, math, foreign language, and psychology departments. The old library had been razed and replaced by a soaring steel-and-smoked-glass structure that looked like an overweight bird straining to take flight.

The state road wound around the outskirts of Cromwell Center toward what students called the Strip. Dreadful little bars, cheap restaurants, and a single tattoo parlor, cunningly named Lou's Tattoos, catered to the student taste and pocketbook. This was the center of off-campus revelry and a frequent target of university outcry. Parents who parted with tuitions that rivaled the national debt did not take kindly to having their foolish, inebriated children marked for life with venomous green snakes, arrow-ridden hearts, or precious little scorpions fashioned in the shape of a sweetheart's initial.

Nicky once had a ladybug tattooed on his left ankle during a semiconscious visit to Lou's. Ben and I were furious. "That's about the stupidest stunt you've ever pulled, Nicholas Spooner. Don't you realize you're scarred for life!"

For life.

Diamond's voice broke through my reverie. "Here we are, Sarah Spooner. The Elms." He pulled into the broad parking lot and under the green-striped canopy marked RECEPTION. I retrieved my bag from the cavernous trunk and bid him what I hoped was a final farewell.

The lobby was deserted. For several minutes I waited at the front desk, reading brochures about the Cromwell Artisans' Collaborative, the summer playhouse, activities for Cromwell seniors, Cromwell's parks and playgrounds, the annual Perkins County Fair.

"Help you, ma'am?" A skeletal man with pale gray eyes and teeth like a Halloween pumpkin appeared behind the desk.

"I'd like a room. I'll be staying for a week or so."

His laugh was vacant and hollow like a dry, malignant cough. "You'd like a room? This week? Bet you're the type who sees the glass as half full. Make that all full. This is senior week, ma'am. Coming up on graduation. After that's reunion. Every room in town's been booked for a year or more. Don't even think you'll find room to pitch a tent."

It seemed there was no end to the sick surprises. "There must be someplace. How about one of the surrounding towns?"

He scratched his mottled forehead. "Maybe if you try Alaska, ma'am. Or Mexico. You don't mind my saying so, your timing's pretty rotten."

With an attempt at finesse I fished in my wallet for a bribe. My fingers found a twenty, which I held, at what I hoped was an effective angle, under the deskman's hairy nose. "You must have something . . . maybe if you looked again?"

He stood picking at a cuticle, staring at me as if I were some faintly interesting zoo exhibit. "So you want to stay that bad?"

"I need a place here. It's important. Very important." The twenty was gaining weight in my hand. I considered my alternatives. I could double the stakes. Or I could hold my ground hoping for the magical vacancy to appear. I had no talent for bluffs and bribery. Those were in Ben's domain.

He turned his palms in surrender. "All right then, honey. If it's that important to you, I bet we can work something out." His smile was stiff, his breath fetid. His few remaining teeth were rotted to splinters and stumps.

I tried to ignore the horror of his abominable dental hygiene and smiled back. "Great. I knew we could."

I stood with the twenty still flapping from my fingers like a flag as he came around the desk. His pants were smeared with dirt, and his nails were almost as black as his teeth. "Sure, honey."

Right beside me now, he reached out—I thought to take the twenty. But he bypassed the bill, grabbed my right breast, and began kneading furiously, as if I were a lump of temperamental dough. For an instant I was too startled to react.

"Mmm . . . nice jugs. Beautiful. Mmm . . ."

He was slobbering like a rabid animal, a trail of spittle straining toward his bony shoulder. His breath was the foul, rancid scent of a dead thing.

Recovered from the shock, I raised my knee in a reflex of defense and forced a quick thrust into the tangle of hardness and mush between his legs.

His smile twisted into a grimace of pain and surprise, and he began to sputter like a fountain with a leak. "You bitch . . . you little bitch. I oughta . . ."

I left him folded over, cursing at the floor, and ran outside for a greedy breath of fresh air. The sun's persistent glare surprised me. Days might have passed in those few seconds of revulsion.

Where now?

My heart and head were thumping in unison. I looked down along the stretch of unpromising road for a phone. Nothing. A lump of anger and weariness burned in my throat. What now?

A horn beeped. I turned, and there was Diamond, stuffed behind the Leatherette dash of his rented Lincoln, smiling.

"Need another lift, Sarah Spooner? I thought I'd wait and be sure you were all set."

Eager to put Jack-o'-Lantern the Ripper behind me, I slid in beside Diamond and threw my bag in the back-seat. "They had nothing I was willing to take," I said. "I don't know where to go now. I understand it's senior week. The town is booked solid."

Diamond drove a few blocks in blessed silence. I began to relax. The shudders of revulsion had played out, and numbness replaced them. Familiar numbness. If only I could drive the few blocks to Nicky's apartment and ring the bell. If only Nick would answer as he used to, frowning in mock annoyance at the intrusion. I could hear his firm voice—a song, a symphony. "C'mon in, Mom. You don't mind waiting in the living room for a few minutes, do you? You see, I've got these three naked girls in my bedroom, and there are all these illegal drugs and booze bottles lying around."

"Take your time, dear. I'm not in any hurry."

Nicky.

"You hungry, Sarah Spooner? That little trattoria up ahead has the best *paglia e fieno* east of the Mississippi. Ever have that? Straw and hay, they call it. White and green noodles with a sauce that is to die from. Wouldn't expect decent pasta in Cromwell. But life is full of surprises."

Before I could answer, he pulled into the narrow drive and parked next to the restaurant's red-striped canopy. The name, Trattoria Maria, was painted on the glassed front in what looked like a single strip of fettuccine.

The floor was littered with sawdust and stubbed cig-
arette butts. In the small front room there was space for
six round tables. Each was set with an anemic red car-
nation in a wax-coated Coke bottle and a white cloth
battle-scarred by the blood of Maria's homemade
marinara sauce. At this hour we had our pick of tables,
and Diamond chose the one nearest the electronic jukebox.

"A double order of *paglia e fieno*," he said in cred-
itable Italian. "A side of mussels marinara, some garlic
bread, a large house salad, a carafe of Chianti, and . . . I
guess that's all for now."

The waitress scowled. "You expecting a famine or
something?"

"Are the snide remarks included? Or do I have to pay
extra?" Diamond said with an air of composure that
made me feel a grudging tug of respect.

"It's your funeral, mister. My old man ate himself to
death. You want to go that way, be my guest."

"Your old man probably died to get away from you,
nosy waitress. How about you, Sarah Spooner? What'll
it be?"

My appetite was nowhere to be found. "Just coffee.
Black."

The waitress tossed Diamond a last look of disdain
and sauntered toward the kitchen.

"Funny place for a spy from Weight Watchers," Diamond said. "Every once in a while we fat people run

into one of those calorie evangelists. Worst sort of people. If you looked at that poor woman's handwriting, I bet you'd find a rotten childhood, an acned adolescence, and at least one abusive husband. You should eat something. The food here is wonderful.''

''I take it you've spent a lot of time in Cromwell.''

''Some. No more than I've had to. The chief of police, guy name of Byron Dexter, is an old pal and something of an admirer. Whenever he gets stuck with a rough case, he calls me in. That's how the university got hold of me.'' He issued a dramatic sigh. ''What price fame. Tell me, what's a class act like yourself doing in a dump like this?''

The food arrived, and Diamond poured me a glass of wine and heaped an extra plate with pasta over my protests. Watching him eat was better than Broadway. With movements that might have been choreographed by a master, he twirled a precise spiral of sauced noodles on his fork, traced a perfect arc between plate and face, arm bent just so, and set his cavernous mouth in an anticipatory oval. Then, as food-laden fork passed through the gummy portals, he curled his tongue and closed his fat lips around the implement in a passionate caress. The fork, mission completed, slid like a figure skater back toward the waiting plate while Diamond made round, graceful chewing motions and rolled his chocolate eyes in pleasure. All the while he kept the beat with a low hum of sensual fulfillment. At times I felt I should look away and leave the lovers alone.

When the last morsel was eaten, the last fatty globule of cream sauce captured on a crusty slab of bread, Diamond folded his satisfied hands and smiled. "Was I right or what?"

I had tried one bite to keep him happy. Noodle-flavored chewing gum in a cheesy Elmer's glue. Each to his own. "It's okay."

He dabbed his lips with the corner of a paper napkin and patted his middle. "Can't abide things you have to chew. That's the problem. Hate meat, never touch the stuff. But I'm not your standard vegetarian, either. Hate vegetables, fresh fruits. Yuck. So I eat the good stuff: noodles, bread, ice cream. Puts the weight on, that's the only downside." He put a hand on his middle as if to tame it. "So, you didn't answer my question. What brings you to this horrid little hamlet, Sarah Spooner?"

"Oh . . . I have some things to take care of. Personal business. But now it looks as if I'll have to make other plans. There's no place to stay."

"Important personal business?"

"Yes. Important to me, anyway. But I'll work it out . . . somehow."

Diamond cast a longing eye at his empty plate and called for the check. "No dessert for me. Gotta watch the old waistline."

"You wanna watch that waistline, you better get yourself a wide-angle lens," the waitress snapped.

"You know, you got a rip there, Miss Buttinsky. Right there under your nose. Nasty rip. You ought to have it sewn up."

While we waited, Diamond took a clean napkin from the metal dispenser and pushed it toward me. "I'd like your autograph, Sarah Spooner. For when you get famous."

"Sorry. I don't do autographs, Mr. Diamond. You know, if I give one to you, I'll be bothered by all my other fans." The thought of being dissected by this odd person frightened me.

"Just write, 'The sly brown fox jumped over the yellow gate,' and your name. Or are you scared?"

"Why should I be scared? Frankly I think you people tend to overestimate your abilities to get information from handwriting. I'll agree you can make some basic judgments, get some idea about stability and basic personality type. But some of it verges on a parlor trick, a magic show. You have to admit you can't know everything there is to know about a person from the way that person writes, 'The sly brown fox . . .' Admit it."

"I admit it. Whatever you say. But tell me, Sarah Spooner, what exactly frightens you about it? What harm can it possibly do? Especially if, as you claim, it's mostly a parlor trick."

"I told you. I am not frightened." I took the napkin and Diamond's ballpoint, which read, "Al's Auto Body. U-wreckem. We Checkem." A tremor threatened to erupt in my fingers, but I managed to hold it back and scrawl the required message.

He perched a dainty pair of rimless half glasses on the broad bridge of his nose and squinted at my writing.

After a few seconds he turned the napkin upside down and looked again. His face drooped gently like a theater curtain. "I'm sorry. You have suffered a tragic loss, haven't you? Nice person like you doesn't deserve that."

"Where does it say that?" I tried to sound light and breezy, but the pain was bubbling up again.

"Hard to explain. There's a disruption in your rhythm. That's the dead giveaway. But there's more. Little blips in the lower register. This space between the loops of your ascenders. I told you . . . it's complicated, but we can tell a great deal. Who died?"

"My son." The words came out a sick whisper, but they seemed to grow until the room was so full of them that I could barely breathe.

"He was one of the suicides?"

All I could do was shake my head. The rest of me was caught in a hideous spasm of grief.

"I had that feeling about you. You'll come with me, Sarah Spooner. I'll find you a place to stay."

I had turned to aspic. Diamond helped me out of the restaurant and into the Lincoln. "Thank you," I managed.

"No problem. That's what nosy strangers are for."

Shadows were stretching over Cromwell, softening the harsh edges. The day was closing in on itself, gathering up its store of failed dreams and broken promises. Could this be the same day that I left Ben, angry and stubborn, in a separate world? Could I be the same person who existed in that world? I felt as if someone had taken enormous shears and cut me away from what I had been.

And I wondered, for a terrifying instant, what I was about to become.

-6-

We entered the university through the north gate and drove past the Plant Genetics School and the College of Veterinary Medicine. For several hundred acres Diamond negotiated the tortuous curves through the Cromwell School of Vocational Agriculture, an experimental dairy farm and large animal-breeding complex rivaling any in the world. At intervals we passed sober, stone-faced buildings that housed research centers for every conceivable agrarian study: the Reisling Center for Pomology. "Apples," Diamond explained. Grimley Hall, Research in Bovine Nutrition ("Cow chow"), Sopwirth Center for Equine Insemination.

"That's where they jack off the horses," Diamond said. "Amazing what some people will do for a buck."

The road dipped suddenly, and we drove into a dense thicket of greenery. The air hung with a sweet moisture that made my eyes water. "Ever been here?" Diamond asked. "Called the rain forest for obvious reasons. Guy who runs it is a Dr. Plante, would you believe? Seems like your basic northern jungle, but from what I understand, they're doing research here into some god-awful germ that could wipe out the whole population in a blink. Have to keep it warm and humid to run some of their crazy experiments. They have heating coils running underground, moisture pumps, costs more than you can imagine. Never could understand why people spend so much time and money trying to figure out how to kill each other. You can ignore somebody for free, I always figure.''

''That's true.'' I breathed in cautious measures until we left the rain forest behind and drove onto the road that wound around the engineering school and the business college. ''I never realized how huge Cromwell was. Nicky . . . my son . . . was in liberal arts, an English major. We saw almost nothing but the center of the campus.''

''Larger than you'd imagine, Sarah Spooner. Lots of secret government stuff goes on here. The rain forest is only one of several centers funded by federal grants. Plenty of people at Cromwell would like to see all the labs torn down and replaced by fraternity houses. Seems there's plenty of disagreement about what a college is supposed to stick its nose into. You listen to some folks, universities should have a hand in anything and everything. I'm with the crew that thinks schools are for learning. Old-fashioned notion, I guess.''

Ancient ivied buildings rubbed elbows with stark, modern structures devoted to space research, astrophysics, computer science, and bioengineering. All so new to me, the names tickled my mind. I felt like a dinosaur frozen in time and thawed to an alien era. "Maybe they learn too much," I muttered. "Or not enough." Strange chant—too much and not enough. What could Nick have been thinking? Could he have been thinking at all?

Diamond screeched into a sharp turn off the main road and drove down a dirt road that bent after several hundred yards through a majestic bower of willow and oak. The Lincoln crept along a narrow cobblestoned street bordered by French lilacs in full blossom and antique gas lamps now flamed by electricity. There were boxy Victorians and country colonials with leaded glass windows and gingerbread trim. Each was walled by a stiff formal garden, shrubs cropped in perfect rounds and ovals, trellised wisteria and rock gardens planted with phlox and border perennials. A vague breeze moved the arthritic fingers of ancient elms and sugar maples.

Diamond clutched the wheel. Maneuvering the Lincoln down this trail made for horse carriages was as tricky as threading a fat lady into a tight corset. Shrubs tore at the car's beef-toned metallic finish as we drove, and the mag wheels shrieked in complaint as they squeezed against the ancient curbs.

"What is this?"

"It's called Parrish Common. Not many people know it even exists, as you might imagine. Seems old man Parrish set this strip aside for exact preservation. Wrote it into one of his mammoth donations. I think it was funds for the undergraduate library or something like that.

"Anyhow, according to the book, this was where the Parrish family used to live. They owned all the houses. Started with the main building, that's the Barrington Arms now. Then every time one of the Parrish clan got married, the old man built a house on this block, each next door to the last. Lucky there weren't more of them. This little street might have gone straight on to Philadelphia."

"Who lives here now?" The houses looked too perfect for human habitation. Windows all opened to a precise level, weedless lawns. Doors inset with polished brass nameplates and knobs glinted in the waning sunlight. I thought I saw a curtain move in a second-story window, but when I looked again, there was nothing but stillness. Probably just my imagination filling in the blanks.

Diamond shrugged. "No one. Pity, isn't it? Such a waste. But no one steps in those places except the cleaning and maintenance people. Parrish forbade it as a condition of his endowment. Nothing gets lived in but the inn. Think of Parrish Common as an old Western ghost town done in shades of early Americana. Wouldn't surprise me a bit if two guys in big hats swaggered down the road and started shooting at each other. Welcome to the nineteenth century."

"I'm having enough trouble with the twentieth, thank you. No time capsules for me."

Diamond exited the quaint mews through a spiked black metal gate. Suddenly we were on a long concrete drive dotted at intervals with copper plaques gone green with age. A red brick building peeked through the towering stands of blue spruce in the distance. "The Barrington Arms," he said, dipping his head in a deferential bow.

As we rounded the trees the building emerged, looming over us like a cold, dead giant. The massive front, ancient brick weathered to shades of parched earth and ash, obliterated the remaining daylight, thrusting us into a chill dusk of isolation. A dark canopy fluttered over a stretch of blood-red carpet leading to the front door. Beside the brass lion's-head knocker, a tiny sign read, THE BARRINGTON ARMS. WINSTON LAWRENCE, PROPRIETOR.

"This is where the big shots stay?" I said, tuning my voice to sound casual. "Is that before or after they die?"

"Relax. I hear it's really lovely inside. And the service is wonderful. They don't get more than two, maybe three vampires a year."

"That's good to know." I tried to find Diamond's ease a comfort. *You are in no position to be choosy*, I reminded myself. If Diamond could, as he claimed, work something out with the manager, I would have a way to remain in Cromwell and find out what I needed to know about Nicky's death.

Nicky's death and mine.

"Come on in, Sarah Spooner. We'll see what we can do. I don't know this Winston Lawrence person, but I know his brother, Wallace. Happens to be president and chairman of the Board of Trustees at Cromwell. Actually there are three Lawrences—triplets from what I hear. Third one is an absentminded professor—a Shakespeare expert. Different as night, day, and Miami. My friend Chip Dexter, the police chief, calls them Lawrence the meek, Lawrence the sleek, and Lawrence the geek. Quite a character, old Chip.''

Diamond tugged open the massive front door and led me into the deserted foyer. The ceilings were vaulted, the walls papered in a dusty rose floral print, the floors carpeted in a deep burgundy plush. Ornate sconces left ragged puddles of light. In the center of the room a crystal chandelier cascaded over an enormous white slatted bird cage. Four fat white doves slept on gilt perches.

Along the wall sketches of stiff, unsmiling children hung in clusters. Thin girls with corkscrew curls poking out from starched bonnets; boys with dour expressions and deep circles under their vacant eyes. There was a child caught in a paralysis of fright and another boy-beast with three heads and a devil's tail. I wondered who would purchase such unappealing images.

A young girl with blond hair and a bored expression was behind the reception desk. She met Diamond's request for an extra room with a horizontal head shake and an extra crackle of her Juicy Fruit. He insisted on seeing the manager, and Miss Amity tossed her blond hair to show the way. I followed Diamond through an archway and down a dim corridor to a room packed with files and storage crates. There was a primitive copying machine, a shelf full of ancient movie cameras and film canisters, a watercooler spitting large bubbles, assorted cleansers, spare rolls of toilet tissue, and a large, utilitarian metal desk. A slight man with a ruddy complexion and thinning gray-blond hair hunched over a yellowing ledger, so still and unprepossessing, I thought he might be just another piece of office equipment.

Diamond cleared his throat, and the man raised a pair of dull, dachshund eyes and a shrill wisp of a voice. "Yes?"

"Aldo Diamond. And this here's my associate, Sarah Spooner. My office goofed up and forgot to tell you she was coming along with me. University business, you know." He winked.

The man looked back at his ledger. He traced the fine spiders of writing down the page. "Diamond. Yes, I see. You'll be with us for several weeks."

"Don't rub it in. So listen, what can you do for my nice friend here? Might have to settle for the presidential suite, I bet." Diamond winked again, at no one in particular. "I know you people always have a room or two tucked away for emergencies. You take care of us. We'll take care of you."

The man pursed his meager lips and wove his fingers into a protective ball. "Oh, my, my. I can appreciate your predicament, Mr. Diamond. But we haven't a single vacancy. It would be my pleasure to accommodate you, sir, I assure you. But . . ."

Diamond thumped his fat fist against the man's desk, startling everyone including himself. ''Now let's cut the games. How much do you want?''

''Oh, my. Please believe me, sir. Money is not the issue here. I would be delighted to offer accommodations to your . . . associate . . . if one were available. Unfortunately this is the busiest time of the year. Graduation. Then reunion. We simply have no vacancies. None at all.''

Diamond banged the desk like a crazed auctioneer. ''Fifty . . . make it a hundred! Here.'' He extracted a thick wad of bills from his pocket and began counting out tens.

The man flushed. ''My, my. Please, Mr. Diamond. There is nothing I can do. I cannot offer you a room I do not have. It is simply impossible.''

''Look, my friend. I didn't want to mention this, but I'm here on important university business. I'm here at the request of Wallace Lawrence himself, if you must know. You know the name, I suppose. Wallace Lawrence? As in Chairman of the Board Lawrence, your boss's brother?'' He loomed over the desk like a storm cloud. ''Old Wally will not be happy if he finds out I had any hassle here. Not happy at all.''

The man seemed to shrink under Diamond's bullying. He extended a limp hand. ''Please, Mr. Diamond. Allow me to introduce myself. I am Winston Lawrence.''

Diamond shook the hand like he was pumping a rusty well. ''Good, then. I like to deal with the person in charge. Let's get down to it, Lawrence. What have you got for my friend here?"

"Believe me, sir. There is nothing I can do. I would be happy to accommodate you, but I simply haven't any vacancies. My dear brother would surely understand. . . . Here is your key, Mr. Diamond. Of course, you are welcome to give your room to the lady if you wish." He cast a nervous glance at the wall clock. "If you require assistance with your luggage or anything else, kindly let me know. I am due to leave shortly, but my assistant will be available to help you."

Diamond turned and stormed out of the office, motioning for me to storm along. He marched to the waiting Lincoln, leaned against the hood, and stretched his lips in a grin. "Now I've got him right where I want him, Sarah Spooner. Did you hear what he said? Give the room to the lady? Perfect. That's what I had in mind all along."

"Thanks, anyway, Mr. Diamond. I appreciate your kindness, but I can't take your room. You have business here, and there's no place else to stay."

"No, no. You don't understand. I'm not going anywhere. We'll stay together."

I could feel the rage rising from the bottom of my feet, hot lava filling me until it took every shred of control to keep from erupting on the spot. Even Diamond. Even this big cartoon of a person . . . and I thought he was just being a nice guy. "I am not interested in staying with you, Mr. Diamond. Not for a room, not for a palace, not for anything! What is it with you men? You think every woman can be bought? You think you can put a price tag on my dignity? My integrity? Well, you've got another thing coming! You can take your damned room and . . .''

His face fell like a chastened puppy, and I felt a swell of guilt, as if I had just committed puppy abuse. "I'm sorry if I misinterpreted your offer, Mr. Diamond. I just thought . . .''

"My people taught me to look out for my fellow man, Sarah Spooner. My fellow person, I mean. I was just trying to help you out in a pinch.''

"That's very noble. And I appreciate it. It's just been a terrible day. A terrible month. And I took it the wrong way. I'm sorry.''

He perked right up like a thirsty plant after a good soak. "No harm done. None at all. Tell you what I had in mind. You see, I've got a suite. Two rooms. You can have one. I'll take the other. I bet we can keep out of each other's way if we try. You snore?''

"Not that I know of.''

"Well, I do. But otherwise I'm real easy to get along with. I was just glad old Winnie suggested I give you the room. This way he can't try to charge you any extra.''

I collected what was left of myself and tried to consider my options, such as they were. This seemed the only available place for me to stay. I had to be in Cromwell. My future, whatever was left of it, was blocked by secrets this town held in its shabby clutches.

"If you're sure it's all right with you, Mr. Diamond, I would be grateful."

"It's all right with me, Sarah Spooner. Wouldn't have asked you otherwise. We can help each other, in fact. I'll keep you up on what I hear at the university, and you can give me the inside track on the details of what happened with your boy. That'll help me get to the bottom of what's going on in old Cromwell."

"I hope you do. Before there are any others..."

Diamond hoisted the trunk lid and pulled out his collection of red plaid luggage. He straightened up and gave me a quizzical look. "Oh, there'll be others, Sarah Spooner. No doubt about that. There'll be plenty of others."

The thought crept over me like a bad chill. "Not if the university gets going with some good crisis-intervention programs. There was a rash of suicides in the Wheldon County high schools last year, and they managed to get it under control with peer counseling, hot lines, high-risk identification, parent groups. It can be done. It has to be."

"Let's hope you're right, Sarah Spooner. Let's hope it's as simple as that."

Diamond hoisted a suitcase in each hand and walked back to the Barrington Arms. The door was stiff and heavy. With all my strength I pulled it open and stepped into the cool, dim foyer. The puddles of light lay ahead, a path to some uncertain place.

"Come along," Winston Lawrence beckoned. "I'll show you the way."

Someone would. Sooner or later I would open a door to the truth about my son. Diamond was behind me, panting under the strain of his luggage. I hurried after Winston Lawrence, proprietor, up a narrow winding stair, and down a long corridor. My footsteps were cushioned by a faded Turkish runner, my form cast in eerie shadow along the pink marbled walls. Winston Lawrence stopped before a carved door and tripped the lock with a jailer's key. With a gallant bow he retreated down the corridor and was gone.

Downstairs, I heard voices raised in argument. The words were muted, but the anger tore at the hotel's careful silence. My breath caught as the fury rose to a frightening crescendo, words hurled in attack. Diamond hauled in the luggage and beckoned to me from inside the suite. With reluctance I followed, and he closed the door.

The battle dimmed to an innocent hum.

-7-

My mother answered the phone on the fourth ring. "I never heard of such a thing, Sarah. What could you be thinking? Going off by yourself like that. A business trip is one thing."

"I'm a big girl, Mother. This is something I feel I have to do." I felt myself shrinking like a middle-aged Alice in Wonderland. My mother always affected me that way, though her appearance belied her powers of intimidation. She was a small, round, bouncy woman with a full moon-face, bat-wing arms, and skin fallen in soft folds like a stretched-out bathing suit. Her body was square and businesslike; her chest plump and firm as a hassock; her voice the steadfast drone of a bloodthirsty mosquito.

"Look, darling. I can't tell you what to do. But you don't want to leave a good-looking, successful man like Ben alone for long. You know how many women are out there who would die for a man like that? Married or no? Don't you watch television?"

"Mom, please. Let me speak to Ben."

"He's out, Sarah. What do you expect? You take off and leave him like this, you can't expect him to sit around like a bump on a log. He's a healthy young man, Sarah. He has his needs."

"When will he be back?"

"Do I know? Can I ask a grown man what time he's coming home? You expect me to give him a curfew? Bad enough I have to look after that daughter of yours who happens to think she's a whole grown-up lady who can do exactly what she pleases without asking anybody. Ben is your problem, Sarah. You take care of him."

"Just tell him I called, Mom. Will you? Tell him I'm staying at the Barrington Arms. Suite 211."

"Sure, darling. A suite, you say? Hoo, hah, aren't we fancy? Listen, you take care of yourself. If you go to dinner, take a sweater. You never know. Most restaurants are just like an icebox. You'd think air-conditioning grew on trees or something."

"You'll tell him? You won't forget?"

She bristled. "I do not forget things, Sarah."

That was true. "How's Allison? Can I say hello?"

"She's out too. Don't ask me where. 'Out, Grandma,' she says. 'That's where I'm going.' I hate to tell you, Sarah, but that child is developing a fresh mouth. What happened to her? She used to be so sweet."

"She's growing up, Mother."

"Now why didn't I think of that? You know, I see where Allison gets it from, young lady. You have a bit of a fresh mouth yourself. Two of a kind, you and your daughter. I said to her, 'Darling, what's gotten into that mother of yours? What does she mean taking off like this?' And you know what she says? 'You don't understand, Grandma. You just don't understand.' Like she's a whole smart grown-up and I'm good for nothing but pureed bananas and removable teeth. . . . Anyway, everyone's out but me. But I don't mind. I'm used to being alone. So I'll tell her you called, darling. Just take care. Remember, you've been under a lot of strain. Get some rest. And don't forget your vitamins. You've been eating like a bird.''

I hung up and searched through my meager store of ideas. Ben was probably in the city holding some corporate hand. Allison must have gone to her friend Clare's. They often spent evenings together, plotting ways to enhance their sex appeal or fantasizing about the untimely death of Coty Wheeler's current flame. It was good she had her friends' support and comfort. Everyone needed that.

Diamond knocked. In an unnecessary show of gallantry he had insisted I take the master bedroom with its king-size brass bed, while he camped on the pullout sofa in the drawing room. The entire suite was done in rose-toned floral chintz with flounces and ruffles and miles of gathered lace trim.

''Come in.''

''You ready to eat, Sarah Spooner? I'm starved. There's a terrific little Chinese place just out past the

Strip, no atmosphere but the lo mein is top-notch and the fortune cookies are never wrong.''

I was still full from watching Diamond eat his lunch, but I could not get myself to take on anything more ambitious for this evening. Maybe Diamond had more to tell me, I thought.

Maybe the sun would come up in the morning.

A chill breeze had risen with the moon. Our shadows stretched across the parking lot as we hurried to the warmth of the waiting car. Diamond whistled a shrill tune as he revved the engine and drove out through Parrish Common.

"So, Sarah Spooner," he said as if reading my mind. "What's your plan? You going to see your boy's friends? Teachers? What?"

"I . . . I guess all those. Anyone who might know what happened. You didn't know Nick, but he was so full of life, so optimistic, ambitious. And he had a wonderful sense of humor. Believe me, he was the last person in the world you'd have expected to commit suicide.'' The word caught in my throat. "I have to find out why—what happened."

"Then you will. I'm a good judge of character, you know. And you are one determined woman. That's clear as day." He drove back along the state road toward the Strip. Traffic had swelled to a modest peak, Cromwell's work force, such as it was, returning to their five-room Cape colonials and split ranches. "See that guy?" He pointed out the Lincoln's window toward a young man in a baseball hat behind the wheel of a small, dilapidated beige pick-up.

"What about him?"

"He's married. Two kids. One on the way. Basically he's a nice guy but not too much on the beam. Low voltage," he said, pointing to his temple. "You get the picture. His wife's a manicurist, or maybe she does facials, works two afternoons and Saturdays. He's got a little tool-and-die business he runs out of his basement. He likes to hunt, only drinks on holidays, has a little trouble with his sinuses."

"Where do you get all that?"

"Trade secret. Does Macy's tell Gimbel's?"

"I don't know."

"Well, I do, Sarah Spooner. That's the whole point. I know things. It's a mixed blessing, believe me. I watch other people floating through life in happy oblivion and I'm jealous. I look at someone, and right away I know things about him. I have feelings about what's going to happen to him, what he's been through. It's not just the handwriting. I have this extra sense. Call it what you like."

My first instinct was to call it bullshit. But I had to admit that Diamond was unusually insightful. Not that I would place his talents on any unique psychic plane. Working in criminal investigation, I often came across people who seemed to have a third eye trained beneath the human surface.

"What do you suppose it means if one person is completely blind to another, Mr. Diamond?" Was it possible for parents not to notice that their child lay bleeding with a mortal wound? Could Ben and I have been that blind to Nicky?

"I suppose it means there's something too ugly to see, or too painful." Diamond frowned and bit his beefy lip. "It's none of my business, Sarah Spooner. But you're not going to get anywhere by trying to go back and do it all over again and again in your mind. Blaming doesn't bring anybody back. Understanding helps, but that's not the end, either. You have to get to the point where you can put it away. I'm not talking about getting rid of it. No one can do that. But you can fold it up and store it where it doesn't keep getting in the way."

I was in no mood for simple logic. "That all sounds very neat and easy."

"No, Sarah Spooner. It's the hardest thing you'll ever do. But it's also the most worthwhile."

We passed a campus sign, and Diamond turned off the road. He pulled up next to the administration building and squealed to a stop. "Where are you going?"

"Not me. You, Sarah Spooner. I know you aren't hungry. What you need is to get started, and this is as good a place as any. I'll meet you back here in a couple of hours."

Familiar numbness was creeping up my legs. "Not now," I said. My voice was lifeless, hollow.

Diamond patted my hand. "It's time. Believe me, Sarah Spooner. It will not be easier if you wait. If it's something you have to do, get started. Now."

I climbed heavily out of the Lincoln. Diamond slammed the door behind me and drove off before I could change my mind.

The campus was nearly deserted. A solitary couple walked arm in arm along one of the worn paths that crossed the main quadrangle like string sculpture. Lights winked from the rows of windows in the library, and I pictured pale, anxious students with thick glasses hunched over ancient volumes in the dusty storage rooms. Nicky had led me through those dismal cubicles on one of our many walks on the campus. "Step this way, ladies and gentlemen," he'd bellowed like a carnival barker. "Right over here. That's it, miss. Don't push, now. There's plenty of room for all of you."

"Shush, Nick. This is a library. People are studying."

"Not studying, miss. What you see is the human species in its most cellulose form, *Homo sapiens cabbagensis*. See that young creature over there? You could stuff him in the feed tube of your food processor, turn him on slow pulse, mix in a little mayo and vinegar, and you'd have the best coleslaw east of the Mississippi."

"That's mean, Nicky. He's studying. Correct me if I'm wrong but you are supposed to be here for the same reason, my son. Though sometimes I suspect you forget that."

I'd seen something in his eyes, a vague flicker of something I did not like. Hurt? Sorrow? But it was gone in a blink. Nothing. Just my imagination. A mother's guilty imagination. Nicky could take a little gentle criticism as well as the next person.

". . . Now, ladies and gentlemen, follow me to the main reading room, headquarters of the world-famous Cromwell Student Panty Patrol."

I could still feel his hand on my wrist, guiding me. The burning started there and began to spread up through my arm until it settled in a sick mass behind my eyes. Not again, Sarah. Not now.

I turned away. Across the campus, a single light flamed in the campus infirmary. I was drawn to it like a mindless moth.

The building was crafted of huge concrete slabs piled at odd angles like a child's block structure. From the outside, I placed the lit window at the center of the third floor. A man's silhouette played against the drawn shade.

The offices were rarely occupied after regular hours. Sick students were housed in rooms at the rear of the building, invisible from where I stood. Nicky had only been admitted once, with abdominal pains that he took for an overdose of Johnny the Greek's pepperoni pizza. In fact, he was felled by a virulent strain of stomach flu that visited Cromwell in the fall of his freshman year. Ben thought I was crazy to fly up and see him. "He's a big boy, Sarah. You'll only embarrass him."

Big boy or no, his eyes smiled when I showed up and clucked over his sweet green face and his fevered brow and called him "poor baby." He made a show of not caring that I was there. But he was glad. I know he was. "I'm not dying or anything, Mother dear. You're welcome to go back home and nag at Dad and Allison."

"Soon, Nicky. As soon as you're well enough to make me."

The building was warm, the air still and scented with disinfectant. I climbed the stairs, worn to a smooth sheen by thousands of ailing student feet. My footfalls clattered in the emptiness.

As I opened the fire door to the third floor I saw the light shining midway down the corridor. Passing the doors that led to Ophthalmology, Ob-Gyn, X-ray and Speech/Hearing, I came to the swatch of light under the office marked, MENTAL HEALTH—DR. PELLECK, DR. MARSHALL, DR. SENDOVER, DR. BARDWIN. Below the names, scratched in the paint in childish block letters, was the legend, WAGE PEACE.

Before I could further doubt my coming to this spooky, empty place, I forced myself to open the door and walk into the waiting room. "Anybody here?" "Anybody home?" I allowed a nervous giggle. "Good, Sarah. Some careless soul leaves a light on and you consider it an invitation." I turned to leave.

"Can I help you?"

For an instant I was too startled to speak. "I . . . I was just— Who?"

A gnomish man with a tolerant smile stood in the entrance to his office. He had kind brown eyes and hair that seemed to have fallen from the top of his head to settle in a soft drape around his face. When he spoke, his mouth appeared in the center of the whiskery mass like a pink flower growing in a bird's nest.

He extended a small hand for me to shake. "You're Mrs. Spooner, right? I'm Ron Bardwin. I don't suppose you'd remember me with all the commotion, all the people. But I was at Nicholas's funeral."

"Yes . . . I mean, no. Not really. I'm sorry."

"Won't you come in?"

I followed him into a small, square office cluttered with books and sports trophies. "I don't mean to intrude, Dr. Bardwin. I was just walking on campus and I saw your light."

Bardwin slumped behind the desk, rubbed his eyes, and yawned extravagantly. "You are not intruding. In fact, any interruption is more than welcome. As you can imagine, things have been more than a little crazy around here . . . I mean, crazy busy, not crazy crazy. Then I suppose you can say it's been crazy crazy too. Forgive me, Mrs. Spooner. I don't do any better under impossible stress than the next guy."

"Aren't most of the students gone for the summer already? I would think things would slow down."

"You would think so, yes. But not this year. I'm working like crazy to wind things up so I can get to my sister's wedding this weekend. Things are completely out of control.''

"The suicides?"

Bardwin closed his eyes and nodded. "It's a nightmare. Then, you know that as well as anyone. Better. I'm terribly sorry about Nicholas. He was a nice kid. Bright.''

"Yes, he was." Is. I still had trouble with the past tense. The fact. "I came to Cromwell to find out what happened. Why Nicky would do such a thing. I don't understand, Dr. Bardwin. Do you?"

He meshed his fingers and twiddled his thumbs. "What exactly is it you don't understand, Mrs. Spooner? The suicide? The human condition? The mechanics of depression? The agony of relinquishing childhood?"

I felt suddenly exhausted, overwhelmed. "All of the above, I suppose. Can you help me?"

"Not officially. I mean, I am not at liberty to discuss specifics of your son's case. Doctor-patient privilege. Or, more accurately, I know Nicholas wouldn't want me to, and I respect his wishes.''

"Nicky was a patient?" The room was wavering like a boat in a storm. "I didn't know. . . ."

Bardwin's voice was a soothing chant. "Nicholas was a very private person, Mrs. Spooner. That was part of the problem. He kept things inside where they could fester and do the most damage. He came in to see me a few times, but even here he found it hard to let go.''

"But he was so happy, so funny."

"On the outside. It was his way of covering up. Not an unusual way, either. The funniest comedians are often chronic depressives in clown makeup."

"Depressive? Are you telling me Nicky was depressed? What would he be depressed about? It doesn't make sense."

Bardwin leaned toward me across the desk. "Illness doesn't have to make sense, Mrs. Spooner. There are no such rules."

The room started to spin, the edges pressing in on me, making it hard to breathe. Bardwin looked odd, his face twisted as if he were trying to solve a puzzle. Nothing made sense. Nothing.

"You okay? Mrs. Spooner?" He was shouting at me from the top of the well, but I couldn't climb out. Couldn't move.

He came around the desk and shoved something under my nose. A sharp blade sliced through my head, cutting away the fog. "Stop it. Stop that!"

"Smelling salts," he said sheepishly. "I thought you were going to pass out."

"I'm all right now." I collected myself and motioned for him to sit down again.

He shook his head in apology. "I'm sorry if it came as a shock. I thought Nicholas might have mentioned me. It was a good thing that he came here. A first step."

"But it wasn't enough."

Bardwin looked away. "No. Not soon enough or long enough to change the course of things. I'm sorry, Mrs.

Spooner. I wish it could have been different."

"So do I, Dr. Bardwin. But—"

He raised a hand. "And I wish I could help you now. The privilege thing is only part of the problem. The fact is, I don't have the answers you want. I don't think you're going to find neat answers."

"I'm going to try. I owe it to Nicky. And myself." I collected what was left of myself and turned to leave. "If at any time there's more you think I should know, Dr. Bardwin, please call me. I'm staying at the Barrington Arms for a few days. After that you can reach me at home."

"Mrs. Spooner, I know it's none of my business, but if you really want to do something for yourself—and Nicholas—you'll do your best to get past this. I know he would have wanted that. The last thing he wanted was to drag anyone down with him."

My hand was frozen on the doorknob. "I am doing my best. This is the only way I know how to get past it, Dr. Bardwin."

"Are you getting any help with this, Mrs. Spooner? Any counseling?"

"That's not the kind of help I need. I have to know what happened to Nicky. I have to."

His face was full of sorrow. "It was his life, Mrs. Spooner. His personal world."

"His to live, Dr. Bardwin. Not his to throw away."

He shook his head. "But that was what he chose. I know it's hard. . . ."

I left the office and retraced my steps through the deserted building. Depressed. Suicidal. Nicky? More than ever, I was convinced there was some other explanation. Years in the D.A.'s office had taught me that the neatest scenarios were the ones that shattered to useless splinters under close scrutiny.

Diamond's car was waiting when I got to the administration building. On the backseat was a bag jammed with paper take-out cartons and the heavy scent of a Szechuan hot spice and soy sauce. I settled on the seat beside him and shut the door. He was staring out the window, so absorbed that he didn't notice my presence.

"Diamond?"

Turning, he blinked away the worry clouding his eyes and pressed his lips together in a determined seam. "Oh, hello, Sarah Spooner. How'd it go?"

"It was a start."

"Good. That's good."

"What about you, Mr. Diamond? How was dinner?"

"Fine. Nothing I didn't expect." He cleared his throat and gunned the engine. His face, reflected in the windshield, was heavy with private concerns.

"You sure?"

He turned on the radio. Blaring rockabilly drowned out my attempt at cross-examination.

A taut silence stretched between us until we turned in the drive and parked in the lot at the Barrington Arms. As he lifted himself out of the Lincoln he spotted the bag on the backseat.

"That's for you, Sarah Spooner. Something told me you might be hungry by now."

The night was drawn in charcoal, the sky burdened with dense black clouds. Diamond walked a few steps behind, leaving me to the silence I needed. The answers were closer. A step closer. But were they the answers I needed?

My stomach grumbled softly. I was hungry. I hoped he had gotten spareribs and egg rolls. Nicky's favorite was moo shu pork with hot mustard. I could see his deft fingers rolling the pancake in a smooth envelope and dipping the edge in the fiery sauce. Ali and Ben liked to share a mountain of orange beef and fried rice. They always made fun of me for piling crispy noodles on everything. The mama bird building her nest.

I stopped at the door. "You were right, Mr. Diamond. I'm starved."

"I told you, Sarah Spooner. I know things."

He stared up at the inn as if it held a dreaded private vision. My mind was galloping over the rough terrain of grim revelations. Depression. Suicide.

"Don't let it get you, Sarah Spooner," Diamond said, as if he had scooped into my brain with a ladle. "There will be more. Much more. Don't try to put the puzzle together until you have all the pieces."

Easy for him to say, I thought.

"I know it's hard," Diamond said. He pursed his fat lips and managed a rueful smile. "I got all your favorites, Sarah Spooner. Wait and see."

-8-

Diamond was hunched over a thick stack of files when I awoke. It was such an odd night. I slept in vague, unsatisfying pulses, snippets of dreams floating through my mind and dancing out of reach when I squinted to bring them in sharper focus. In the background there was Diamond's odd snore. A stark trumpet blast followed by the weak putter of a lawn mower in low gear. Then a silence. A thick, oily silence that made my back bristle. Several times I snapped awake, listening for the relief of the next trumpet toot. I could imagine a vicious assassin, suffocating poor Diamond by torturous degrees. How could he survive such a night?

Still, he seemed alert and ambitious this morning, dressed in oversize Army fatigues, seated at the carved mahogany drawing-room desk, peering through a dense magnifier at a page of student writing. A bold, definite hand, I thought, peeking over his shoulder as I passed. Thick ovals in the *L*'s and *T*'s. A triumphant dot over the lowercase *I*'s. A capital *E* so balanced and sure, it might have been emblazoned on the writer's sweatshirt as a badge of perfect adjustment.

Diamond clucked and shook his head. He took a small red candy bear from a paper bag beside his chair and pressed it on the page with the thick ball of his thumb. Picking through the bag again, he stuffed several orange bears in his mouth and chewed in broad, determined swirls.

I coughed to steal his attention. "It must be frustrating for you when the writing is so clear and sure that you don't have anything to report."

He scratched his head. "I only wish for that kind of frustration, Sarah Spooner. It's unbelievable how much pathology I've found. Why, in this stack alone, we have six possibles and a dozen or so wouldn't-surprise-mes. What's with these kids, anyway? So much unhappiness, so much self-doubt . . ."

"Not this one." I picked up the red-beared paper and looked closer. Bold, certain. "I can imagine the type who wrote this, one of those insufferable young diplomats with a ten-year plan, an investment portfolio, a tidy little love life, and a closet full of three-piece suits just waiting."

He pinched the paper from my hand. "Let me explain my system, Sarah Spooner. Green gummy bears stand for good adjustment, blue ones mean a little personal isolation but nothing to really worry about. The yellow bears are a warning sign. I'm going to go to the dean and see if I can get more samples from those students, see if I find something more definite on them. Yellow-bear students may be going through some temporary crisis. For example, if they filled out these application forms around the time of the SATs, you'd see more yellow-bear tendencies that might clear up after a nice pizza and a mindless movie.''

"And the red bears?"

He held up a puffy hand. "I was just getting to those. Red bears are your basic candidates for the butterfly net. I plan to send the nutcrackers to round up this crew and get them some help before it's too late."

Again I stared at the powerful, sure penmanship atop the pile. A smiling, strong-boned face stared back at me from a passport-size snapshot in the upper left corner. "This one?"

Diamond clicked his tongue. "I wouldn't buy that fellow any magazine subscriptions, if you know what I mean."

Turning the page upside down or backward made things no clearer. "What is it? What do you see here that I can't?"

He unfolded himself from the desk chair and allowed a loud, leonine stretch. Peering over his half glasses, he poked a thick finger at the first line of writing. "See that? The rhythm is choppy, like an EKG after a bad heart attack. And the slight backward slant indicates a very introverted state. This guy is all boxed in, like a pacing prisoner with nowhere to go. Then you get to the N's, and that's the dead giveaway. You see these two

N's in the word *intend*? See how the first has a notch before the second bump and the second one doesn't? This guy doesn't even know who he is anymore. Doesn't know if he's a thinker or a doer. Feels like he's lost touch. I can almost see him jolting awake in the middle of the night wondering what the hell's the point of getting up in the morning.''

"Because of a couple of *N*'s? I don't believe it."

"Suit yourself, Sarah Spooner. Misguided skeptics make the world go round."

I looked at the page again. "What's the point, anyway? Knowing someone is at risk can't stop anything, not if the person is determined. . . . Nothing helps, not even being in therapy." Anger bubbled up in my gut. Bardwin should have done something for Nicky—before it was too late.

Diamond bent a chunky knee until it crackled like a wishbone. "You're right. Therapy is no guarantee. Neither is my pointing out risky cases. There are no guarantees, Sarah Spooner. So I guess we should all go home and stick our heads in the sandbox until we put down a nice set of roots."

"That's not what I meant."

He popped several licorice bears in his mouth. "I know it isn't." Leaning over the desk, he tapped the piled folders in a neat stack and pressed a yellow bear more firmly in place. "I could use some breakfast, Sarah Spooner. How about you?"

Downstairs, a slim young man with oily brown hair and a pitted complexion had replaced Miss Personality behind the desk. He directed us to the dining room, set at the end of a long, lush-carpeted corridor punctuated by wooden-bladed ceiling fans and oversize parlor palms in huge wicker pots. A tall woman with curious eyes and a permanent, tight-lipped smile plucked two menus from a bronze holder and led us through the dim, deserted main room to a table on the terrace overlooking a golf course and a graceful pond.

Diamond ordered in the commanding voice he reserved for food issues: a three-egg omelet, griddle cakes with raspberry syrup, Belgian waffles, raisin muffins and apple butter, strawberries and heavy cream, cranberry juice.

My meager appetite dissolved as he ordered, as if filled with his words. "Just coffee for me. Black."

Diamond frowned. "You eat like a bird, Sarah Spooner. Why don't we get you a nice little bowl of seed and gravel to start the day? Heh, heh. That's what I always told my wife."

"Wife?" Hard to imagine. I could picture Diamond at the helm of a troop of Eagle scouts or locked in a neurotic relationship with a domineering mother. But a wife?

His face closed like an automatic door. "I'd rather not talk about it, if you don't mind."

Odd. It never crossed my mind that Diamond might be a real, multifaceted person equipped with pain and secrets. But then, my mind was too full of self-pity to accept other people's realities. "I'm sorry."

The food arrived, and I fell into a gentle trance, hypnotized by the pleasured rhythm of Diamond's eating. He was the liveried guard at the castle door, scrutinizing each culinary visitor in turn and preparing each for the regal presence. The griddle cakes were carved in perfect triangles and crowned with raspberry tiaras. The waffle was divided into syrupy coins and delivered to the royal storeroom atop a fluffy egg carpet. Neat muffin slices were festooned with brown butter and chased back with a swallow of cranberry cocktail. The strawberries, hulled and dissected, were twirled in the sweetened cream and made to disappear in a gesture worthy of a court magician. The performance was exhausting.

"So," he said at last, capturing an errant raisin from the rim of his plate, "what's on the docket for today?"

I shrugged. After last night's unpleasant surprises I began to doubt if I could see this through. "I'm pretty tired."

He swigged the last of his cranberry juice and motioned for the check. "You going to your son's apartment? That should probably be next on your list."

I resisted his impeccable guidance. "I don't know, Mr. Diamond. Nicky only lived there for a couple of months before. . . . He moved in with a Mike somebody after his last roommate transferred out of Cromwell. I doubt if I'll find out much from talking to him."

His smile was tolerant. "I guess you're right. How much can you learn about a person after living with them for only a couple of months? What's sixty days? Sixty nights? You wake up, eat, study, hang out with a person for a couple of months, and you probably don't even know their name for sure."

"I intend to see this Mike person. I'm just not sure if I'll go today."

He clucked his tongue. "Right. Wouldn't want to see you rush into anything, Sarah Spooner. Maybe if you wait another day or so, Mike will be gone for the summer and you won't have to hear anything unpleasant."

"Maybe."

"So that's why you came all this way? To hide?"

Diamond's face was a warm, satisfied pink, his expression inscrutable. "I'm not planning to hide, Mr. Diamond. There's too much at stake."

He scrawled a broad squiggle on the check and scraped his chair back along the wooden terrace planks. "You're sure about that, Sarah Spooner. There is a lot at stake. A whole lot."

I followed him back through the dining room and out to the hotel lobby. The doves were fast asleep, curled in on themselves like feathery snowballs. Behind the desk, the pockmarked boy was talking on the house phone. Two guests sat on twin flowered sofas, reading sections of the local paper. I raced to keep up with Diamond, who was ambling in double time. "Where are you off to in such a hurry?"

"Can't put off what has to be done. I have some unpleasant business to get over with myself. Same as you. You need a lift to your boy's apartment?"

"No, it's not far," I lied. Parrish Common was set squarely in the heart of downtown noplace. I had no idea how far it was to Nicky's new apartment on West Highland Avenue. But I needed to get there on my own. And I could use the time on the way to recharge my failing courage.

"Whatever you say, Sarah Spooner. All I'd suggest is you try not to get in your own way." He shoved three thick fingers into the crystal candy dish on the front desk and filled his mouth with sour balls. "Go see that Mike person. You never know."

I watched him scurry across the parking lot to the Lincoln and brush the morning mist off the tinted windshield with his sleeve. Folding his girth behind the wheel, he backed out and away from the hotel parking lot.

I set out at a walk down the shaded drive leading out of the Barrington Arms and into Parrish Common. The somnolent street was caught in a chill silence. I lengthened my stride and kept my gaze forward, trying to ignore the strange sense of menace that pursued me down the narrow mews. Nervous lights still flickered in the electrified gas lamps, and I caught the stale smell of a spent hickory fire.

With relief I turned onto the main campus road and tried to judge the shortest route to West Highland. Unpleasant business to get over with. I hoped it was nothing worse than that.

-9-

West Highland Avenue lay across the manicured campus in a pocket of spent elegance known as the Homestead. Large colonial houses, once home to champions of Cromwell commerce and industry, now served as school-year residences for motley bands of students and the most frugal faculty. Nicky's apartment was in a battleship-gray three-story house complete with all the off-campus amenities: peeling paint, missing shutters, and warped wooden steps rising to a dilapidated veranda. An odd array of makeshift mailboxes were nailed beside the front door—everything from wicker bicycle baskets to an old black leather purse. I arrived breathless and dripping perspiration from my brisk jog through the main quadrangle.

Climbing to the third floor, I was taken by the whimsical patchwork look of the place. The doors were painted in a show of individual mood: brilliant primaries, oversize blue dots on a crimson ground, rainbow stripes. One hallway boasted a childish mural depicting crude,

stump-legged people picketing some unnamed social in-
justice. Another was crowded with pilfered street signs.
All silly foolishness. Why didn't Nicky see it that way?

Outside the apartment door marked "N. Spooner, M.
Erdman," I brushed the rivulets of sweat from my forehead and took a minute to catch my breath. Pressing the
button, I half hoped this Mike person would be out.

"Yes?" A diminutive, dark-skinned girl with silken
ebony hair and wide almond eyes answered the door.
Her fine features were drawn in a frown—half leftover
sleep, half confusion. "Can I help you?"

"I'm sorry if I woke you. I'm looking for Mike Erdman."

"I'm Mike. Michelle, that is. And you are?"

"You can't be Mike. Nicky never said . . ."

Puddles of feeling collected under her eyes and she
bit her lip. "You must be Mrs. Spooner. Nicholas spoke
of you often. Come in, please."

She wore a man's white shirt and slim faded jeans.
Tiny, I thought. A tiny wisp of a girl. Were she and
Nicky . . . ?

"Sit down, Mrs. Spooner. Would you like something?
Some tea?"

Her delicate fingers fluttered as she talked. There was
something vaguely Oriental about her—just enough to
give my mother palpitations, I thought, without the ac-
tual heart attack. "No, nothing. You're . . . Mike?"

Her laugh was a gentle trill. "I gather I am not what
you expected, Mrs. Spooner. Nicholas was reluctant to

tell you about me. I think he felt you might not approve.''

"You were . . . living together? You and Nicky?''

"Yes. We were living together. He didn't say anything because he assumed you would object to me, to our relationship. Sometimes it is easier for a son to practice a bit of innocent deception. Nicholas was careful to step around other people's feelings whenever he could.''

My eyes were fixed on her, glued to this impossible twist of events. "You and Nick were . . . lovers?'' The word stuck in my throat like a bone.

"Yes.''

Lovers. The word flapped around my mind, unconnected to any form or logic. "For how long?''

"We were together for . . . almost a year. It was a drifting together, Mrs. Spooner. For many months we refused to see the strands of attachment knitting us into one piece. When we made the discovery—that we were connected, I mean—we were already married in a way.''

"Married?''

She laughed again. "Not literally married. I mean bound together, a unit.''

My mind skidded over the icy hazards. "Did you know how unhappy he was, Michelle? Did you know he was depressed?''

"Depressed.'' From her lips it sounded like a soft, harmless breeze. She looked around the apartment as if she were seeing it for the first time: brick-and-plank bookcases, draped mattresses propped to mimic sofas and chairs, an old door set on sawhorses for a cocktail table. She sighed. "In a way Nicholas was a sort of living mummy, Mrs. Spooner. There were layers of him wrapped in other layers, and still other layers inside. He would allow little hints of himself, small fragments, to pass through. No more."

"So you didn't know? You were as shocked as I was?"

She sat on the floor, crossed her sparrow legs in a perfect lotus, and stared at the rag rug. "No, Mrs. Spooner. I was not shocked. Saddened, terribly saddened, but not shocked."

"But why? Why would he do such a thing?" I was crumpling in on myself like a used paper bag. "Why, Nicky?" The pain came in a flood. There I sat on a worn plaid bedspread in the presence of my son's lover, bawling like a wounded infant. She came and sat beside me, her fingers tracing vague circles on my heaving back.

"I know, Mrs. Spooner. It's okay."

We sat that way for what seemed to be hours. Slowly I found the shredded remains of my lost control, and the crying muted first to a slow whimper then to syncopated pulses of grief. "I'm sorry . . . I'm so embarrassed."

"No. We both loved Nicholas. It's right for us to cry together."

She took me by the hand like a helpless child, handed me a damp cloth to wipe my eyes, and seated me at the tiny, round kitchen table. The tea was fragrant chamomile sweetened with honey. She buttered a thick slice of warm wheat bread and ordered me to eat. "It was hard not to love him, Mrs. Spooner. Believe me, I tried. Nicholas was not easy."

Odd, beautiful girl. "Were things okay between you? Did you two have a fight?"

"Many. We fought over everything. Was it better to breathe in or out? Was I shorter or was he taller? Which side of the world was up? And was it possible there was no up side at all? We agreed on nothing. I suppose that was part of the attraction."

My hand was trembling. "I . . . I hate to ask this, but I need to know, Michelle. Could Nicky have been depressed because of the fighting? Because you two didn't get along?" I held my breath, wanting and not wanting her to say yes.

She stared at me as if I were some difficult puzzle. "I did not kill Nicholas, Mrs. Spooner. He killed himself."

"No, I didn't mean—"

She held up a hand. "I know you didn't. And I think I know what you are searching for. I, too, wanted to understand why he would do this terrible thing to himself—and to the people who loved him. I still try to understand. At times I can hardly believe it is true."

My mind raced up another leg of the maze. "There has to be a reason, some explanation for Nicky's death . . . Could it be that maybe he was . . ."

"Murdered? It crossed my mind." She rose and refilled her flowered cup with steaming water. "But I let it go. Where is the logic, Mrs. Spooner? I can't imagine why anyone would want to kill Nicholas. He was a gentle, frightened, harmless person.''

"But it is possible," I persisted. "I've worked on murder cases at the D.A.'s office, and you wouldn't believe the crazy motives. He could have been caught in the middle of something that had no connection to him at all.''

"At first I wanted to think this was something beyond his control, that he did not do this dreadful, stupid thing to himself. But I don't believe it any longer. Nicholas killed himself, Mrs. Spooner. We have to find the way from there. My way is to start again. I am leaving Cromwell tomorrow. Transferring. In fact, it is good you came now, a happy coincidence. Many of Nick's things are still here. I was planning to put together a package to send to you, but now that won't be necessary. You may take whatever you want. All of it.''

I sipped my tea, not ready to change the subject. "What if . . . let's say Nicky caught someone cheating from his test paper and threatened to report the incident.''

She frowned. "Given Nicholas's casual attitude toward his studies, I hardly think he would be the target of a cheat, desperate or otherwise. The only time I ever saw him expend any effort was on his writing. He had talent, as I'm sure you know. And the passion to shape that talent.''

More surprises. "Writing? In high school, getting him to finish a term paper was like pulling teeth.''

"I don't mean that sort of writing. Nicholas showed considerable ability in creative areas—personal reflection essays, short stories. One of his English professors talked of having some of his work published. Before . . ."

"It's so strange. The more I find out, the less I understand. He was my son. How could there be so many things I didn't know about him?"

"A child becomes a separate person. I imagine that must be very difficult for a parent to accept."

Tiny, wise woman-child. Serene and strong. As delicate as a Dresden doll. Graceful. "In a way it is difficult. . . . When Nick was a baby, I loved to watch him. Just sit and watch all the miraculous things he could do: stretch, yawn, make funny rubber faces. He was reminding me how the world could be discovered a piece at a time, leading me through all the brilliant, simple truths I had learned to overlook. Then, one day when he wasn't even two years old, he announced something he had learned without me, when I wasn't looking. I can't even remember what it was anymore, but I felt this tremendous sense of loss. He was beginning to leave me behind, to create his own world. I suppose a child's first obligation is to become a stranger to his parents."

"Would you like to see Nicholas's writing? You may find some of what you are looking for."

"Yes. I guess so." The thought made me shiver. I was not at all certain what it was I was looking for, and even less certain what I would do if I found it.

She carried one of the painted ladder-back chairs from the kitchen table and set it inside the door of a closet crammed with clothing, books, and papers. Nicky's things and hers jumbled together in a carefree, crowded heap. With feline grace she climbed on the chair and retrieved a thick stack of colored files.

Back at the table, she thumbed through the pile and extracted a folder marked "English" in Nick's round, fluid handwriting. "This cannot be," she said. "There's nothing here."

"Maybe in one of the others?" I felt relieved in a way; the truth was safely lost where it could not threaten my comforting illusions.

She cast her delicate fingers into each folder in turn. "No, nothing. I know it was here, Mrs. Spooner. Nicholas was very careful with his writing."

"When did you see it last?"

She kept looking in the folder as if she could make the papers appear. A shrill edge crept into her voice. "Not since before the suicide. I haven't been able to look at his work. Not yet. But I'm sure it was here. The only time Nicholas removed his papers from the folder was to show them to his professor."

"Then maybe the professor still has them," I said soothingly. How lovely to be the sane one. "Which professor was it? I'll go see him."

She sighed and bit her lip. "I'm not certain. One of his English professors. You know how Nicholas invented names for people? Dr. Tooth, the dentist; Mr.

John Fixer, the plumber. He was taking several English courses. I remember him speaking of someone he dubbed Milton Dickens Swift, who taught British literature; another he called Huckleberry Schwartz, an ethnic Twain buff; and his Shakespeare professor, known to Nicholas as 'Rose,' because he claimed he would still smell by any other name.''

I could see Nicky standing at his imaginary podium, decimating the entire English department with a single round fired from the muzzle of his automatic wit. "Which one talked about submitting his work for publication?''

She released a tremulous sigh. "I don't know, Mrs. Spooner. He didn't say.''

"Don't worry, Michelle. I'll find out. I'm going to get all the answers. That's why I'm here.''

She set the cups in the tiny, chipped porcelain sink and wiped the table with a sponge. When she looked up, I could feel the frost that had settled over her. "First, Mrs. Spooner, you must be certain you have all the questions.''

A dense heat had blanketed the day. Tar fumes rose from the pavement and hovered in the shimmering air like a swarm of determined insects. My head ached, and a stonelike laziness crept up my legs.

The Barrington Arms seemed a lifetime away. I set out at an optimistic jog that faded in a breath to the plodding shuffle of a bed-worn convalescent. Why hurry? I was moving in slow, useless circles like a fat honeybee buzzing over a plastic plant. My life was reduced to false starts and impossible endings.

Damn you, Nicky. Damn you for doing this to me.

-10-

"Hello. May I speak with Ben Spooner? This is his wife."

"He's not in, Mrs. Spooner. You know how busy he is. I don't expect him for the rest of the day."

For no extra charge my husband's secretary was willing to perform rebuking services. Remarkable in this age of reluctant help. "Didn't he leave a number? It's important that I speak with him."

Deep, disgusted sigh. "I'm sorry, Mrs. Spooner. He's on the road, in and out of meetings all day. You know how it is. If you tell me where you can be reached, I'll ask him to call you when he gets a chance."

"No. Don't bother. I'll try him later at home."

Diamond was still out. The suite was crisp with conditioned air and a soft, artificial breeze from the broad-bladed ceiling fan.

I lay back on the cool comforter, allowing my sweat and frustration to evaporate in the silence. How lovely to drift outside myself where the weight of my own helpless foolishness had no meaning at all.

Mike Michelle Loveliness Petite placed a slim, soothing hand on my forehead. Mike. Nicky's lover. The word danced on my tongue. Nicky and Mike, Mickey and Nike—odd little playground chant with no sense or meaning.

Nicky's lover. I tried and tried not to picture them together, locked in the breathless pleasure of youthful passion, the slim, young bodies straining to escape their separate bounds and blend together in a fluid whole.

My mother appeared and clicked her tongue. "You think this is the girl for Nicky, Sarah? Where does a girl like that come to a boy like Nicky? She doesn't compare, Sarah. Let's face it. He's head and shoulders above her. I don't like to say it, sweetheart. But I bet she's after him for his money. . . ."

Bodies. Ben's and mine, twisted in a familiar knot. I saw Ben's serious love face and felt the seeking pull of his familiar urges. With the ease of years he played me like a pinball machine until my head floated above my contented body on a raft of pleasure.

Ben.

But where was Nicky's face? Struggling back up to reality, I felt the sick horror of loss. I couldn't find my son's face, could not remember the look of him. The memory was wiped away, leaving a raw, empty wound in my mind.

Try, Sarah. Try to picture the unruly halo of curly hair, the twin cowlicks sticking up from the sides of his head like devil's horns. Remember when Nicky was a little boy and Ben always teased about his hair?

There he is in the kitchen, rubbing the itch of sleep from his eyes. And there's Ben at the table, taking tentative sips from a cup of sweet, scalding coffee. "Well, look who we have here, Little Satan Spooner. Now there's a surprise. Sar, did you know the devil wore Dr. Denton's to sleep?" I could picture the delighted mischief creeping up behind Nick's expression as he curled his slim fingers into mock claws and growled his high-pitched devil growl.

The chin. A strong, square, near imitation of his father's that trembled when he had his fill of fear or disappointment. How well I thought I knew the little boy behind that tremulous chin. The rules were so clear and definite then: how tightly shut the closet door had to be to keep the monsters safely inside; how open I had to leave the door to his room to test but not strain his bravery; which demons frightened him the most and how to hug them away. Always the same routine, every night for a million nights. "Good night, Nickel Pickle Gooner Spooner Molloy. Sleep the tightest tight there ever was."

" 'Night, Mommy. See you in the morning."

"First thing."

"First thing, you promise?"

"Before I'm even awake. I promise." And I would pull the covers up under that smooth, square little chin and touch my lips to the velvet forehead.

Nicky.

Diamond's knock brought me back. "You in there, Sarah Spooner?"

"Yes."

"You decent?"

Decent. "Sure, come in."

Diamond looked a fright, his hair disheveled, one shirttail hanging over his belt like a flag of surrender. "You want to go out for something? A bite to eat?" He plucked a Heath bar from his deep front pocket, peeled it, and seemed to suck it into the giant vacuum tube of his appetite.

"Is something wrong? You look upset."

He waved the thought away. "Me? I'm fine. I could just use something to eat. You want to go out?"

All the meals were blending together, making me sick at the notion of food. I was even beginning to dislike flatware and china. "I'm really not hungry. Not right now. How about a nice long walk?"

He looked as if I'd suggested something illegal. "It's hot out there. How about a ride? Good air-conditioning in that car. The finest." Digging in his deep front pocket, he extracted a Hershey bar with almonds, inhaled the contents, tossed the wrapper in the wastebasket, and moved on to a Chunky.

"All right." I checked my watch. The day had dissolved. Allison would be home from school by now and I felt a sudden pang of guilt. Was I overlooking my daughter? Was Ben right that I was a onetime maternal failure about to go for the daily double? "Just let me call home first."

He left the room, chewing faster than he walked. I heard the crinkle of candy wrappers and his nervous muttering through the closed door. Dialing my house, I realized how far I had moved from any semblance of a normal life.

The phone rang at the other end—a relentless bleat . . . bleat. I let it sound for some time in the emptiness. Nothing. No one home.

"Okay, Mr. Diamond. We can go for that ride now."

I found him pacing the front room, shaking his head as if arguing with some invisible adversary. For an instant he seemed not to know who I was.

"You okay?"

"Fine, Sarah Spooner. I'm just dandy."

He drove like someone pursued. We were out of Parrish Common in a harrowing blink and riding in aimless circles through the main Cromwell thoroughfares. Crowds of proud parents were shepherding their reluctant graduates on shopping expeditions through the trendiest downtown boutiques. Others, unaccustomed to the whimsical fits and starts of college-town traffic, pressed their outrage on their horns until the area sounded like a convention of mournful sheep.

Diamond's mouth was in perpetual motion, lips moving in silent argument or working over some confection plucked from the bottomless pit of his pocket. "Are you sure you're all right, Mr. Diamond? You don't seem like yourself.''

He turned to me in a start, nearly hitting the car in front of us in the process. ''Really? No, nothing wrong. Nothing at all. I'm fine. Don't you worry, Sarah Spooner. Everything's going to work out. You'll see.''

''Exactly what is there to work out? Exactly what is going on? You said you'd keep me informed.''

He tried to sound offhanded, but there was a shrill edge of hysteria in his tone. ''Well, sure I will, when there's something to tell. But there's nothing worth reporting yet. You know, I bet I'm just out of sorts from working too hard. That must be it. All-work-and-no-play syndrome. You play tennis, Sarah Spooner?''

''No.''

''Me neither.''

He drove around and around until my head started to ache. ''Mr. Diamond, why don't we go get something to eat, after all.'' Anything had to be better than circling the wagons until the Indians died of boredom.

He allowed a pinched smile in my direction and slipped into a tight parking space in the crowded municipal lot. ''There's a terrific little English pub in the Cromwell Sheraton. They have the best Yorkshire pudding you ever tasted. And a decent blueberry trifle. Decent. Nothing to write home about.''

''How's the roast beef?''

He made a face. ''I told you, I don't like eating meat, Sarah Spooner. Something so . . . primitive about it. You eat macaroni and you never have to think about some sweet, dumb, four-legged wide-eyed macaroni being fattened up and driven to slaughter just so you can have a meal. Macaroni doesn't have a mother or any love life to speak of. I can eat without picturing little macaroni orphans or money-grubbing macaroni farmers willing to forcefeed poor little penned-up macaronis for profit. Eating macaroni becomes almost a moral obligation when you think about it. The same for Yorkshire pudding.''

The maître d' accosted us at the entrance. He was a coat hanger of a man, so slim that his tuxedo hung from his shoulders like a table drape. ''I am sorry, sir. But we insist on jackets for the gentlemen.'' He pointed at a sign that read, PROPER ATTIRE.

Diamond shrugged. ''You have one I can borrow?''

Frowning a doubtful frown, the hanger disappeared into the coatroom and emerged with a long-sleeved horse blanket. ''The largest we have, I'm afraid.''

Diamond managed to wedge his bulk inside the oversize plaid. I tried not to laugh. And I hoped the other diners wouldn't assume he was the entertainment.

As soon as we were seated, he began drumming his porky fingers on the glass slab covering the lavender linen cloth. The table shook with the rhythmic force of his nervousness. His face was lost in a fog of distraction as he chain-gobbled buttered breadsticks.

''Please, Mr. Diamond, tell me what's troubling you. Maybe I can help.''

"What? Oh, no, Sarah Spooner. You stay away. Far away if you have any sense. You don't need any of this aggravation. Believe me." He bit his lip.

"I can't, Mr. Diamond. I came here for some answers. If you're on to something, I have to know. Please."

He pinched a breadstick between his fingers like a cigar.

"This has nothing to do with you . . . with your problems. You don't want to take on extra worries, Sarah Spooner. Makes no sense. None at all."

He ordered two servings of Yorkshire pudding, a trio of baked, stuffed potatoes, and a large, baked butternut squash with brown sugar and a maple-syrup glaze. While he ate, shoveling in the creamy carbohydrates with a determined spoon and a showy flick of the wrist, my anxiety climbed like a child's fever.

If Diamond found something about the suicides, it had to have some bearing on Nicky—on Nicky's death. But what could it be? He was disturbed enough at the number of unstable psyches in the Cromwell student application pool. Could there be something more? Something worse?

"Mr. Diamond. I must know what's going on. How else can I finally figure out what happened to my son? You yourself said I shouldn't try to piece the puzzle together until I had all the information. And here you are, keeping something from me." I was pleased at the even, sane lilt in my voice. "I need to know."

He tore his gaze from the vast, bumpy landscape of Yorkshire pudding and stared at me. "Look, Sarah Spooner. I'm not a bad guy, am I? If this was something

for you, I'd tell you. I'd be the first to tell you everything . . . if it had any bearing on your son at all.''

There was sincerity in his eyes. And a desperate
pleading. ''All right. I guess you would. You know how
important this is to me. I'm sure you would tell me what
was going on if it had anything at all—no matter how
farfetched or difficult to hear—to do with the suicides.
Wouldn't you?''

''Of course. Of course, I would. You can count on it,
Sarah Spooner. I'll always make it my business to do
what's best.''

''I'm sure you try, Mr. Diamond.''

I watched him eat, mesmerized by his total absorption
with the act. Each bite seemed to carry him a comforting
step away from reality. If only I could join him in his
wonderland. Too much was happening. There were too
many new fragments of truth to step over, too many
question marks. And through it all I was more alone than
I had ever been, so alone that I thought I could disappear
and leave no empty spot in the universe.

His plate was nearly empty. He slowed, savoring
every morsel. I waited until the last of the Yorkshire
pudding had disappeared. ''Diamond,'' I whispered, ''is
it about the suicides?''

He wiped his mouth with great deliberation and set
his napkin beside his denuded plate. With a grand
sweeping gesture he motioned for the check. And then,
turning half away so I might not notice, he put a finger
to his eye and wiped away a tear.

-11-

I forced myself to think beyond the storms and secrets of Cromwell and tried calling home again. My mother sounded breathless, as if she had just done some very strenuous shopping. "So, it's the prodigal daughter. Nice of you to think of us, dear."

"I've been calling all day, Mother. No one was home."

"Oh? Well, you certainly can't expect a mature, sophisticated, important lady like your daughter to spend her time with a miserable, stone-age old grandma like me, can you? I swear, Sarah, someone should give that child a good talking-to. Someone should help her right down off that high horse of hers."

"Let me speak to her."

"You want to speak to Princess Allison? I'm sorry, dear, but you'll have to make an appointment with her secretary. Allison Spooner is entirely too important to speak to every Tessie, Dolores, and Hortense who calls."

"Please, Mother. It's been a long day."

"Oh? And mine has had fewer hours than yours, I suppose? You think it's a picnic taking care of a fresh mouth? Well, it's not, I have to tell you, Sarah. She's up in her room with some girl who has hair like a porcupine and so many holes in her ears, you could put her right in one of those loose-leaf binders. I said to her, 'Darling, what kind of a friend is that for a nice little girl like you?' but she didn't even answer me, Sarah. What's gotten into that child?"

"Let me speak to her, Mother."

"I'll try, Sarah. But I'm not making any promises. I don't know what's with that girl. You know what she said to me? 'Don't make a big deal, Grandma.' Is that the way for a girl to talk to an old woman?"

"Hi, Mom."

"Hi, sweetie. Is everything okay? Are you okay?"

"Fine, sure. Gram thinks I'm the scarlet woman or something, but no big deal. You managed to live with her for all those years. I guess I can handle a week or two."

"Thanks. I appreciate it."

"No big deal. Have you . . . found anything?"

"Not yet, but I'm working on it. I'll let you know as soon as I have anything to report."

"Is everything all right? You sound a little funny."

The child knew me too well. "Just tired, I guess. Is Daddy home?"

My mother was back on the line. "Ben? You mean that man you married? Hang up, Allison. It's not nice to listen in." Her voice dropped to a whisper. "I'll be honest, Sarah. I haven't seen him since you left except two days ago when he stopped in for two minutes to pick up a couple of clean shirts. For all I know he could be sick—or worse. He doesn't even call to see how everybody is. Ben used to be such a nice boy, Sarah. What's happening to everybody?"

"He's probably been called out on the road, Mother. He travels a lot. It's part of his job. You know that."

"Call it what you will, Sarah. You leave an attractive, charming man like Ben alone and you can't expect him to just wait around for you to come back. If he finds someone else, don't come crying to me. You'll have no one to blame but yourself."

"Please ask him to call me if you hear from him. It's important. . . . I forgot to ask Ali about school. Has she been studying for her finals?"

"Do I know?"

"Good-bye, Mother."

Her words lay on me like a stone. Where was Ben? The last thing I needed now or ever was a replay of his brief, but classical, fall from grace. The whole thing, had it happened to someone else, would have seemed like a trite little plot for a soap opera: She was an office temp with blazing black eyes and a "come-hither" build who could type eighty words a minute with one hand otherwise occupied. He was the vulnerable (though ever well-intentioned) victim of an unruly mind and a willful body. The attraction was instant, intense, and meaningless— like strong, hot, decaffeinated coffee, I supposed. It was over, he assured me, almost before it began. But I had to know about it in great, gory detail to salve the poor man's beleaguered conscience. Bad enough he had to deal with the fragrant, juicy, lascivious, fleshy memories without having to put up with all that messy guilt.

So I listened. And when he was done with it, I tried to be done with it as well. Really I tried. But for months I could hardly think of anything else. Ben and little Miss Rapid Temp with the excellent "skills" would writhe into my mind at the most inconvenient moments—in the middle of a difficult summation, during a heated conference with my boss. They would appear in my mind's eye, grunting and slurping and hyperventilating at each other, making it very difficult for me to concentrate on such trifling matters as serial murder or child molestation.

The last thing I needed was for Ben to toss me that kind of boulder when I was treading for my life.

I couldn't even think about that possibility. There were enough wrong, troubling things to deal with right here.

Diamond had spent the whole evening pacing the front room. Long after I turned off my light I could hear his feet slapping their anxieties against the floorboards. Later I awoke to the thunder-hush of his snoring, mingled with the plaintive sleep moans of someone pursued

by devilish dreams. However hard he tried to deny it, I
was sure Diamond knew things he was not willing to
tell me. Terrible things.

As soon as the first fingers of light crept through the
shuttered windows, I gave up trying to sleep and tiptoed
out past Diamond's thrashing, unconscious body. I was
driven by a growing sense of urgency. What he refused
to tell me, I would have to find out for myself. Cromwell's dark secrets had to be linked in some way to
Nicky's death. I could feel that as the one certainty holding together the shreds of my sanity. All of it was connected: the suicides; the missing papers; Diamond's
increasing agitation over some hideous knowledge he
would not reveal.

The campus was still shrouded in damp morning stillness. A pair of disheveled students tossed a Frisbee
across the lawn. Another pair lay as still as bookends on
an old Army blanket, recuperating from an overdose of
revelry. I was nearly upended by a hunched, tight-lipped
biker, whizzing too close as he passed me on a ten-speed
Schwinn.

"Pardon me," I said.

He glared as if I had some nerve standing where he
might wish to ride, and whizzed off in a righteous huff.

The English department was housed in Greenville-
Day Hall, an imposing, ivied brick building with stern
little windows and a copper roof gone green with age. I
entered a front hall redolent of mildew and the stubborn,
nervous scent of students beleaguered by exams. "It's

so ridiculous, Mom," Nick always said. "They make you sit on a little wooden seat and write in a little blue book. Then they look at the little blue book and decide if you've been bad or good. Like Santa Claus, I guess. Only, if you've been a bad little boy, you get a bad letter on your transcript instead of a lump of coal in your stocking."

"It's the system, Nick. For better or worse, you're a part of it. Why not make the best of the situation?"

"It's not as simple as that."

Even as a little child, he hated being told what to do. Nick was never one to perform in the name of approval. His drummer had a particular offbeat only Nicky could hear. Some called it original, others eccentric. I, in typical mother fashion, called it individuality and thought it gave my son a particular shield against the pain others might try to inflict. I guess mothers were invented to insure the world a steady supply of purblind fools.

The glassed directory was blank. Classes had ended the week before exams, and the summer session would not begin for another two weeks. In between, I supposed, professors did something professorial like dusting their reference books or arranging their lives in alphabetical order. I walked the empty corridors, wondering what to do next.

"Might I be of service?"

The voice came from a disembodied head poking out from an open office door halfway down the hall. "I'm looking for an English professor . . . I'm not sure about the name.''

He chuckled. ''You have come to the right place, madam. We have English professors of every form and feature you might imagine . . . and some entirely beyond human imagining altogether.''

As he stepped out into the corridor I recognized him as the mad biker who had nearly run me down. He seemed not to remember. ''My name is Sarah Spooner. My son, Nicholas, was an English major. I'm trying to locate the professor who might have some of his papers.''

His face crumpled, and he stepped forward to sandwich my hand between his sympathetic pair. ''Ah, yes. You poor, dear lady. The loss of a child, a tragedy of incalculable proportions. I am truly, truly sorry. Please accept my heartfelt sympathies.''

''You knew Nicky?''

He stiffened and ran a self-conscious hand over the shiny surface of his scalp. ''Not well, I regret to say. Such a large department, you know. English is Cromwell's most popular major. Nearly one thousand students in all, over a hundred in honors alone. Not to mention all the youngsters who enroll in our survey courses and electives. Staggering, as you might imagine. Still, I do make an effort to meet as many as I can. Your son was not, as we say, one of our more involved young people.''

''I know.''

He slapped a hand over his mouth. "Do forgive me. That was a terribly tactless remark. I certainly didn't mean it as a criticism. I only meant—"

"Not important, Professor . . ."

"Miles." He stuck his hand out like a tollgate. "Hardy Steppington Miles."

Milton Dickens Swift. "You're the one who teaches British literature?"

"Yes. How did you know?"

I shrugged. "Just a lucky guess."

He clapped his hands together. "So. How might I help you? We all felt terrible about your Nicholas, of course. Terrible tragedy. And the others. So many from our department . . ."

"Really?"

"Ah, yes. Didn't you hear? The whole campus was abuzz with the dire statistics. Seven of this year's suicides were from the English department. We were the butt of some rather perverse humor, as you might imagine. And some rather uncomfortable scrutiny."

He led me into his office as he talked—a charmless cubicle crammed with books, papers, and wall-to-wall files. Tossing a stack of notebooks on the floor, he motioned me to sit on a green-webbed lawn chair in the corner.

"Seven from one department does seem like an awful lot."

"Now, now. There you go jumping to conclusions like everyone else. Keep in mind, madam, that we are the largest department on the campus. Our students tend to have keen, inquisitive minds and a sort of restless intelligence that can generate the best, or the worst, reactions. It's only logical.''

''Maybe there was too much pressure in the program. Too many demands—''

He smashed a fist against his littered desk, startling me. ''Nonsense! Are these students here to be pampered or to learn? Pressure is the spark that ignites the fires of intellectual hunger.''

''That's fine for those who are up to it. What about the kids who aren't?''

''Our job is to teach an appreciation and understanding of our magnificent language, Mrs . . . uh . . .''

''Spooner.''

''Spooner, of course. As I was saying, our job is to foster literary ambition and the furtherance of the full range of skills, from technical communications to belles-lettres. We are not mental health professionals. And we certainly can't be expected to function as surrogate nannies.''

My rage boiled over. ''And that's it? That's all you have to say on the subject? Too bad if beautiful, young lives are thrown away like so much garbage? Too bad if your so-called job leads to seven wasted lives?'' This man was not just a pompous jerk. He was a dangerous, pompous jerk.

He watched me rant and blinked his beady eyes at me as if I had just touched down from another planet. When

I finished, he straightened his bow tie and ran a hand over his cheek as if to make sure all was still in place. "I can understand your dismay, Mrs. Spooner. Your son's death . . . all the deaths . . . have been tragic. Just terrible."

The storm was waning. "Then how can you sit there and tell me you have no responsibility? How can you live with the knowledge that your program was so crazily demanding it led children to kill themselves?"

He cocked his head like a curious dog and peered into my eyes. "Tell me, Mrs. Spooner. Did you hear your own words just then? I have entirely too much faith in the human spirit and the mortal imperative for survival to believe that anyone would commit suicide over a heavy reading list or too many term papers. Does that make sense to you?"

"None of it makes sense."

He dug a box of tissues from the rubble on his desk and held one forth as a peace offering. "I wish it were that simple. We make our courses easier and the suicides stop. But I'm afraid that would be no solution."

"Then what is? Are you trying to tell me you just allow it to keep happening?"

Leaning back in his chair, he blew a noisy stream of air. "We still have much to learn, I'm afraid. I assure you we are all putting forth our best efforts to achieve an understanding and a prompt resolution of these terrible events."

"Look, Dr. Miles. You may be trying. But trying is hardly enough when lives are at stake."

"Yes, true. Of course, I do see your position. The whole issue is most perplexing." He looked around the office as if he suddenly noticed something missing. "Well, then . . ." Abruptly he stood, cleared his throat, and emptied his face of all expression. "Please do accept my sympathies, Mrs. Spooner. All of us in the English department share your concerns and your grief. If there is any way I can be of personal service, any way at all, please don't hesitate to call on me. I do understand what you must be going through."

No, you don't, you arrogant creep. You have no idea. Not unless you've ever lost a child. Why is it that people who see you drowning insist on jumping into the water with you and pretend to drown along?

"There is one thing, the reason I came to the English department. Nick's . . . friend told me one of his English professors was considering having some of his work published. She can't find his papers in the apartment, so we assume that the professor, whoever it is, has them. Do you know anything about that, Dr. Miles?"

He stiffened and looked away. Eyes skyward, he hummed for a moment in reflection. "No, I can't recall any talk of publishing your son's work. Of course, so many of our students have the misguided notion that having works published is a simple matter. They haven't the slightest idea how difficult it is to be accepted in print. One of the major professional challenges, I assure you. I can't tell you how often one student or another assumes his work is worthy of such recognition. It is rare, mind you, Mrs. Spooner. Very rare indeed that a mere student displays that level of skill and development.''

"I'm only telling you what I heard from his friend. I'm sure she wouldn't invent such a story. And neither would Nick.''

He shook his head. "Very rare indeed, though it is a common delusion.'' He reddened and twisted his lips in an apologetic grimace. "There I go again. Please, Mrs. Spooner, I didn't mean to imply that your son . . . If he said it was so, I would not doubt his veracity for an instant. Perhaps there was some misunderstanding. Then, quite possibly, he was one of those rare exceptions—a student with precocious literary talent, though a rather uninvolved student, as I mentioned. Anything is possible. I am certainly not privy to every bit of departmental intelligence. That would be rather difficult, as you might imagine—what with one thousand majors, one hundred in honors alone . . .''

"Yes, I guess it would. Would you happen to know where I might find the professor who teaches the Shakespeare course for majors? Or the one who teaches Twain?''

"There, now. At last a request I can fulfill. Dr. Goldenberg, who teaches Twain, is out of town undergoing medical treatment. Poor old fellow is feeling the weight of his years, I'm afraid. A heart condition. He's had several attacks in recent years. As far as I know, he should return by midweek.

"Dr. Lawrence, who not only teaches the Bard but lives, breathes, eats, and, I suspect, sleeps Shakespeare, is available. In fact"—he upended his wrist and squinted at an ancient Bulova—"it is precisely ten twenty-one. If dear Professor Lawrence is running true to form, he should appear posthaste—ten twenty-five, to be precise. The man has something of a fetish for punctuality."

Hardy Steppington Miles whistled a nervous little tune as he straightened the stacks of papers on his desk and generally avoided my eye. "Any moment now."

I stood to leave. "If you happen to remember anything else about Nick or hear anything about any papers of his, Mr. . . . Dr. Miles, I would appreciate a call. I'm very anxious to find out all there is to know about my son's death."

He cleared his throat. "Of course, Mrs. Spooner. Who would do otherwise?" He rose and offered a stiff, reluctant hand. "So sorry I cannot give you information regarding the papers you seek."

"That's all right. Thank you for your time."

I walked down the hall as Hardy Miles had directed, relieved to be away from him. My reaction could best be described as instant dislike of the brash, self-important man. I'd had professors like that in law school, snoot-brained, humorless, walking word factories who seemed to consider it a sacred duty to make the mere mortal student feel suitably inadequate.

My footsteps clattered in the stillness, and the corridor seemed to echo with my breaths and heartbeats. As I walked, a chill of realization crept up through my feet. Nicky had walked over this dingy stretch of corridor. Back and forth a thousand times. I could almost see the imprint of his long narrow foot, the loping stride, and the rhythmic swing of his gangly arms. My head filled with the thought of all the minds and bodies he might have touched in this place. Why hadn't anyone been there for him? Why hadn't anyone recognized his pain?

"Hey, Spooner, you look like hell. What is it, kid? You thinking of doing something drastic? 'Cause there's help, kid. People who can talk, listen, hold your hand. Whatever it takes, whatever's broken can be fixed. It never has to come to anything as drastic as . . ."

I could see his face, the pain and torment hidden behind the clown mask. "Hey, you kidding? I'm the last person in the world you have to worry about. The last. If I had suicidal tendencies, I would have eaten the dorm food years ago."

"P-pardon me!"

In my reverie I came within inches of bumping into a little man bustling down the hall in a nervous flurry. "I'm sorry. I didn't see you."

"Never mind. 'They say the b-best men are molded out of faults. And, for the most, become much more the b-b-better. For being a little bad.' That's *Measure for Measure*, Act V, Scene i. I t-t-tend to walk t-t-too quickly at t-times."

"No. It was my fault. Dr. Lawrence?"

"Warren Lawrence. And you are?"

"Sarah Spooner. I'm Nicholas Spooner's mother."

His pale face sagged. "Nicholas. Ah, yes. 'Night's kuh-candles are b-burnt out, and jocund day stands tiptoe on the m-misty mountaintops.' *Romeo and Juliet,* Act III. I was so suh-sorry to hear. Nicholas was a f-fine young man." He held up a finger as if testing the wind. " 'Framed in the p-prodigality of nature.' *Richard III,* Act I, Scene ii. A sorry, determined b-boy, it seems, under the m-m-mask of joviality. Or, as it is said in *Julius Caesar,* Act I, Scene iii, 'So every b-bondman in his own b-bears the p-power to cancel his captivity.' " Lawrence shook his head, displacing a gray-blond tendril over his rumpled forehead. "I enjoyed your son's p-presence in my classroom, Mrs. Spooner. He was a sp-spark of intelligence awaiting the flint of inspiration. Mine." He giggled in self-appreciation. "Not b-b-bad, eh? Would you care to c-come in?"

He fumbled with the lock on his office door, his fingers dancing nervously on the molding as he worked.

The whole musty building seemed to be closing in on me. "I'm sure you're busy, Dr. Lawrence. I just wanted to ask if you knew anything about some papers of Nick's. He kept a creative writing folder, but the work seems to be missing. His roommate told me one of Nick's professors talked about publishing some of his writing. Were you the one?"

With a triumphant little flourish Lawrence pushed open the door and motioned me inside. His office was pin-neat, in stark contrast to Hardy Steppington Miles's. The obligatory sea of reference books was ordered by shape and color, the matching walnut desk and chairs arranged in a perfect rectangle. He set his brown mock crocodile briefcase beside the desk and flicked an invisible dust speck from the polished wood surface. As he sat in the oversize green swivel chair, he adjusted his tweed sport coat so the lapels lay in a precise parallel to the rungs of my straight-backed chair. Satisfied, he sat back and molded his hands around an imaginary beach ball.

" 'Tell me where is f-fancy bred, Or in the heart or in the head? How b-b-begot, how nourished? Reply, reply.' III, ii, *Merchant of Venice.* I must say I know nothing about any of your son's p-papers. I never discuss p-publication with my students. In my opinion, any meaningful move toward p-professional status would have to come from the students themselves. Can I offer you a c-cup of tea?"

He twirled his chair to face the wall and extracted a dual-burner hot plate and a carafe of water from a hidden cabinet. As he fussed over his preparations I tried to imagine how this expansive oddball could possibly be one of the triplets of Winston Lawrence, the little mouse at the Barrington Arms.

Since Diamond and I checked in several days ago, I had only seen Proprietor Lawrence a few times. He skulked about in the shadows of the hotel, appearing at odd hours to rustle a few papers, attend to some mysterious business, and disappear, it seemed, in a puff of smoke.

True, there were physical similarities: the ruddy complexion; the fine, salted honey hair, though Winston wore his without a part and Warren's was scored down the center like a road. Professor Lawrence shared his brother's small stature and slight build, but he was generous in his movements whereas innkeeper Lawrence was stuck in the straitjacket of his spare personality. Even the voice was a stark contrast. Warren boomed his stammered stock of Shakespearean quotes like a frustrated Olivier, while Winston sounded like a transistor radio whose batteries needed replacing.

"C-chamomile, Lemon Lift, Red Zinger? What is your puh-pleasure?" He held out a tin full of tea bags.

"Nothing for me, thanks. I just came to ask about the papers. If you don't know anything about them, I won't take any more of your time."

With grand theatrical flair, he extracted a tea bag from the tangle in the canister, tinted his steaming water a pale copper, plunked in two sugar cubes, and released a squirt of flavor from a plastic lemon. His first sip was followed by a sigh of profound relief. "I'm s-sorry I c-can't help you, Mrs. Spooner. I'm sure the m-missing papers will t-turn up."

"I hope so, Professor."

He squinted at me and frowned. "I hope y-you are n-not jumping to unfortunate c-conclusions, M-mrs. Spooner. I have heard all the idle w-words. There is 'n-no hinge nor loop to hang a doubt on,' III, iii, *Othello*. Please b-believe me."

"Look, Professor, I don't know what you're talking about. My son's papers are missing. I assume one of his professors has them. I'm not concluding anything. . . . What idle words are you referring to?"

His face fell. "Stuh-stupid rumors, no more, Mrs. S-spooner. M-malicious g-gossip. N-not a shred of t-truth to any of it."

"Gossip about missing papers?"

I watched his hands curl into determined fists as he pushed his words through iron-clenched teeth, " 'Slander, whose edge is sharper than the s-sword, whose t-t-tongue outvenoms all the worms of Nile, whose breath rides on the p-posting winds and d-doth b-belie all corners of the world.' N-nasty, baseless accusations. I w-will have n-none of it, M-mrs. Spooner. N-n-none. And n-neither should you."

"I told you. I don't know what you're talking about. All I want is to find Nick's papers, Professor. It's strange that his work seems to have disappeared. If you've heard anything that might help me locate it, I would like to know."

" 'Our d-doubts are traitors, and make us lose the g-good we oft might win, by f-f-f-fearing to attempt.' *Measure for Measure*, I, iv. I suggest you t-turn your m-mind t-to loftier p-purpose.''

In no mood for more of his ranting, I stood to leave. ''I've taken enough of your time, Professor. I'll be going now.''

''Mrs. Spooner, I s-sincerely hope you will n-not be swayed by v-vicious rumor. 'Rumor is a p-pipe b-blown by surmises, jealousies, conjectures, and of so easy and so plain a stop that the b-blunt monster with uncounted heads the still-discordant m-multitude can p-play upon it.' *Henry IV,* Act V. P-please b-believe me, the p-papers will t-turn up. W-why assume they were st-stolen?''

Good question. I felt a shiver of discovery. ''Is that what the rumors were? Why would anyone want to steal a student's papers?''

''P-precisely. A foolish n-notion p-promoted by foolish, m-malicious men. I d-don't know why anyone would s-say s-such a thing.'' He shrugged. '' 'The art of our n-necessities is strange, that c-can make vile things precious,' III, ii, *King Lear.*''

''Do you mean you think someone has been spreading rumors about stolen work to make trouble? But why would anyone—?''

Professor Lawrence drew an imaginary lance from his scabbard and pointed it at an invisible adversary. '' 'Though this b-be madness, yet there is m-method in 't.' ''

''But why? Accusations like that would have to be proven. No one would believe such a thing without evidence.''

"I've s-said too m-m-much already, Mrs. Spuh-spooner. I'm sure N-Nick's puh-papers will turn up."

"I hope so, Professor. It seems Professor Goldenberg is my last hope. Maybe he has them."

"M-m-maybe he d-does."

I shook his hand and left him still sipping at his tea. Back in the dark, dim corridor, the feeling came back to me—stepping in Nicky's footsteps, breathing the same musty air that filled his lungs. Could I also be sensing some disturbing presence that Nicky felt? Something wrong in this place that drove him—or pulled him—to his own destruction?

A shiver assailed me. "Something wrong," I whispered. And the sound of my voice echoed in the emptiness like a wind of warning.

Somewhere behind me a door was slammed shut and a chair scraped against a cold wood floor. Frozen to listen, I tried to make out the muffled sound of a single voice. Something familiar about the tone, but the words were lost in the distance. I hurried downstairs and out toward the sunshine.

A dense cloud of summer heat settled over me, and I squinted against the furious glare of the morning sky. The campus was coming alive. Families moved in chattery clumps. Pairs of graduates strolled the meandering paths, reveling in their lack of purpose.

Gaily patterned tents had sprung up overnight, and in one a Dixieland band costumed in red-striped shirts, gartered sleeves, and straw hats was warming up for the evening's festivities. A rickety truck bumped over the grassy quadrangle delivering kegs of beer.

That voice. I rummaged through my memory for a connection. Why was that voice so familiar? So disturbing? The fog lifted little by little. The office . . . no. But work-related.

Then it came to me. How could I have forgotten? I was back in the interrogation room of the forty-eighth precinct. It was a dim, airless little cubicle with barred windows. A scarred table in the center lit by a garish bare bulb in a wire cage. Cold metal chairs. Desperate messages scratched into the faded green walls.

Across from me sat a burly gorilla of a suspect with gnarled fingers and a slash scar down his cheek. Pat Scofield was at my side, tossing questions with me as if the man were the center pit in a game of horseshoes. The ape man sitting stone still, no movement for hours except the thick features working in a nervous, unyielding silence. Until . . .

Explosion. Before my mind registered anything, I felt the steel fingers pressing around my neck, choking off the air. My head filled with panic and the sick, scared, animal scent of his body. I could feel the life in me growing, expanding until it threatened to burst and fade to nothing on the stale air. Everything was too big, my tongue, the veins distending in my temples, my eyes bursting from their pods like ripened peas.

For an instant I was dead, unaware, floating in a cool yellow sea of light. Somehow Pat called the guards and got him pulled away. The life flowed back into me like warm soup. A minute and it was over. But I would never forget the look on his face or the words he spat as they dragged him out of the room: "You're dead meat . . . both of you . . . the whole fucking lot of you, dead meat!"

And I would never forget the tone of that voice. It had the same odd cadence that pulsed from behind some closed office door in the English department. The desperate, mad sound of that voice.

"Try to forget about him, Sarah. He's crazy." Pat sat beside me until I'd stopped shaking. "Try to remember that it has nothing to do with you. That man is one sick, crazy person. You could tell by listening to him. It's that rage, that crazy, groundless rage that comes through in his voice. I've heard it before in suspects like him, ones long gone over the edge. You get so you can hear it in your sleep, in your worst nightmares. The words don't matter. It's the tone. That particular tone of voice. I call it the voice of lunacy."

The voice of lunacy. And now I had heard it again.

-12-

Diamond was still in the suite, clad in a faded beige T-shirt and giant jeans. With vague, puffy eyes he blinked at me and shook his head as if to clear it.

"Mr. Diamond . . . are you all right?"

He flushed and looked away. "It's nothing, nothing at all. . . . Graphologist burnout. That must be the problem. You read a lot about it these days. Not hard to understand, either, Sarah Spooner. Handwriting can be a pressure cooker, believe me."

A nervous tic was dancing at the corner of his eye. "Maybe you need some time off, Mr. Diamond. You can't be very effective when you feel so pressured. That's why I haven't gone back to the office yet. I'd be useless."

"Office. Glad you reminded me. You had a call from your office. Someone named . . . Snowfield, I think." He frowned. "I wrote it down somewhere. . . ." His porky fingers dove into the mass of folders and paper scraps on the desk.

"Pat Scofield?"

"That's it. Said it was urgent. That's the problem with this world, Sarah Spooner. Everything's urgent. One big emergency after another. Gets so I want to crawl under the bed and hide."

Now that would be a trick. "Is he in the office, did he say?"

"I guess. I wrote down the number. It's here somewhere."

The desktop looked like the aftermath of a blizzard. Diamond's meticulous record keeping had gone the way of his tranquillity. What was tormenting him? What could be so dreadful that he refused to tell me? How could I work my way under his defenses? "Don't worry about it. I'll track him down."

There was no room in my muddled head for office urgencies. I pressed a finger in my ear as I dialed. Diamond's munching was the sound of elephants dancing in a roomful of balloons.

"Hi, Pat. What's up?"

"The Harper case, I'm afraid. I moved for another postponement, and the judge said we must go ahead immediately or he'll dismiss for failure to prosecute."

"Not now. It can't be."

"I'm afraid it is. We're on for this coming Tuesday, Counselor. That gives you just enough time to get your suit pressed."

"I can't, Pat. I'm not finished here yet. You'll have to take the case."

"Now come on, Sarah. Be reasonable. You've been on Hot Lips Harper's case from the beginning. I don't know anything about it. I'm glad to help you out, but I can't get a case this big together in three days, not without you to brief me at the very least. We may as well let old Judge Jerkwater dismiss."

"No. We can't do that. The Harper case means too much—the grant from People Resources may turn on this one. You told me that yourself. . . . Listen, I can't leave Cromwell. But you can come here and I'll brief you. I know you can handle it, Pat. You're the best."

"Hold the applause, Counselor. If I agree to this foolbrained scheme, it's only because my boss is a wonderful woman who has been very good to me and almost never asks me to do crazy, unreasonable things."

"Thanks, Pat. I won't forget this."

"I just hope I'll be able to forget it. You get me a room and I'll fly out first thing tomorrow morning."

"Great. I'll get right back to you with the details." The phone was settled happily in the cradle and a smile was painted on my face before it dawned on me. A room.

"Diamond? I have a colleague coming to Cromwell for a couple of days. Any suggestions about where I might find him a place to stay?"

Still munching, he surveyed the suite. "It'd be a little crowded here. . . ."

"No, I didn't mean here. I've imposed on you enough."

"Well, then I suppose the nearest town that might have something is Vesna. Tiny place about thirty minutes from here. Blink and you miss it. Don't blink and you'll wish you did—heh, heh. Only kidding. It's not a bad place, really. Quiet. No good restaurants to speak of . . ."

"That's not important. They have a hotel?"

"Motel . . . motor inn, they call it. Vesna-by-the-Sea is the name. Stayed there once on an industrial job. Vesna is, believe it or not, the world capital of plastic liners for disposable diapers."

"You think they'd have vacancies?"

Cheek distended with potato chips, he made a victory sign. "Can't imagine why they wouldn't. No one in his right mind would vacation in Vesna, and there are only so many overflow relatives at a given time. Don't be fooled by the name. Vesna-by-the-Sea isn't. There's no water for two hundred miles. It's a tiny little nothing of a factory town. Disposable diaper liners—imagine."

I reserved two rooms at Vesna-by-the-Sea and agreed to meet Pat at the motel for a two-day cram session on the Harper case. Gratefully, I accepted Diamond's offer of his car. Rentals, he explained between fistfuls of Ridgies, were as hard to come by as rooms. "It'll be good for you to get away from this hellhole, Sarah Spooner. You have any sense, you won't bother to come back."

"I'll be back, Mr. Diamond. I'm not finished here."

"Will you know it when you are, Sarah Spooner? That's the question."

Restless, I left Diamond to his puzzles, papers, and potato chips and retrieved my suitcase from the closet shelf in the bedroom. I packed a change of clothing, my jogging wear in case Pat was inclined to conference along the Vesna streets, and a favorite Mickey Mouse nightshirt, a gift from Nicky for my last birthday. The phone rang as I was debating over whether or not to pack a sweater (my mother's conscience making house calls).

"For you, Sarah Spooner."

It was Ben. "Who the hell was that, Sarah?"

"Didn't my mother tell you? It's graduation week. There wasn't a room in Cromwell. A very kind gentleman is allowing me to share his suite."

"A likely story."

His face, complete with supercilious smirk, appeared in my mind. "Now, wait a minute, Ben. You disappear for days, not a word to me or anyone, and suddenly you're the injured party? I assure you, my dealings with Mr. Diamond are strictly humanitarian—one kind person helping a fellow human in need. He saw how important it was for me to find out about what happened to Nicky. That's more than I can say for you."

"I'm busy dealing with what happened to Nicky my own way. Your Mr. Diamond can afford to be a big hero, Sarah. He didn't lose his son."

I felt myself deflating. "You're right. I'm sorry, Ben. That wasn't fair of me. I know you loved Nicky. I just need your support right now. And it hurts that you won't, or can't, give it to me."

"Listen, I really can't get into this now. I have a meeting in a few minutes. I heard you wanted me to call. Anything important?"

"Now, wait a minute. I haven't spoken to you in days. Where have you been, anyway? You didn't say anything about a business trip."

"I . . . it came up at the last minute."

His voice was dripping with guilt. I felt a familiar sinking sensation, and the words fell out like things dropped from overfilled hands. "Who is she, Ben?"

There was a long, thick silence. "It doesn't matter. She doesn't matter. I needed to get lost for a little while, Sarah. Try to understand."

My mouth was chalk. "You picked a fine time."

"Look, Sarah . . . these things just happen. You left and I went a little crazy. Look. We all have our ways of coping."

A sick pool of emptiness was settling over me. My voice was dead hollow. "Of course, Ben. I understand. Some of us cope horizontally, some cope vertically."

"It doesn't mean anything. Please believe me."

"No . . . it doesn't. Nothing means anything. Maybe it never did." All of it was building in me until I felt ready to explode. Too much. "Look, Ben. I don't want to talk about this now. I can't deal with our problems until I have this thing with Nicky straight in my mind."

He sounded like a small, frightened child. "I love you, Sarah. I'm sorry."

"Not now, Ben."

"I'll call you. . . ."

Numb, I went back to my packing. None of it mattered, I told myself over and over. Nothing mattered. Maybe my world was broken in too many pieces. Maybe I would have to turn my back on the wreckage and start again.

I tossed in a few extra things and shut the valise. Diamond was still munching in the front room. He looked up from his *A Concise History of Cromwell* when I walked in. "Jeez, Sarah Spooner. You look like you just took a direct hit below the waterline."

No point burdening him with my worries. It was obvious he had more than enough of his own. "I'm all right. I was just trying to figure out what more I can do today. . . . I went to see two of Nick's English professors this morning. The third is out of town for a couple of days. Any suggestions?"

The empty bag of potato chips lay crumpled in the garbage. He struggled against the seal on a party-size sack of beer pretzels. "Hmmm. You might want to go to the lecture this afternoon at Trinity Hall. Chairman Lawrence is giving a talk on the suicides."

Anything was better than having time to think. And I was curious about the official university line. The adverse publicity had to be a problem for Cromwell. But did they deserve better? How could they stand by and do nothing while several of their students were suffering from terminal despair?

To kill the intervening time I sipped on a tall iced tea while Diamond had lunch at the campus commissary. An enormous plate of thick, gummy institutional spaghetti seemed to drain directly into the bottomless cavern of his appetite. There was a low, groaning slurp, followed by a sound like insincere applause, and *voilà*, the plate was empty. Diamond wiped the corners of his mouth for form. No morsel of food would dare attempt an escape.

Pausing before dessert, he sat back and surveyed his midsection. "Food is my downfall, I'm afraid. If not for food . . . Ah, well. How about a nice slice of that Boston cream pie for you? My treat."

He came back with a trayful of small, sweet-laden dishes, chunks of fruit pie and frosted cake, glazed cookies, sugar doughnuts oozing jelly, custard tarts.

"Maybe you should try to cut down, Mr. Diamond. All that can't be good for your health."

He spoke between mouthfuls. "Can't. It's hard to explain, Sarah Spooner. I've got this hole—here." He poked his middle with an index finger. "And if I don't keep it filled up, it starts to get bigger and stronger until I'm sure I'm going to turn inside out like a shirt."

"What is it that's worrying you? Maybe if you talk about it . . ."

Chewing faster, he waved me away. "Nothing. Nothing at all. Who says anything's worrying me? Don't you even think about it. Not for a minute. Some things are better left alone. Believe me."

"But . . ." A photographer from the campus paper came over and started snapping pictures of Diamond and his calorie collection.

"You get the hell away, you nervy twit."

The boy darted away from Diamond's flailing arms and kept snapping, the automatic advance on his Nikon crackling and hissing.

"You leave me the hell alone. Give me that camera!" Rising as quickly as his bulk allowed, Diamond tried to grab the photographer, or the camera, or both, but he could not keep up with the boy's lithe darting and feinting.

"Diamond, ignore him."

His face was beet-red, his breath coming in stertorous pulses. "Diamond, please."

Too outraged to hear me, he waited for what seemed the right moment and lunged at the photographer, hurling his body like a crazed bull. The boy paused, grinned in amusement, and danced out of the way. Diamond crashed into the row of wooden benches and tables, overturning several and smashing a bench to unrecognizable fragments. He emitted a loud, tortured gasp and collapsed.

"Diamond. Are you all right? Mr. Diamond?" I turned to the startled paparazzo.

"You idiot! Look what you've done. Go call an ambulance. Quick!"

The boy was terrified. "I didn't mean anything. I never saw anyone eat like that. I thought it would make a good story."

"Go call!"

By now a small knot of people had gathered to watch. I bent over Diamond and whispered in his ear. "Are you all right? Diamond?" His face was as pale as death, his breathing shallow and uneven. Please be all right, Diamond. Please.

A baby-faced ambulance attendant raced into the cafeteria and pulled up short when he saw Diamond's inert form. "Jeezus H. Christmas. Someone should've asked for a forklift."

"Is he going to be all right? He took a terrible fall."

"We'll take real good care of him, lady. Don't you worry." He leaned over Diamond and spoke directly into his chubby ear. "Hey, Slim? You hear me? Tell me if anything hurts." He pinched up and down the lengths of Diamond's arms and legs and slapped his cheeks. "You in there, Slim? Anybody home?"

Diamond grunted softly and opened a rheumy eye. He glared at the attendant. "Kindly back off, young man. Your breath is bad enough to cause a person grave bodily harm."

"You sure you're okay?"

"I'm fine. And I'll be even better when you back away and allow me some air."

"Thank the lord. If we had to lift you, we'd need an ambulance for ourselves." Slowly he helped Diamond to sit, and then to stand. "You sure you're okay, Slim? 'Cause the floor will never be the same."

"Go away and leave me alone. Tell them to go away, Sarah Spooner."

"You sure? Maybe you should go to the hospital for an examination—to make certain everything's okay."

"I'm fine." He narrowed his eyes and stared at the photographer, who stood cowering in the corner. "The film."

The boy placed the exposed roll in Diamond's waiting palm. "I'm sorry."

"You would have been. Sorrier than you can imagine."

He pulled the film from the plastic case and held it up for the light to ruin. "That was my right to privacy you were attempting to violate, young man. May I suggest you find yourself a more suitable profession? Something hazardous might be nice."

Diamond straightened his clothing and smoothed a stray hair from his forehead. Ignoring the gawkers, he turned to me with a forced smile. "Well, Sarah Spooner, we'd best be going. Don't want to miss the lecture."

"Are you sure you're up to it?"

Grasping my elbow, he squared his shoulders and steered me out of the cafeteria and into the blazing midday heat. A crowd was already milling through the carved wooden entrance doors of Trinity Hall, the campus chapel. Waving makeshift paper fans and complaining about the weather, a steady stream of people slipped into the dim, stuffy main hall of the old stone building and filled the rows of polished pews.

Inside, columns of light streamed through the stained-glass windows and tinted the heat-flushed faces of the crowd to an eerie burnished copper. A mahogany dais with a portable microphone and a pitcher of water had been placed next to the pulpit. Beside it, a white-robed priest with a beatific smile and folded hands stood waiting for the assemblage to be seated.

Diamond and I managed to find separate vacancies in the back. I watched as he wedged himself between two disconcerted women. They exchanged disapproving glances and seemed to shrink away as Diamond settled back to listen to the lecture.

The priest cleared his throat. "Ladies and gentlemen, it is my great privilege to introduce the guiding force behind our great university—Chairman of the Board, Wallace Lawrence."

An overheated assemblage managed a polite show of enthusiasm. Chairman Lawrence appeared from a rear door and walked his regal presence to center stage. His stance was all control and confidence; his face radiated wisdom and self-possession. He seemed somehow larger than his brothers. His hair was slicked back from the stiff set of his forehead, and he kept one brow raised, giving him a look that was somewhere between supercilious and sinister. This was obviously a man at home with power. Taking time to position himself to advantage, he adjusted the microphone and set a pair of black-framed half glasses on the bridge of his nose. Ready, he looked out at the crowd, commanding a rapid, respectful silence with his eyes. His accent was New York British.

"Father Brown . . . members of the faculty . . . friends. I thank you for being here. Were it not for a matter of gravest importance, I can assure you I would not be speaking today. All of us would much prefer to concentrate on celebrating the accomplishments of our graduating class. Hopefully future commencements will not be marred by dreadful events such as those that have cast a cloud on Cromwell during the past several months."

He gazed skyward as if seeking divine intervention. Then he fixed the crowd with a cold, determined gaze. "My topic, as you know, is suicide. But make no mistake. I am not going to speak of suicide as a tragedy or of its 'tragic' victims."

His face narrowed. "If there are victims, they are not the unfortunate young people who chose to resolve their personal problems in this deplorable manner. I know the majority of so-called mental-health professionals pity and grieve over the person who takes his own life. But those of us who sanctify human life and revere the promise of youth and intellect must deplore such an act. We cannot pity and grieve. Suicide makes us angry. Angry and resentful."

There was a stiff smattering of applause. But looking around, I saw shock registered on a number of faces.

Lawrence held up a hand. "I can imagine what some of you must be thinking: How can Chairman Lawrence be so insensitive? So uncaring? Please be assured, no one cares more than I; no one feels more deeply the pain and suffering from these desperate events.

"During the past several months it has fallen on me to answer the tormented questions of abandoned friends and family. It has fallen on me to ease the suffering of countless students, faculty, and parents touched by these horrendous incidents. I have shed tears with them, wept openly for the waste of human gift and promise. I am not a cold man. I am an angry man."

Fists clenched, he seemed to grow as he spoke. "I am angry for the hideous waste. And angrier still for the black stain these unnecessary deaths have cast over our beloved institution. By choosing to end their lives in this manner, these young people have threatened the life of a legacy that has nurtured the minds, souls, and futures of countless young people for over a century."

Murmurs rose like an insect swarm. Lawrence waited for them to subside. "I suppose few of you have considered the broader consequences. To be honest, at first I was too distressed to consider them myself. Today, Cromwell University stands at a dangerous crossroad. The small-minded bureaucrats are out in force, beating the bushes for that most coveted prey—the scapegoat."

Beside me, two women whispered. One rolled her eyes.

"This great university, this venerable institution of higher learning, is being asked to pay for the misdeeds of a handful of spoiled, selfish, immature individuals. It seems we must all suffer for the shortsighted misdeeds of the few."

My face was burning. How could he speak like this?

"The young people who chose to end their own lives did not consider the consequences for themselves or for the rest of us. Now it seems we may all pay a tragic price for the self-absorption of these selfish few."

Furious, I rose to leave and climbed over the packed knees and feet to the aisle. "We stand to lose millions of dollars in endowments alone, not to mention the loss of something far more valuable—our reputation. For the first time since Cromwell's inception we have a shortfall in applications. We face underenrollment and the dreadful consequences: staff cuts, program cuts, the very lifeblood being drawn from us."

Out of the row at last, I raced toward the exit. A few other offended listeners were straggling out beside me. His voice boomed out at us. "Leave. Go on! If a thing is unpleasant, close your mind to it. That is a privilege you retain. But there are those of us who cannot walk away, no matter how unpleasant things become. There are those of us who have given our lives to this university—to excellence. And we will not stand idly by while the unconscionable deeds of a few bleed our beloved

Cromwell to death! We shall fight back! And we intend to triumph!''

Closing the chapel door behind me, I heard a vague pulse of approval as he finished speaking. The crowd began to file out behind me. I waited off at the side for Diamond.

"Guy's a real sweetheart, isn't he, Sarah Spooner?"

"How can he dare to blame Nicky and the others? What sort of a human being would say such things?"

We walked along a narrow dirt path. Diamond still seemed distant, almost dazed. He shrugged. "What sort? Good point. I guess he went over the edge when he heard about the accreditation board."

"What about it?"

"They have Cromwell under review. Seems they're threatening to pull the school's accreditation if the suicides keep up." He dug into his pocket and peeled the foil off a large chocolate-crunch bar. "They lose their accreditation, they might as well hang out the for-sale signs."

"I can understand why he'd be upset, but that doesn't give him the right to attack Nicky and the others."

His chocolate-filled cheek moved in determined rhythm. Popping the final square in his crammed mouth, he dug into his pocket for another bar. "From what I hear, Lawrence—pardon me, *Chairman* Lawrence— thinks he's got all the rights in the world when it comes to Cromwell University. Thinks he owns the place."

"Frankly I don't care what that man thinks. He has no right to talk like that, and I'm not going to let him get away with it. I think I'll write a strong letter to the board. . . ."

"Sure, Sarah Spooner. That's your privilege. You have to do what you have to do. Wait here." We were outside the campus store, a grey concrete slab of a building plastered with countless posters, ads, and announcements. Diamond rumbled down the stairs toward the glass-fronted entrance. I watched him dash to the candy counter to replenish his supply. With a sheepish grin and lumpy pockets he joined me again. "All set."

At the end of the main quadrangle we crossed out of the campus toward the footbridge leading over the Sachem gorge to the area of the Barrington Arms. It was a reasonable walk but the oppressive heat seemed to stretch the distance. Diamond's breath was labored and a sweat stain spread over the front of his shirt.

He wiped his face with a large hankie and gazed back at the campus. "Who would have guessed hell would have a library with a million volumes, Sarah Spooner?"

Trying not to be obvious, I checked him over as we walked. Diamond's fall had left no obvious mark, but the change in him was getting more and more pronounced. Over the past two days he had grown more and more nervous and distracted, bearing the solitary burden of some awful knowledge. No matter how he tried to cover it up, his attempts at humor were strained, his offhandedness unconvincing. It had something to do with Nicky. No matter how Diamond protested, I knew it had something to do with Nick's suicide and the others. If only I could creep inside his mind and find what he was hiding there.

"Look at that. I wonder what's going on."

Diamond pointed to the footbridge. A knot of people were gathered at the side of the road beside the start of the guardrail. They all seemed to be speaking at once, a frenzied blur of chatter. Above it all, a siren screamed its approach as the blinking face of an ambulance raced toward us.

We hurried toward the crowd. Diamond tapped a man's shoulder to catch his attention. "What happened?"

The man turned slowly, his face vague with disbelief. Extending his arm, he pointed a single finger down toward the base of the gorge. "Someone spotted a kid down there. Crazy kid jumped in and killed himself."

Diamond put his hands over his eyes and turned away. "Not again. Not another one."

Even as I vowed not to look, my eyes were drawn to the craggy base of the gorge. There was the vague outline of a human form, cradled in a spreading scarlet pool. The tremor started in my legs, weakening them until it took every scrap of my strength to stay upright. "No."

Diamond caught me in a firm grasp by the elbow and led me away from the crowd. Two men from a rescue team were scrambling down the steep face of the gorge, carrying a stretcher. Campus police were working to disperse the spectators. "Go on home now, folks. The show's over. Nothing you can do here."

Nothing.

Diamond's firm hand kept me from falling to pieces. "Let's get out of here, Sarah Spooner."

I let him direct me, placing one wooden foot in front of the other like a puppet. Numb. Blessed numbness.

Somehow we made our way back through the odd, quiet world of Parrish Common and into the cool, peaceful lobby of the Barrington Arms. Winston Lawrence was bustling about, as nervous as a cat. Despite the air-conditioning, his face was dripping perspiration, and his mouth moved in agitated silence. Seeing us, he clasped his hands and feigned a pleasant smile. "I do hope your stay is proceeding well, Mr. Diamond? Mrs. Spooner? Kindly do let me know if you need anything. Anything at all."

He bustled away without waiting for an answer. An overwhelming sense of exhaustion settled over me. "I think I'll go up and rest for a while, Diamond. It's been a tough day."

"Yes, you do that, Sarah Spooner. That's a good idea."

I climbed the stairs and settled on my bed like a stone. My eyes wavered out of focus and I felt myself dropping off into welcome oblivion. Floating through the blackness, I tried to sweep past the thoughts tormenting me like mean children: Ben and his "sweetie"; Nicky; Chairman Lawrence with the nasty fire in his eyes and the icicles running through his veins; Diamond. Diamond trying to drown himself in food, trying to kill himself.

There was a black place at the edge of the dream. I reached out for it, something to hold on to, but it crumbled in my seeking fingers and fell away. Useless, Sarah Spooner. You can't change what happens; nothing in the world you can do about it.

I stood with my hand outstretched, desperate. And as I watched, terrified young faces screamed in futile protest as they plummeted in turn off the end of the world.

-13-

Cromwell was still asleep when I drove Diamond's rented Lincoln out through the center of town and onto Route 387, a narrow, discouraging stretch of pitted blacktop bordered by drab countryside and billboards advertising products I would never use. An occasional sixteen-wheeler bore down on me before zooming past with a loud flourish and a determined tug on the surrounding air. Otherwise I had the road to myself. Enjoying the blessed peace and monotony, I tuned the radio to soft, boring music and leaned my head against the plush headrest.

On the way to Vesna, I passed a string of nondescript towns: shabby main streets centered around vintage movie marquees and store signs done in blinking neon. Clotheslines, burdened with sturdy, shapeless wash, connected row after row of colorless clapboard houses bordered by overgrown boxwood hedges and picket fences in desperate need of paint.

Vesna was no better. Entering town, I noticed the obligatory trio of toughs assembled outside the local tavern, though it would not open for hours. A vagrant wrapped in a newsprint blanket slept on a rickety bench, his breath rising in pale, uneven clouds on the chill morning air. On the corner, small children played, shouting mysterious pairs of initials in shrill, excited voices and racing across the street in some ritual of hazardous fun.

Slowing to a crawl, I passed the Vesna Hall of Records, the public library, and police headquarters—a squat, converted brick schoolhouse fitted with window bars and an emergency buzzer for crimes committed after regular business hours. The remainder of the commercial district consisted of a hairdressing establishment fronted by a hot-pink and sky-blue barber pole; two small clothing shops; a florist featuring desiccated houseplants with yellow-tipped leaves; a funeral home; a meat-and-potatoes food mart; and a small diner.

At the end of the main road a multitiered sign pointed the way to Vesna's churches, clubs, and other dubious points of interest. I followed the wooden finger labeled VESNA-BY-THE-SEA.

True to Diamond's word, the motel was no more promising than the town. A low line of faded yellow units were set in a horseshoe around a littered parking lot. The office was in the center, marked by a hand-lettered sign and a plastic hanging fern in a mock wicker basket. I registered and went to wait in the room for Pat. He wasn't due for a while, plenty of time to count the holes in the stained acoustical tile ceiling and do the crossword puzzle in the Vesna *Weekly Mail* (compliments of the management). One across . . . two words (seven letters) for a road with no exit.

Dead end.

Restless, I paced the room. In a way I welcomed the diversion of the Harper case. And Pat. Who could be a more comforting contrast to the bleak emotional landscape at Cromwell? Thinking of him, I realized how much I had missed our morning runs. The solid feel of his presence in the adjoining office. His steady smiling logic that seemed such an easy bridge between calm and chaos.

"Sarah?"

The blond, aristocratic head was poked through the adjoining door. "Pat." I raced to the comfort of a long, lingering hug. "I'm so glad to see you."

He laughed. "So it seems."

"I've missed you."

A vague flush rose in his cheeks as he gently tried to disentangle himself. "No one to pick on, huh?"

"No one worth the trouble." I clasped my hands behind his neck and felt the press of my chest against his. Nice.

"Sarah. Come on. Cut it out. This isn't funny. . . ."

I was transfixed by the soft center of his mouth, wondering how it would taste. Wondering hard enough to pull that aristocratic face down on mine and find out.

"Sarah . . ."

These things just happen. Ben's words. Just . . . happen. Smooth sensations carry you off on a wave of pleasure. Strong pulling sensations. Too strong to fight. Why bother? Too nice. Nicer than any I could remember. Didn't mean anything . . . just happens. I could sense Pat giving up . . . melting with me.

"Sarah." He broke my grasp on him and pulled away. His lips were puffy from the intensity of my kiss. And he had the confused look of a sleepy little boy. "I don't understand."

"What's to understand? Old lady meets boy, old lady wants boy, old lady makes a fool of herself."

He took my hand. Dear Pat, gallant to the end. "You're no fool, Counselor. And you're no old lady. Nothing would delight me more than if I thought your invitation was genuine and sincere."

"What makes you think it isn't?"

"I know you better. Maybe too well. Something happened with Ben."

"Nonsense. This has nothing to do with Ben."

He stared into my eyes. "Okay. If you're sure . . . because being dishonest with me and yourself wouldn't really be fair, Sarah. Not to either of us. I mean, here we work together, have to be able to look each other in the eye. . . ." Slowly, he placed his hands in the small of my back and pulled me toward him.

Without thinking, I pressed my hands against his shoulders. "So you're right. Partially right, anyway. Do you know how obnoxious it is to be right all the time?"

He put a finger on my chin and forced me to look at him. "I just think there's too much at stake here for us to make a mistake. But if you ever really want to . . . for you. Or for us. Keep in mind that I've had a chronic case for you for a very long time. Just don't play with me, Counselor. I'm a sensitive soul."

"I know you are, Pat. I'm sorry." I felt a satisfied smile tugging at the edges of my mouth. "Did you mean that? About that 'chronic case' you mentioned?"

His lips caught mine in a very sexy little nip of feeling, and his tone turned husky. "Yes. Now let's go out to lunch and talk about the Harper case."

The diner was packed. Harry's Charcoal Hearth appeared to be the social hub of the community. The air was thick with tinny country songs played over a worn jukebox and the mingled scents of griddle grease and dime-store fragrances. We found a small, vacant booth with a speckled Formica top and torn vinyl seats near the kitchen and slid in opposite each other.

Pat picked up the oversize, plastic-coated menu. "So, Counselor. What'll it be? 'The succulent Salisbury steak, Harry's favorite, with a generous side of golden-brown home fries and our famous eat-all-you-want portion of coleslaw'? Or 'the country fried chicken dripping with a succulent honey glaze and served up with a succulent side of candied sweet potatoes'? Or . . ."

I watched Pat's face as he read from the list of daily specials. Steady, open face. Honest blue eyes. Good bones. Again I felt an overwhelming ache of desire for him. "Why don't we just go back to Vesna-by-the-Sea and . . ." I caught his knee between mine.

He bit his lip. "Tell you what. I'll make you a deal. First you tell me what happened with Ben and how making love with me when you don't really want to will make it right, and then, if it makes sense, we'll go back to the room."

"I do really want to."

"I don't believe you."

I squeezed his knee again and walked my hand halfway up his thigh for good measure.

"You're not being fair, Counselor."

"I didn't hear you object."

"I don't object. I told you." He put a hand over mine. "I just want to be sure that this makes sense—for both of us. I know it isn't my business, but what the hell's going on?"

"Nothing's going on. . . . Nothing and everything. Ben is handling things his way, and I'm trying to find my own solutions."

"Whatever he did, you can't pay him back, Sarah. That's not the answer."

My control was slipping. "I'm not trying to pay him back, Pat. I don't care what he does. So what if he takes other women like most people take two aspirin? So what if he's a two-timing shithead with the moral fiber of a brussels sprout? That's his problem. I don't care what he does. Ben is not the issue here. We are. You mean a lot to me, Pat.''

"And you mean a lot to me. But I don't believe you. Ben is the issue. You're not being honest. Whether you realize it or not, all this is an attempt to retaliate.''

"How could he do this to me at a time like this? What kind of a person is he?''

Pat shrugged. "Misguided. Vulnerable. You're right. It's really unthinkable for him to go seek physical comfort from someone outside of his marriage just because he might have been feeling confused and angry, maybe even abandoned. Infidelity is unpardonable under any circumstances. I agree with you.''

I caught the little twinkle in his eye. "You're trying to tell me something.''

"I don't have to tell you anything. You know you love Ben—even though he's a mere mortal and you're a mere mortal and you're both capable of making mistakes.''

Chastened, I felt my erotic energies pulsing their last. "I'm sorry. I guess I'm behaving like a jerk.''

"An attractive jerk.''

"Well, you're an attractive jerk, too, Pat. I guess that's what makes us such a fine team.''

Our coffee came. Pat plunked two sugar cubes in his and tapped the cup against mine. "To Hot Lips Harry Harper: May we put him away where he belongs for a long, long time.''

"May everyone get what's coming to him.''

"Once we figure out what that is."

I clinked my cup against his. "Here's to smartass lawyers and all the people they save from themselves."

"Let's get down to business, Counselor. We're running out of time."

Working on the Harper case was like recovering from a long illness. At Cromwell I was all raw nerves and reactions, running in place in a desperate attempt to find the misplaced shards of my broken life. Here, I was a flesh-and-bone person of worth and substance, connected to the world by my particular strengths and abilities. Pat noticed the change.

"It's funny, Counselor," he said with a yawn. "Here we've been beating our brains out for about a million hours, and you keep looking better and better."

"I feel better and better. You can't imagine how nice it is to get away from Cromwell. Everywhere I turn at that place, I see Nicky. And all anyone talks about is suicide. You walk along the campus on a beautiful, sunny afternoon and you can almost see the tortured spirits flying over the place."

"Then why not come home? Give it up?"

Why? "I ... I can't, Pat. I'm close to something. I can feel it. You know, at first I thought I could never learn to live with what happened to Nick. I remember lying in my bed, thinking, 'If he's dead, I may as well be dead too.' Now ... I'm beginning to believe I can find a place in my life for Nicky's death. I know I want to survive, to love, to feel happiness again. I'm not ready to give any of it up, Pat. Does that sound horribly selfish?''

"No. It sounds healthy."

"Whatever it is, I think I can get past this. But I need a few more answers first. Nicky didn't give me the answers. For a while I couldn't forgive him for that. Now I have the feeling he didn't have them to give."

Pat looked grave. "Are you saying you suspect there was more to Nick's death than a simple suicide?"

"I don't know—yet."

He tapped the pages of the Harper brief into a neat stack and slipped them into his briefcase. "You listen to me, Sarah. If there's funny business going on at Cromwell, you run quickly in the other direction. Give what you've got to the police and let them take care of it. You just said you're interested in survival. Poking your nose into suspicious circumstances can be hazardous to your health. You know that better than anyone."

I had told him too much. With difficulty I kept my tone even and offhanded. "Don't be silly, Pat. I didn't say anything about suspicious circumstances. Good old paranoid Pat Scofield, always jumping to wild conclusions. There are just a few things I have to clear up about his . . . suicide. Then I'll come home."

His eyes were like the penetrating probe of a microscope. "You're sure? Because I could have Hodges call someone in Cromwell and make sure they get on the case."

"No, Pat. There is no case for them to get on." Exactly what I feared. If Pat started the wheels turning on an official outside investigation of Cromwell, I would have no chance of finding out what really happened to Nicky.

From long experience I knew that an invasion of blue-coats and badges could change the face of a case until it was all but unrecognizable. Our most successful investigations were the ones where the suspects had no idea anything was going on. Like the Harry Harper case. There were no uniforms nosing around to turn Hot Lips into Saint Harry. No battalions of pistol-packing police to tip him off. We kept everything under wraps until he played his entire act for the hidden cameras with the help of a decoy cop.

"You handle the Harper trial, Pat, and don't worry about me. I can take care of myself."

"If Nick's death was in any way suspicious, Sarah, you could be in danger."

"Come on now, Sherlock. You're letting that imagination of yours get the upper hand."

Pat peered at my face again and then gave up the discussion and went back to studying the brief.

Danger. The word crawled up my spine. Maybe I was in danger. Dreadful, inexplicable things were happening at Cromwell: odd dissonant notes that added up to some very frightening possibilities.

"Time for us to go over the summation, Counselor. Then I guess I'm on my own."

"Yes, Pat." Soon we would both be on our own. Pat in the real, predictable world. And me off sifting through the menacing shadows at Cromwell. Resting my eyes, I leaned back in my chair and listened to the relentless scratching of Pat's pen against the legal pad until I was lulled into a dreamy half sleep. Drifting.

Floating images. Undulating water draped with the sparkle of a brilliant summer sun. Children splashing and screaming with the pleasure of a shocking chill on sun-toasted flesh. Then a black stain—growing overhead. Bigger. Plummeting toward them . . . danger. Pleasure screams pierced with fright. Faces turned to masks of grimacing terror. Running.

The stain gaining speed—form. And landing with a sick groan of finality. Spreading. Bloody scarlet, spreading until the water is blood, the children frozen statues. And at the center—a dead body bobbling in the water. A mischievous death smile on its face.

Nicky.

Nick!

Hands shaking me. "Sarah, Sarah. You okay? Wake up, Sarah. You had a bad dream."

Slowly I pulled up out of the fog. Just a dream, I told myself. Another stupid nightmare. Nothing more.

"You want to tell me about it?" Pat said. "Sometimes that helps."

"No. Nothing to tell." Just a dream. So many dreams. So many black notions working their way to the surface of my mind. I walked to the bathroom and splashed my face with cool water. Nothing but dreams, I assured my frightened reflection.

Or was Nicky trying to tell me something?

-14-

Graduation day had left its electric imprint on downtown Cromwell. Merchants posted signs congratulating the graduates and encouraging them to spend in celebration. An enormous banner was draped across the main downtown street: CROMWELL SALUTES THE CLASS OF '87, and fat clusters of red and blue balloons bobbled from tree trunks and telephone poles.

On the main campus quadrangle, thousands of stern gray metal folding chairs were set out in neat rows. They faced a makeshift metal beam platform and a wooden podium from which the commencement speeches were slated to boom forth over a portable public-address system. The ivied buildings were festooned with sober lengths of scarlet and navy blue fabric—Cromwell's colors. And the granite likeness of Isaiah Cromwell astride a rearing palomino sported a scarlet and blue patchwork sport jacket and a blue bowler hat with a scarlet feather and band. Someone had even painted a scarlet smile and a navy-blue handlebar mustache on old Isaiah's sober granite face.

I parked in a sliver of a spot at the edge of campus and made my way through the crowds. Much as I dreaded it, I had to hear Chairman Lawrence's graduation speech. If he took off after the suicide victims again, I intended to register a formal protest with the university. I was even toying with a wrongful-death suit against Cromwell. The nerve of that pompous, insensitive blowhard. How could he possibly blame Nick and the others for the faults of humanity? The frailty of the human spirit? The complexities of pain and survival? How could he ignore the school's failure to stop the hideous waste?

The graduates had already assembled along the back street leading to the main campus. The women wore deep red gowns and matching mortarboards; the men were robed in rich royal blue. In the dense heat, they turned their programs into paper fans and passed contraband flasks and bottles of cheap, chilled champagne. There was a steady stream of animated conversation punctuated by loud bursts of giggled excitement. A tipsy walleyed boy in blue motioned to me as I passed and said in a faked Mexican accent, ''Hey, preety theeng. You want to buy a deeploma? Special deescount today. Two for a dollair.''

I allowed a tolerant smile and looked beyond him at the flushed faces of his classmates. All youth and promise, energy and expectation. The weight of it settled on me like a stone.

''Nicky,'' I whispered.

"Yeah?" My breath caught as a boy turned in response. For an instant he was Nick. Same dimpled, crooked grin. Same curious tilt of the head. His green eyes walked over my face until he was satisfied I was no one in particular.

"Sorry. You looked just like . . ." I muttered. But he had already turned his attention to more interesting issues.

Swarms of observers were filing into the long rows of folding chairs. I looked around in vain for a familiar face. But it seemed I was doomed to sit through this alone. I wrestled my way over several impassive legs and took a stiff seat in the center.

The school band struck up a hesitant prelude to "Pomp and Circumstance" as the first self-conscious pairs of graduates filed down the center aisle. I stared back through the sea of red and blue robes until my eyes could no longer focus. Looking, searching for something that no longer could be.

Rising to a brass crescendo, the tune repeated in endless chorus as thousands of robed paraders shuffled self-consciously past. In small bursts of enthusiasm family groups marked the appearance of their squat son or hawk-beaked daughter, all but lost in the yards of mock silk. By the end of the procession, a dull ache of jealous longing had overtaken me.

There were the usual speakers: The valedictorian, a swarthy, unsmiling boy with a penchant for fifty-dollar words, made a lengthy plea for his classmates to shift their professional goals from the almighty buck to concerns for nature and humanity. He made the point that if all of these budding entrepreneurs and investment bankers insisted on wearing crocodile shoes and toting snakeskin briefcases, their children's world would be devoid of those creatures altogether. Imagine.

A retiring government professor accepted an honorary degree and offered a long-winded diatribe against what he called the pitiful state of the academic salary. "Think of it," he said. "Were we able to dunk a lay-up shot or roll over two thousand pounds of padded defensive linemen, we would be wealthy beyond imagining. But since all we do is insure the future of our country, we are doomed to a life filled with cents-off coupons and charter flights. . . ."

Finally Chairman Lawrence mounted the podium in a voluminous black robe and puffed Elizabethan cap and took over the audience with a commanding sweep of his eyes.

"Distinguished visitors, friends of Cromwell, graduates"—he faced down someone chatting in the front row—"it is with a terrible confusion of pride and sorrow that I stand before you on this occasion." His eyes ambled along the rows of seated spectators as if he spoke to each of them in turn.

"There is pride in your growth and accomplishments. Pride in the emergence of your individual talents and your collective promise. Four long years ago, when first we assembled on this site, I sensed that among your ranks would be many young men and women who would go on to distinguish themselves and their university. And so you have . . . most of you.''

His face assumed a stilted smile, and he smoothed the polished surface of his hair. He was careful to affect that mush-mouthed, strangle-nosed London twang, even when clearing his throat.

There was a polite, insincere smattering of applause and laughter.

Lawrence allowed his plastic smile to fade in slow motion and held up a flowing black wing for silence. ''But there are the others. And the cowardly deeds of those selfish few threaten to undermine your accomplishments and blemish your bright futures. Over the past several months we have watched several of your number dash the precious gifts of their promise against the destructive rocks of despair. Most of us were shocked at the outset, shocked and dumbfounded at the meaning of these acts of self-destruction. But in time, shock yielded to discomfort and discomfort to disgust.''

Chairs creaked as the crowd began to squirm. The sanctimonious creep was going to do it again. I would lodge that formal protest. I owed that much to Nicky. And myself.

Lawrence stared down at the crowd, waiting for his indictment to take full effect. His face settled in a satisfied sneer. ''You have triumphed over the triple threat of cowardice, conceit, and selfishness. Those who fell in ready surrender to life's challenges committed those threats to the integrity of the very institution that sought to nurture and fulfill them. They threatened you and the future you have worked so hard to achieve. They have shaken the very foundations of Cromwell. And we shall not find easy forgiveness in our hearts.''

A low chant rose from the seated graduates. In seconds it built to a furious boom. ''Bull—shit . . . bull—shit!''

Most of the spectators sat in shocked silence at first. But a few began to snicker and several took up the cry. ''Bull—shit . . . bull—shit!''

Lawrence's face grew deadly pale as he tried to shout down the taunting, but the crowd went on, fueled by the pleasure of release. ''Bull—shit!'' Months of fear and frustration reverberating in the air. ''Bull—shit!''

I watched Wallace Lawrence, biting his lip and wringing his hands in despair. Good for you, I thought. Good for you.

After several jubilant moments the band struck up the university alma mater and a timorous, moon-faced girl stepped to the microphone to sing in a thin soprano. ''In harmoneee . . . we sing our praise to theeeee . . . our storeee . . . one of glor-eee. Everlasting it will be—ee.''

Slowly the chanting subsided. Lawrence, his composure restored, began calling names, and the graduates stepped forward on cue to receive their diplomas. ''Samantha Abrams, Jonah Ackbar, Lawrence Barry Ackerman . . .''

I settled back and watched the new procession. Cameras flashed and crackled as the moment was recorded for family posterity. And I noticed a few professionals snapping shots and scratching notes on steno pads. Good, I thought. Let the world hear about Chairman Wallace Lawrence and his repugnant attitudes. Let him be the final nail in the coffin of his beloved university.

At the end of the ceremony I stood at the edge of the crowd, looking for Diamond. Families passed, linked together in easy chains of pride and pleasure. I tried to think past the envy gnawing at my insides. Would I ever have that feeling of simple belonging again?

"Sarah?" I felt the hand on my back.

"Ben? What are you doing here?"

I stiffened in his hug, and he drew away. "I wanted to see you. To talk."

"I'm not so sure we have anything to talk about."

"Please, Sar. Don't shut me out. Not anymore." His eyes caught mine. "I love you. I know things have been a god-awful mess, but we can work it out if you want to, if you still care."

His eyes were pleading, pulling at me until I needed all my strength to hold on to my failing resolve. "I care, Ben. But I don't know if I have the strength to pick up the pieces."

"I'm not ready to let it go, Sarah. We can't do that. We've been through too much together to give up over a rocky time and one stupid mistake."

"Is that the way you see it? One stupid mistake?" I snapped my fingers. "That's it?" All so simple.

"What can I say? I'm sorry. I'm so terribly sorry about everything."

I looked in the murky pool of his expression—sad, sorry man-child. Little boy looking for the salve of sympathy. Part of me wanted to give him what he wanted. But it wasn't as simple as he wanted to believe. There was a curious void between us. I shivered in the heat. "How do you know when a marriage is dead, Ben? How do you know what's worth trying to save and what's too far gone?"

He wove his fingers into mine and led me away from the crowd, out past the line of stately buildings toward the road. "Ali was invited to go to Clare's summer place on Martha's Vineyard for a couple of weeks. I thought it would be good for her to get away. Anyway, your mother's had about all the adolescence she can take."

"That's nice. Clare's been good for Ali. They can talk to each other."

"I guess. I think she misses you."

"She understands. She understands a lot of things I wish she didn't have to. In a way, she's more grown-up than I can stand for her to be."

There was a hollow place in his voice. "I want us all together again, Sar. I want us to be a family."

Poor Ben. He really could not see the giant chasm between wanting and what was. "How long are you planning to stay?"

"Just a little while. I have to go to London for a few days, Sarah. The marketing conference, remember?"

"Yes." Echoes from a different life. We had planned to go together. London, Paris, Amsterdam.

"Please, Sar, come with me. Maybe if we have some time alone . . ."

In the shade of a towering elm I stopped and looked at him. So familiar I could trace the fine lines of his face with my eyes closed. Without looking, I could draw his body, line for line, planes and ridges, soft and firm places, secrets and sensitivities. If I had the strength, I could jump into his thoughts and swim with him through the thickest pains and pleasures. "Not yet, Ben. I'm not ready to leave here yet, and I'm not ready for the two of us." My voice was an irresolute whisper.

"You're sure?"

"I'm sure."

He smoothed the back of my hair as he had a thousand times, and a tickle crept up my neck. "All right, then. Whatever's right for you, Sar. Maybe by the time I get back . . ."

"Maybe."

He tugged up the tight corners of his mouth and shrugged. "Can't blame a guy for trying. Anyway, if you're not going to join me, I'll be back right after the conference. Next Saturday."

"I don't know when I'll be through here, Ben."

"I'll wait."

I pulled back from a wave of feeling. "You have a good trip."

He checked his watch. "I guess if you're positive about not coming, I'll drive up to Syracuse and catch the five o'clock."

"I'm positive."

With an awkward kiss, he backed away and toward his rented car. I watched him settle behind the wheel, adjusting his square shoulders against the seat. Breath held, I waited for the plaintive whine of the engine as he pressed his eager foot against the accelerator. Then he turned to look back into the line of traffic and pulled away from the curb.

He raised a hand as he passed, and I waved in return.

Suddenly weary, I walked back to Diamond's car and drove to the Barrington Arms. He was waiting for me in the lobby, his porky hand working like an oiled piston as he dipped into an oversize box of strawberry-colored popcorn.

"I missed you at the graduation, Sarah Spooner. Quite a crowd, huh? Quite a scene. You ready for some dinner?"

Ben was gone. Allison. Pat. There sat my portly partner, my friend, his face taut with effort, cheeks working in a fury of nervous need.

"I missed you too, Mr. Diamond. Where shall we go?"

The town was crawling with celebrants, but Diamond had made a fortunate reservation at The Inn at Lake

Pequod, an ancient, milk-white farmhouse with warped plank floors, faded floral wall coverings, and spotty air-conditioning. The graduation hordes had filled the bar to overflowing and spilled out into the entrance foyer to wait in the shadow of a wall hung with farm collectibles: rusted milk cans, ancient wooden plows and worn leather tack, county fair prize ribbons, quaint homilies embroidered on linen samplers.

Diamond burrowed through the crowd and worked some magic on the maître d'.

"Right this way, Sarah Spooner. Our table's ready."

I tried to ignore the disgruntled stares on my way into the dining room. We were led to a prime center table festooned with a candy-striped cloth and a centerpiece of red and blue flowers and matching balloons.

Diamond shook out his large red linen napkin, tucked it into the starched collar of his white shirt, and shook his head in mock apology. "That's always the way. He who gives, gets. He who hesitates, waits. I'm starved."

The bread basket arrived, and Diamond started eating with a vengeance. Ripping off thick chunks of warm, spongy rye, he slathered each bite with a hillock of soft herb butter from a porcelain crock and popped it in his mouth. When the basket was almost empty, he motioned for a fresh supply of bread and attacked the crudités, buttering the radishes and carrot sticks and depositing them in his mouth like a trainman shoveling coal into a fuel-starved engine.

When the waiter came with a second loaf of bread, Diamond opened the menu and began to chant like a religious zealot: a bowl of clam chowder and one of cream of celery soup, Duchess potatoes, two of the dinner portions of cheese tortellini, two fettuccine Alfredos—extra sauce . . .

After the waiter left, shaking his head in disbelief, I tried simple reason. "Please, Mr. Diamond. You're going to make yourself sick."

Still stoking his boiler with crusty chunks of bread, he looked up at me. "Don't you worry about me, Sarah Spooner. I'm not worth it."

"Of course you are. You're a caring, sympathetic person and a talented professional to boot."

A faint blush rose in his cheeks. "Thank you. But that isn't enough. I'm a total failure—as a human being."

"No, you're not."

He held up a hand. "Yes, I am. You want to hear what a wonderful person I am, Sarah Spooner? I stood by and let my whole family die. What kind of a person would do that?" His eyes filled.

"What are you talking about? I don't understand."

He bit his beefy lip. "It's a long story."

"I've got time."

He blotted his eyes with the corner of his napkin. "You remember how I said I know things? How I have these feelings?"

"Yes."

"Well, I had this feeling about my family: my wife, Emma, and my little boy, Willy. I was off testifying at a murder trial in Peoria, Illinois. They hired me as a witness for the defense. Alleged perpetrator had the handwriting of a choirboy—not a violent blip in his body. The smoothest, roundest ascenders you ever saw. And rhythm as sure as the kick line at Radio City. . . . The case was all circumstantial. The D.A. was grasping at straws. The crime was done, therefore somebody had to do it. Might as well be this guy as the next. He was handy. You know the way.

"Anyhow, when it was my turn to take the stand, I got this awful feeling something was about to happen to Emma and Willy. My Em was a fine woman, Sarah Spooner. Bright, funny, kindest soul you ever met. We met in high school. Senior year, we wound up on the yearbook committee together. Identification was our game. You know where you look at the pictures and tell who's who underneath? We fell for each other like a ton of bricks and that was it. I think it was while we were identifying the boys' gymnastics team. Or maybe it was girls' field hockey.

"We were married for about a year when Willy came along. Em did natural childbirth, the whole business. Wasn't even in style then. But Em wanted everything just so. You can't imagine how we doted on that little boy. He was something special, my Willy, a real little ball of sunshine. Smart as a whip. And cute. Boy was a regular comedian. Used to leave us in stitches with his

Jack Benny imitations and his Henry Kissinger. Had the moves, the face, everything. Real talent.

"I used to love to go in and watch him sleep at night—all curled up and cozy, his hair all mussed up and his little brown teddy tucked under his arm. Had that teddy from practically the day he was born and wouldn't think of going to bed without it. That is, except if he had a friend sleep over. Then Teddy had to hide under the mattress. 'Teddy understands, Daddy. Don't you, Ted?' he used to say. Can you imagine?"

Diamond sighed. "You know how the air in a child's room gets to smell of talcum and sleep and you can get hypnotized watching that little chest rise and fall?"

"I remember."

He took a deep tremor of a breath. "Anyway, I was sitting in the courtroom, about to testify, and I get this feeling. It's so overpowering, it almost knocks me off my chair. And I know it's about Em and Willy. Something bad. And I have to warn them. So I raise my hand like a school kid and tell the judge I need a recess. But the son of a bitch starts asking me questions. 'Are you sick, Mr. Diamond? What do you need a recess for? Don't you realize it's highly unusual for a witness to request a recess? Do you have any idea how much it costs the taxpayers every time we take a recess?'

"So the feeling is getting worse and worse. Like I'm drowning. Holding my breath until my insides are ready to burst. And I start to feel so dizzy and sick, I can hardly answer the questions. Still the judge won't quit.

'You are a professional, Mr. Diamond. Surely you must recognize that we cannot recess for every little request. Can you imagine what that would do to an already over-loaded calendar?' ''

His face was twisted in pain, his eyes glazed. ''Finally, I couldn't take it anymore. I ran out of the courtroom with the bailiff chasing after me. When he tried to keep me from the phone, I decked him. I was crazed by then, the feeling was so intense—screaming inside me like a pack of trapped animals . . .

''I was shaking so hard, I could hardly dial. I tried twice before I got through. The phone rang and rang. But no one answered. I knew they had to be there. It was just the time Willy got home from school. Emma was always there waiting for him. Like clockwork. 'Those first few minutes after school are the most important,' she always said. 'A boy needs his mother and his snack.' Emma was a wonderful mother, Sarah Spooner. The finest.

''I couldn't wait any longer, so I called our next-door neighbor, Mrs. Hammernick. When she heard my voice, she got hysterical. 'How did you know, Aldo? How did you find out already? It just happened a couple of minutes ago. They were just taken away. My God, Aldo. I never saw such a thing. I liked to go blind from how awful. Willy was running across the street from the school bus, and Emma must've seen the car coming. She tried to save him, Aldo. She ran right out there. But it was too late. The car hit them both.' ''

Diamond was pale and trembling. I patted his hand. "That's awful. Terrible. But you shouldn't blame yourself. It's not your fault."

He shook his head. "I knew, Sarah Spooner. I was warned." He blew his nose and took a deep breath. Then he wrestled his wallet from the distended pocket of his slacks. "Willy and Emma were my life. All I had. Look."

I took the picture, a rumpled snapshot of a young couple standing with a little boy. All of them were smiling stiff camera smiles. The woman had a gentle child's face and large, wondering eyes. The boy's front teeth were missing, and there was the shadow of a chocolate mustache under his upturned nose. My eyes kept returning to the man, reed-thin with a thick mass of wavy, brown hair and a clear, steady gaze. I looked from the picture to Diamond and back again.

"Yes," he said. "That was me. Believe it or not. Amazing what can become of a person after a few years of wading in dog poop."

The first courses arrived, and Diamond turned his attention to an attack of hunger lust. I wished for something wise and soothing to say, but I knew the pain of such loss could not be eased by well-intentioned words. Healing took time and resolve. Maybe we all needed to take hazardous wrong turns along the way.

I wondered if there was really any way to warn a person away from his own destruction.

-15-

At dawn, dressed in red nylon shorts and a white mesh running top, I crept past the sleeping swell of Diamond's body in the front room and set out to jog along the somnolent streets. The air was misty and scented with the damp perfume of blooming flowers; the street lamps dimmed to a gentle haze in the first stage of their surrender to the daylight. A plump cinnamon cat, perched on the concrete steps of a large stone fraternity house, lifted its head as I passed and mewled a lazy challenge. Trucks clattered on some distant road. In a house at the corner, a baby screamed for attention and was still.

The rhythm of the run filled my head, displacing the jumble of worries that jolted me to consciousness at intervals during the endless night. Awake, I heard Diamond's heavy pacing, his footfalls hacking against the wood floors until the boards groaned in protest. Then he would sit, the bedsprings straining under his bulk, and the night's silence was broken by munching sounds, the crisp crunch of Diamond's teeth against a mouthful of beer nuts or a Dutch pretzel, the relentless glug of Diamond's throat as he downed a half gallon of lukewarm Dr Pepper or a tepid can of carbonated chocolate fudge.

Asleep, his silhouette resembled a beached whale or a sand dune rising and sinking with the whimsical shifting of the winds and tides. *A Concise History of Cromwell* lay open across his chest, covered by a protective hand. He was never far away from that book, I noticed. Then, I suppose he had to cling to something.

As the pavement melted under my feet, I pictured him lying there in the front room, curled and cozy like the image of his dead son, Willy, his free arm clutching some familiar comfort—the phantom of his dead wife, Emma, or the lost substance of his home and family.

Cool perspiration licked the backs of my knees and slithered down my cheeks as I crossed the rickety bridge over the gorge connecting the outlying streets to the Cromwell campus. I kept my eyes straight ahead. Below, in the inky chasm, my imagination could detect the bloody shreds of failed lives. In ghoulish slow motion I pictured falling bodies, faces distended with the shock of final knowledge as they fell. Falling as shrill screams of horror rose like a maniac's machete to slash the stillness.

The buildings were dark except for the occasional haze of a blue light illuminating a fire alarm box or the yellow glare of a desk lamp left on by some careless academic. Trees cast their ample shadows across the deserted quadrangle, and a bossy crow squawked in dismay at my intrusion.

I kept running, past the flying concrete form of the undergraduate library, past the cafeteria and the ancient stone chapel. The law school complex dissolved in a blur to my left, and I caught a glimpse of the engineering buildings—chemical, mechanical, electrical, electronic, civic, physical, and aeronautic. The seven docks, Nicky called them. "Hold your ears as you go by, Mother, dear," he said. "The roar of the calculators is deafening."

Out past the school on the south side, I jogged down the gentle hill to the seedy collection of shops and apartments known as Campusville. This was the preferred living space for Cromwell's tradition busters and trendsetters. Beatniks in the sixties replaced by seventies hippies and eighties punks. The area was imbued with the smell and feel of rebellion: buildings sported angry splashes of sprayed silver-edged graffiti, and the air hung with the stale aromas of burned incense and exotic cooking.

At the corner of Ivy and Vine, I recognized a building Nicky had pointed out several times with shining eyes and a voice full of childish pleading. This was the Hotel Ponderosa, home to a dubious pack of campus legends Nick had come to hero-worship, makers of crazy mischief that appealed to my son on some inexplicable level. The Ponderosa cowboys once invited Nick to join them on the range, and he flew home for an unexpected weekend visit to make a personal pitch. "They're very careful about who they ask to live with them, Mom, Dad. Do you realize what this means?"

"It means you'll flunk out by the end of the semester," Ben said.

"It means we might as well shred your tuition money and feed it to the pigeons," I added.

We were typical parents in that way, confusing our own fears and wishes with our child's self-definition. Nicky wasn't so much Nicky as he was Ben's chin or my flat feet or Grandfather Joseph's penchant for one-liners or my sister's tendency to academic sloth. We had no other way to explain his separateness, his distance. And they had to be explained or left to frighten us to death.

So we denied him the Hotel Ponderosa. Another disappointment added to the list: no Hotel Ponderosa, no year off to backpack across Europe, no cap guns, no camping out with Jimmy Landerson behind the Waverly Theater on a frigid January night for the chance to secure two tickets to a concert by the fabulous Slime Buckets. Disappointments, I wondered if they were cumulatively deadly—like X rays. I wondered if I could protect Allison from the dangers of despair by offering her an endless supply of indulgences. Tempting.

I turned back up the hill and made my way toward the Barrington Arms. I had an appointment to meet with Diamond's friend, Byron "Chip" Dexter, chief of the Cromwell police. I wanted to hear his views on the suicides. The police perspective tended to cut through any blinding emotions or mawkish sentimentality.

In the hotel lobby I found Winston Lawrence behind the desk, pondering a supply catalog. When I entered, he looked up for a brief instant. "Good morning, Mrs. Spooner."

"Good morning, Mr. Lawrence. It's a wonderful day. Clear. Cool."

He looked dubious. "Hardly a wonderful day for Cromwell, I'm afraid, Mrs. Spooner. Haven't you heard?"

"Heard?"

His lips were pursed in dismay. "My, my, it is dreadful, simply dreadful. There has been another suicide. A most tragic, ironic one. The valedictorian of the graduating class was found at the bottom of the Mahkeenac Gorge before dawn. He left a note saying he was afraid to go on. My, my, can you imagine? Poor fellow assumed he could never match his accomplishments at Cromwell." Lawrence's mouse voice had dimmed to a breath. "Oh, my, where will it end, Mrs. Spooner? The valedictorian no less."

Where would it end? My legs turned to rubber and an odd buzzing started in my head. "How did you hear?"

"Oh, the radio, the local television. Bad news travels quickly, as you know."

I climbed the stairs and rapped on the door to the suite. Diamond was swaddled in a gigantic white terry cloth robe, his sparse hair dripping wet from the shower.

His face was mottled pink, and his eyes were bloodshot from a restless night. "Well, you're the early bird, aren't you, Sarah Spooner. Must be hard running like you do. You look all done in."

"There's been another suicide, Mr. Diamond. The valedictorian of the graduating class."

Diamond sank on the pullout couch. "No." He raked his fingers through the wet ribbons of hair. "Another jumper?"

"Yes. They found him at the bottom of the Mah-keenac Gorge."

He shuddered. "What was that boy's name again? Something Greek wasn't it? Archimedes?"

"Atsedes, I think." I retrieved my program from the wastebasket in the bedroom. "Anthony Atsedes, that was it. Look at these credentials: 4.0 average, champion gymnast, editor of the school paper, senior class president. He had a scholarship for a deferred law degree at Harvard and a fabulous position lined up as a junior White House aide in the meantime. Hardly sounds like a life of despair."

Diamond was leafing through a giant stack of file folders on the desk. "Aspetuk, Atkins, Atsedes, here it is." There was a flat, green gummy bear on the front cover. The application was typed with a clear black ribbon. Diamond flipped through the pages until he came to the signature line at the end.

Cradling the document on outstretched palms, he sat in the flowered armchair and stared at the signature. His mouth worked as he studied, and his head tipped and swiveled as he tested the writing from varied angles.

"Thick point . . . twenty, twenty-five-degree forward slant. Unconnected medial *E*. There's a little odd downstroke on the embedded *S*. And the *Y* . . ."

"You see abnormalities?"

His knees crackled as he stood. Tying his robe tighter around his mountainous middle, he returned the Atsedes folder to the pile and fished a bag of chocolate kisses from the desk drawer. "All I can tell you is that Anthony Atsedes had some fool teacher who changed him from lefty to righty. Used to believe it was a strain on the heart to be left-handed. So they'd tie the left hand to the child's chest and force him to use his right. Pretty oldfashioned. Almost barbaric, if you ask me. Made some kids so nervous, they developed tics or started wetting the bed. But most handled it. Odd for today, I'll tell you that much. Most teachers gave up trying to convert lefties forty, fifty years ago."

"What about instability? Emotional disorders?"

Diamond shrugged and affected a crooked smile. His voice was a nervous flutter. "What can I tell you, Sarah Spooner? You, yourself, said it was a parlor trick. I can't know everything by looking at a person's signature, now, can I?"

"But you said—"

He stopped me with the flagging of his palm. "I know, I know. My words come back to haunt me. Well, I admit I was wrong. I don't know everything.

Sometimes I wonder if I know anything at all. I'm a big dope, Sarah Spooner. I ought to keep my big mouth shut. That's what I should do.'' He tapped the folders in a pile and began depositing them in an oversize briefcase. "You know, I've had it up to here with all this. I'm about ready to pack it in and move on. No point hanging around anymore. No point for you, either, believe me. Cromwell just happens to have more than its fair share of loonies and loonies-to-be and sub-loonies. We can't do a darned thing about it. May as well go on home. I've had enough, Sarah Spooner. More than enough.''

He stuffed the briefcase with one hand, his mouth with the other. When both were full, he took a momentary break to retrieve another briefcase from the back of the closet and yet another bag of chocolates from the desk.

"Mr. Diamond, I have the feeling you are not telling me everything.''

"Now, now, Sarah Spooner. Why would I keep anything from you, for Pete's sake? You're a grown-up, I know that.'' He looked up from his stuffing and managed a strained, unconvincing wink. "Bottom line is, there's nothing to say. Cromwell's having a run of suicides and that's that. You put a bunch of unbalanced kids in a pressure cooker and that's what happens. Terrible but . . .''

"Simple as that.''

"Not simple at all, but that's the way it is. You can spend the rest of your life in this god-awful place and not change a thing. It's a waste of time, yours and mine.

A big, dumb, foolish waste. Take my word.''

"I'm not convinced, Mr. Diamond. I think you know more than you're saying. Please. If you think Nicky's death might have been in any way suspicious, you have to tell me."

"Now, now. There you go jumping to more conclusions. I told you, Sarah Spooner. It's just a horrible, unfortunate, tragic bunch of events. The university has investigated. I have, the police, the—"

"Sometimes you have to dig to get the answers from the police. I'm going to see Chief Dexter at two, as a matter of fact. Maybe he knows more than he's saying."

As he spoke, Diamond tossed peanut M&Ms back in his churning mouth. "That's plain foolishness, Sarah Spooner. You can take my word for it. Chip Dexter has nothing to tell you. He's ready to cash it in too. You'll see. We've been tossing this thing around since I got to town. He's convinced everything here is on the up-and-up. Don't even bother to go. You're wasting your time."

"I don't care. I want to see him."

"Well, be my guest, then, Sarah Spooner. Go on and see him. I can't stop you. You satisfy yourself. But I'll tell you, there's nothing to be gained by all this digging around. In fact, it's a good way to get yourself in trouble."

"If nothing suspicious is going on, what have I got to lose?"

I watched him shrivel. His tone was pleading. "Look, even if there was some fishy business going on here, it wouldn't have anything to do with your boy. I promise you that.''

My insides turned to ice. "How do you know? You have to tell me.''

He just stood there, his hair sticking out in foolish points, his face hanging slack and pendulous like a water balloon. A murderous rage began to build and boil in my gut. "You have to tell me.'' In a trance of fury I grabbed hold of Diamond's thick shoulders and tried to shake loose the words. "Tell me ... tell me ... tell me!''

He did not move. Impassive, he stood and waited for me to retrieve my senses.

Slowly I absorbed the horror on his face. "Oh, God, Diamond. I'm sorry. I'm so sorry. I don't know what's the matter with me. I must be out of my mind.''

"It's all right. I understand.'' He turned from me and fished in his briefcase. "Anyway, I was wrong to try to protect you. You should know.''

He extracted a folder and opened it on the desk. I recognized Nicky's writing—large, bold stokes and slashes. He pulled the flowered armchair beside the dainty maple ladder-back at the desk. "Sit here, Sarah Spooner. I'll show you about your son.''

His voice was a chant. "I didn't think it should come from me, Sarah Spooner. I mean, who am I, for God's sake. But whatever might be happening at Cromwell, your son's situation was different. Look here.''

As he pointed and expostulated, my ears rumbled with a sound like waves pounding the hull of an old wooden ship. Struggling past the noise, I tried to hear, to somehow absorb what he was saying.

"The sharp slash of the strokes indicates a desperate kind of anger. You see it in violent or extremely chaotic situations. And the way the crossbars tilt up and down, almost at random—that's a clear sign of emotional turmoil. The last time I saw anything this disorganized was in an old man accused of killing his wife of sixty years. Poor old guy couldn't stand to see her suffer any more. She was riddled with cancer, taking enough morphine to kill a horse, but it didn't touch the pain. She begged him to help her, to put her out of her misery."

My head seemed to rattle as I shook it in protest. "There were no major traumas like that in Nicky's life. He had a family, a girlfriend, a future—"

Diamond set a restraining hand over mine. "Just listen. Then we'll talk." His finger traced the base of a line of writing. "See here? You know how I talked about rhythm? Your son's rhythm was choppy and uncertain. That's what happens when you feel like your life has been turned upside down and you're hanging by your thumbnails. Despair, Sarah Spooner. If I took a sample of my own writing after what happened to my Emma and Willy . . . or of yours right after your son's death, you would see this kind of dangerous choppiness. It settles down after a time, when the crisis has passed."

I couldn't stand any more of it. Rising, I took Nick's papers from Diamond, pried loose the red gummy bear, and replaced the folder in the briefcase. "You said yourself, you don't know everything, Mr. Diamond. In this case you're wrong. I knew my son. He was no more desperate than you. Or me."

"I rest my case."

"I'm serious. Nicky might not have been the world's best adjusted human, but he was happy enough. And he was certainly able to roll with a few little trials and disappointments. So he had rotten handwriting. He always got *C*'s in penmanship, Mr. Diamond. Does lousy penmanship mean a person is suicidal?"

He stood and stretched. "Have it your way, Sarah Spooner. You can't accept anything until you're ready. I know that as well as the next person. In the meantime, try to let it go. There's nothing more here for you. Go home and concentrate on what you have left. You'll be better off."

"You sound like you've been talking to my mother." I tried to smile. "It doesn't work, Diamond. I can't forget."

"No one expects you to forget. You're never going to do that. It's just that Cromwell has nothing more to tell you, Sarah Spooner."

"You know, Mr. Diamond, there is one fatal flaw in your logic. That was Nicky's college application, right?"

"Yes."

"He applied to Cromwell more than three years ago. If there was that much turmoil and instability three years ago, why didn't he kill himself then? And how do you know his handwriting, and Nicky, didn't straighten out completely in three years? You said yourself that hand-writing, and the emotions it reflects, is fluid—in constant change."

He held up a hand. "All right, Sarah Spooner. Nobody ever accused you of not being a smart person. Of course, you could be right. His handwriting might have changed. And if we had a sample of his writing just before his death, it might give me a whole different picture. But from this . . ."

I glanced over at my purse. Nick's note was folded and zipped in the inside compartment. The words echoed in my mind: Too much and not enough. . . . Not enough. The note might give us a whole different picture. Or . . .

Diamond folded his hands and chewed thoughtfully on his lower lip. "As for your other question, I don't know the answer. Why does a person manage to cope for so long and then snap? What makes someone choose a certain time to put an end to the challenge, hope, and misery we call life? I don't know. I wish I did." He went to the closet and fished a tin of butter cookies from behind his clothes. Prying off the metal top with a key, he hummed in thought. "Maybe there are certain things we aren't meant to know, Sarah Spooner. All the biggies are mysteries, aren't they? Think about it: life, death, birth, success, failure, clear summer skies, perfect French pastries. Some things have to be accepted as given. On faith.''

''As you said, a person has to be ready for such acceptance, Mr. Diamond. I'm not ready yet.''

He shrugged in surrender and placed a stack of round sugar-studded cookies in his mouth. ''That's up to you, Sarah Spooner. No one can stop you from beating your head against the bricks. All I can tell you is what I see in your boy's writing. I can understand if you don't want to hear it. As a parent, you think you should be able to protect your child, kiss the pain and make it go away. Nothing is worse than thinking you somehow failed your own family—your own son. That's too big a load of guilt for anyone to haul around. Way too big. So you find a way out. Each of us finds a way. You investigate; I eat. Same difference.'' He moved on to the pretzel-shaped stack, lifted the pleated paper container, and poised the trio of cookies on the tip of his tongue like a trained seal.

A weight of weariness settled over me. ''Part of me knows you may be right, Mr. Diamond. But another, stronger part isn't satisfied yet. Why so many suicides all at once? Why the odd feeling around this place? I can't quit until I find exactly what's going on here.''

''You wouldn't be quitting. You'd be going back to your home, your family, your job. People need you, Sarah Spooner. What about *them*?'' He fished for crumbs in the empty tin with a moistened fingertip, then crumpled the paper cups one by one and tossed them in the wastebasket with the fluid moves of a star center taking foul shots. Between tosses, he looked over at me. ''I'm not getting anyplace with you, am I?''

I felt a tug of affection. ''No, but you get good grades for trying. And for helping me get through this.''

He shrugged. ''I haven't done anything. Point is, there's nothing to do. There's nothing more for you to find out here. Go home, Sarah Spooner. Be sensible.''

''No one ever accused me of being sensible.''

He tapped an impatient foot against the floor. ''What can I say to convince you? How do I get through to you?''

My stomach was in a knot. ''You can help me. Tell me everything you know and help me sort through what I've found. If we work together, we can get to the bottom of what's going on here. I know we can. Then I can be done with this place, once and for all.''

His forehead settled in a wrinkled drape, and his eyes clouded over. ''I don't know anything. Nothing at all. Haven't found a thing. You want to play cops and robbers, you're going to have to play by yourself. Dumb if you ask me. A dumb waste. Go home, Sarah Spooner. Don't be a fool.''

''I can't. I have to see this through. I have no choice, Diamond. Don't you see?''

He tossed the last crumpled paper cup. It landed with a satisfying swish in the center of the trash. ''You're a grown-up. I can't tell you what to do. You won't listen, no matter what I say. Why should I waste my breath?''

He fished in the back of the closet for food. When he came up empty, he crossed to the dresser and worked in a frenzy, pulling out shirts and underwear, peering in the corners of the drawers for stray snacks. "Damn."

"Why are you so upset, Diamond?"

"Upset? Who's upset? Not me. Why should I be upset? What you do is your business. Doesn't mean anything to me. Not a thing." With a loud, exasperated whoosh of breath, he tossed the empty tin in the basket. "You insist on wasting your time, go ahead. Why should I try to stop you? What's the big deal?"

"Exactly. What is the big deal?"

"Look, I have a few things to clear up, a few errands to run, and you have your appointment with the chief. I'll meet you back here later on."

I went to shower and change while Diamond got himself in order. I was sure his errands would include several purveyors of empty calories. Without food he seemed to be desperately lost. I thought about the impossible hole he was trying to fill. Lost loves, lost lives. There was no filling such a void.

As I stepped out of the shower I heard the door to the front room open and squeak shut. Diamond's heavy steps retreated down the carpeted hall and were lost on the staircase. Outside, a dog barked its suspicions, and there was a flutter of running feet. Someone in a hurry. The barking built to a furious howl as the intruder passed. Then there was a curious, expectant pause before the world settled back into an uneasy silence.

-16-

A maroon checker cab deposited me at the curb fronting the imposing steel-and-glass headquarters of the Cromwell Police Department. Inside, a chinless muffin of a woman with lacquered lemon hair and a bulging blue uniform sat at the front desk studying a soap opera magazine by the glare of a fluorescent lamp. Several cops stood around with the hangdog look of weary travelers awaiting an overdue bus. A smooth-cheeked rookie peeked up as I entered, then shook his head in dismissal. Another looked me over before turning to aim a violent kick at the belly of an obstreperous vending machine. The machine gurgled in response and spat a thick stream of watery cocoa on the polished black tile floor. The cop flashed a toothy grin and a victory sign at the lethargic onlookers as he swaggered out the door.

The desk clerk, clearly miffed at the interruption, eyeballed me through a tarantula fringe of artificial eyelashes and sighed the directions to the chief's office. I went through the door she indicated with her eyes and followed a confusing maze of identical corridors to the opposite end of the building. Dexter's name was etched in the bubbled glass of his office door.

The chief was perched on the edge of the bronze-toned desk like a torch singer, his square, jowly face set in a scrupulous smile. His teeth were thick, rutted squares and the comb tracks still showed in his sparse, oily gray hair.

"Mrs. Spooner? Nice to meet you. Please sit down. Al Diamond has told me a lot about you."

"He has?" Diamond had made a point of ignoring my frequent requests to arrange an audience with his buddy, the chief. "Then I guess you know that I've come to Cromwell to uncover the circumstances of my son's death. Mr. Diamond assured me the police have been conducting a thorough investigation into the suicides."

He pursed his lips. "Al Diamond said that? Well, I guess that's good news. I've been trying to convince him all week that we've looked under every rock and around every corner. But he never seems to be satisfied. I mean, what more can we do? We've interviewed virtually everyone on campus—students, faculty. Brought in experts. Al, himself, as you know, and others. We all but hired a psychic to check out Cromwell's aura. Right from the beginning I've had several of my top men on it, full-time. The deaths at the university have been our number one priority since they began."

"And?"

His smile faded, and he began tapping the stacks of notes and memos on his desk into neat little piles. "And, and, and. What can I say? Cromwell has had an unfortunate rash of suicides. Nothing mysterious about it. That's the bottom line."

"I'm not satisfied with that, Chief. Why Cromwell? Why now? Diamond didn't think the latest one, the valedictorian, looked suicidal at all from his handwriting. Aren't you the least bit suspicious?"

"Now, now, now, Mrs. Spooner." He waggled his finger. "I am an officer of the law, not a TV detective. It's not my place to be suspicious. My job is to seek the facts and examine those that I find."

"But the facts don't add up in every case, Chief Dexter. Diamond said—"

He folded his hands and trained his beady eyes on me. "Look, Mrs. Spooner. I'll be frank. Al Diamond is an old friend and colleague of mine. I've used him on a pack of puzzling cases. Man was always sharp as a tack. A nose like no other in the business. That's why I suggested he be brought in on this one. But he's not what he used to be. I guess it's on account of what happened to his family."

"Diamond is not the issue here. Even without the handwriting analysis, all these suicides don't make sense. Your 'bottom line' is not enough. I don't buy it."

He held up a hand. "Now, now, Mrs. Spooner. I understand. I can imagine what you must be going through.

And I didn't mean to sound pat and uninterested. You must believe me. This has been the most comprehensive investigation I've ever worked on by a long shot. Come. Let me show you the rest.''

I followed him out of his office and down the cold, gray tunnel of a back stairwell. Two flights down. Three. He moved with surprising agility, taking the steps in twos and threes, springing lightly on the balls of his black-loafered feet. I watched the reflected light glisten off the bouncing bald spot atop his head as I hurried to keep up.

In the basement he put his shoulder to a matte black fire door and stepped into a cavern of darkness. I followed his silhouette inside and waited in the cool silence for him to flip on the light.

He danced his fingers over a control box on the wall, and the room sprang to life. There was a wash of warm, pinkish light and the smooth hum of a generator. Awakened, a row of computer terminals blipped and blinked and flashed disparate series of code words and numbers. A fan of message paper spewed from the slack jaw of a laser printer, and a large copy machine flashed instructions and idiot warnings: ''Remove your original'' and ''Close cover before activating copier.'' Along the wall a bank of silent electronic phones were poised for action.

Dexter crossed to the nearest keyboard and typed a nimble message. The computer flashed, ''Case file loading—please wait'' in vivid green on an ebony background. He motioned me to sit.

In a few seconds a series of names scrolled across the screen. I recognized them as the suicides, and my breath caught as Nick's name joined the others. Dexter tapped again, and the names were grouped and regrouped, split and rearranged in a dizzying array of possibilities.

"Demographics?" he typed.

An outline map of the United States appeared on the face of the screen. The names leapt onto the outline in random placement. "Two from the East Coast. Three from the Midwest, four from the West Coast and Rocky Mountains. Two from overseas. Both nonaligned countries, by the way."

"Affiliations?" he typed.

"One Episcopalian republican moderate; one Lutheran conservative independent; one reformed Jew with liberal democratic leanings. Shall I go on?"

I still stared at the screen.

He tapped again. "Social, academic? Spooner, Nicholas."

Nick's name appeared on the screen. Michelle's flashed up beside it, and I recognized an exhaustive list of his friends and acquaintances. There was a complete record of the clubs and organizations he had joined since junior high school: Future Businessmen, Key Club, the school paper, debate team, three years of soccer, cross-country. The machine scrolled through his high school record and his college transcript.

Dexter winced. "Not fond of the front of the alphabet, your boy."

"Nick always considered grades a foolish imposition, Chief Dexter. In high school he did well despite himself. He didn't need to try. But here. . . . He was very bright."

"I don't doubt it for a second. Cromwell only took the cream."

Scrolling further, I watched a parade of unfamiliar names. "Who are they?"

"Those are your son's"—he cleared his throat—"your son's intimate acquaintances since he came to Cromwell. About an average number these days, I'd say. Lots of the kids want to take their sex ed with a lab." His face flushed. "I told you, Mrs. Spooner. We left no stone unturned."

I'd had enough of looking. "What's the point, Chief? I can see you have examined every wart on Nicky's life, and the others. But what does it prove?"

"Linking ties?" he typed.

"Insignificant," the machine responded.

He substituted, "Patterns? Conclusions? Modus? Status?"

Each time the machine refused to commit to anything. "Insignificant . . . none."

On and on he went, putting the data through every conceivable process. "Insignificant."

Rising, he walked over to the far wall and pressed a button to expose a sliding panel. At the press of another button a series of graphs and charts appeared on a recessed screen in vivid color. The data was processed and juggled in a dizzying array of possibilities.

"Nothing," he said. "Nothing, nothing, nothing. When we realized that seven of the suicides were in the English department, we thought we were on to something, but even that fizzled. You can take my word for it, Mrs. Spooner. These suicides were the result of mass hysteria, contagion. One of those dreadful psychological scourges we can't do anything about. There is nothing to indicate any foul play or criminal possibility in a single one of these instances. And there is no evidence whatsoever that Cromwell is falling under the spell of some mysterious curse—no matter what Al Diamond says."

"Curse?"

"The Cromwell curse." He stood and looked out the window. "You mean, he's spared you that piece of nonsense? Well, good. I'll tell you, Mrs. Spooner. Old Al is not what he used to be. It's sad, really. Diamond was tops in his field, the best. Made a believer out of me, I'll tell you. But now . . ."

"Wait. He did mention something about Cromwell having a run of bad luck. Do you mean the fires? The epidemics?"

He shook his head. "No, I'm not talking about those things. Al's got it in his head that there was some crazy curse placed on the university many years ago and that it's all coming true. Poor guy rants and raves about a prophecy of doom and how the suicides are part of it. He's got a few screws loose if you ask me." He shook his head and wiped his damp forehead on the sleeve of his uniform. "Not surprising, I guess, after all he's been through."

I watched the parade of shifting charts on the screen, possibilities smashed against a cold wall of logic. "A curse. Where did he get an idea like that?"

Dexter started switching off the displays. "Some dumb book he's been reading. Beats me how an intelligent person would believe such nonsense. You want to know why Al is sold on it? You'll have to ask him. I'll be honest, Mrs. Spooner. I think Al's gone over the edge. In fact, I spoke to Chairman Lawrence about him and this curse business. Please keep this between you and me, but Lawrence is planning to take him off the case before all this goes any further. Not that I wanted to see Al get canned, but I think he's got to be turned off before he blows a fuse, or worse."

I followed him back up the stairs and out into the waiting room. At the station door he offered a stiff handshake and a political smile. "Nice meeting you, Mrs. Spooner. Do me a favor, will you? Talk to Al Diamond. He thinks the world of you. Try to convince him to get some help or something. Maybe if he takes a vacation. The guy is really hanging on by a thread."

"I'll do what I can."

The same taxi was still waiting outside the station. As I climbed into the backseat, the driver turned his jutting jaw over his round left shoulder and studied me. "Geez, you look familiar. Wait . . . let me guess. P.S. 32, right?

No. Wait. Lincoln High . . . ninth-grade social studies. Am I right?''

''You drove me here an hour ago.''

''I knew it. I never forget a face.'' He whistled bird-calls as he drove up the town road toward the Barrington Arms. Shrill blips and warbles, guttural caws, and angry vulture shrieks. I could hear my mother's voice chanting a favorite refrain. ''There are more nuts on the street than in Brazil, Sarah. More nuts than Planters.''

Turning into Parrish Common, he fell silent. The dead monument of a street had the same effect on me whenever I passed through. There was the embarrassed sense of intrusion. We did not belong in this private, forbidding place. I held my breath until we entered the gate leading to the hotel.

With a few tentative notes the driver resumed his warbling as he came to a stop at the front door. He kept whistling in a nervous little trill as I counted out the fare into his outstretched palm. Stuffing the money in his pocket, he took a final look at me and clicked his tongue. ''Supposed to be real fancy, the Barrington. Not real friendly-looking, though. I'll tell you that.''

He gunned the engine and pulled away before I was halfway to the door. Looking up at the cold, somber facade, I knew what he meant. Not real friendly-looking at all. The windows were shuttered, and the air-conditioning issued a shrill, relentless whine. Gnarled trees cast a web of harsh shadows over the face of the building as the sun was swallowed by a dense gray cloud.

It had the look of a place where terrible things might decide to happen.

-17-

Diamond was pacing the length of the lobby, stopping once each cycle to thrum his porky fingers along the slats of the bird cage before continuing to plod back and forth, back and forth, between the walls. His head was bowed like a battering ram, and I could hear the rumble of his insistent muttering as he argued with himself. From the sound of it, neither side was winning.

When she noticed me, the blond desk girl caught my eye and rolled hers in a dramatic circle. She motioned me to the front counter and cupped her hand over my ear to tell me, in a warm, unpleasant breath, that Diamond had been pacing like that since I left, and that she, for one, would like to see him removed like so much rubble. Every third or fourth word was punctuated by a sharp crackle of her spearmint gum. The syrupy scent of it, mixed with her bug-spray cologne, left me dizzy.

I walked over to Diamond and laid a gentle, restraining hand on the pillow of his shoulder. "Are you okay?"

His eyes had the pleading, frightened look of a child waking from a bad dream. There was a sick emptiness behind the terror as he searched my face for something. "Dexter told you about it."

"It? You mean, the curse? He mentioned it. Diamond, what's the matter?"

"God, no." He put a finger to his lips. "Not here."

"Are you okay?" I asked again, but the words seemed to bounce off the invisible wall he was hiding behind.

I felt the desk bimbo's curious gaze burning at the back of my head and heard the loud, contemptuous whoosh of her breath between gum crackles. "Come on, Diamond. Let's get out of here."

My fingers wedged in the valley of elbow between the fleshy mountains of Diamond's arm, I led him outside and watched him sink into the passenger seat of the Lincoln. Without speaking, he handed me the keys and stared straight ahead, as if a movie were playing on his side of the windshield.

The giant engine leapt to life, and I pulled out of the Barrington lot and threaded the car through the narrow stretch of Parrish Common. Nearing the main road, I slowed to a stop. "Which way, Mr. Diamond? Where would you like me to go?"

He pointed a fat finger toward the campus and blinked away some private horror.

"You say when," I told him, and drove as slowly as the car allowed. He could pick anyplace he liked to fill me in on his secrets.

I stared over at him as I poked along the shoulder of the road. He sat as stiffly as a portrait model, unblinking. My heart jumped at my chest, and a sick sense of dread worked at my stomach.

"Here," he said. The word was a strangled whisper. I pulled up against the curb right in front of a no-parking sign and stood on the sidewalk, waiting.

He lumbered out of the car and worked his cloudy gaze over the campus. Scratching his head, he nodded at some sudden decision and took off at a clumsy sprint toward the clock tower. I hurried to keep up.

In front of the building that formed the base of the clock tower, he stopped dead and looked around. A cool, light drizzle had settled over the campus, raising vaporous swells from the heated ground that blurred the edges of the world and gave the day a dreamy quality.

Not much was happening. An olive-skinned man in a yellow rain slicker rode a giant mower over the main lawn, trailing soggy clumps of shorn grass. Across the quadrangle, two painters in soiled canvas hats and spattered overalls worked on a wooden scaffold that dangled from the roof of the psychology building, scraping sodden curls of paint from the peeling window frames outside the top floor. At the steps of the main library a giant mail truck disgorged stuffed green sacks of packages and letters and drove away, etching deep, muddy tracks in the softened ground. A solitary figure in a mold-colored trench coat strode away from us, his head turtled into his upturned collar.

Satisfied, Diamond turned and led me in through the heavy wooden door to the base of the tower. The floor was thick with damp soil and a layer of decayed pigeon droppings. Green moss spread like seeking fingers over the crumbling stone walls and filled the air with the cloying aroma of decay. Slowly he ambled to the center of the room and began to ascend the tall, circular staircase, moving his hand by degrees up the rusted metal banister and clutching the clammy rail for safe purchase. His knees made harsh, snapping-twig sounds as they bent, and from below, through the cut metal steps, I could see the weight of effort in his weary face.

"Diamond?"

"Ssh." He turned for an instant and pressed a trembling finger to his lips. "Soon."

As we climbed, the air thinned and was fired by the trapped heat baked into the tower stones. Diamond's breath came in short, whistling gasps, and he stopped for a moment in mid-flight to wipe the dampness from his face with his shirt sleeve.

"Diamond? Are you all right?"

With a distracted shake of his head he began climbing again, a plodding step at a time, until he arrived at the final landing. Overhead, giant gears whirred and clicked their weary progress as the clock approached the half hour. The chimes shifted in the wind, charging the air with a deep, vibratory wave. Diamond squeezed sideways through a narrow arch and was gone.

I followed him out onto a tiny metal platform fronting the base of the clock. The rain had stopped, but a sturdy wind had risen in its place. Fighting back a wave of dizziness, I held the rail and looked around. From below, we were hidden from view by an ornate iron grating inset with some ancient Latin motto. The giant clock face loomed overhead, its huge, blackened hands advancing in jerky pulses. I followed Diamond's gaze out over the misty landscape, taking in the broad expanses of abandoned farmland and the angry, ragged gorges—rips in the land in which desperate people could toss away their lives.

His voice was a breathless shrill. "Seems crazy to you, I imagine. But this is the one place on campus I know we can't be heard. Or followed."

"Why would anyone want to follow us?"

"Why? I don't know the reason. I only know someone in this place keeps a close eye on things. I've had a tail on me since I got here. Wouldn't surprise me if you did too."

"What makes you think someone has been following you, Mr. Diamond? Maybe it's just your imagination. You've been under a great deal of strain."

"Doesn't matter. No point even discussing it." His eyes glazed over as he stood. "You can take my word or not. That's not important now. What's important is your safety. Chip Dexter shouldn't have told you about the curse. I warned him. But now that he has, you'll have to leave Cromwell—right away. Today."

"I'm afraid I don't understand."

"I'll explain, then. I explained to Chip Dexter, but I guess I didn't get through. Chip never was long on gray matter, if you want my opinion. Knew how to get the help he needed, but that doesn't take a genius. I told him to keep his mouth shut, not to tell you or anyone, but Chip's always had loose hinges on those lips. Flap in the breeze and whatever comes, comes."

"He only said . . ."

Diamond waved away the protest. "Doesn't matter how much he said. It's dangerous to know anything at all. That's part of it. Always has been that way. Anyone who knows about the curse tends to have a run of bad luck. Very, very bad luck. That's one of the reasons the books were destroyed—all but a few copies folks had hidden away."

"Look, Mr. Diamond, I have to be honest with you. I'm not a great believer in curses. But since you say I'm hopelessly doomed anyway, you may as well tell me about it."

He chewed his lower lip. "I guess there's some sense in that. In for a penny, in for a pound. I'll tell you, Sarah Spooner. But then you're going to have to leave. Right away. No arguments."

With a grand sigh he reached in his bulging back pocket and pulled out his dog-eared copy of *A Concise History of Cromwell.* "It's all in here. The whole, horrible truth about this place and the demon who founded it."

"Isaiah Cromwell?"

"You remember Charles Manson? Ted Bundy? That Son of Sam fellow, what's-his-name? Cromwell was like them. As bad or worse. Born without a conscience. Got his jollies doing harm to people, especially the ones closest to him.

"Started with his own mother. The Cromwells were society folk, bluebook types. Isaiah took up with one of the kitchen maids just to stick it to his mother. Bettina Molloy was her name. Pretty thing. Old lady Cromwell all but had an apoplexy when Isaiah announced their engagement. But there was nothing she could do about it. He was that type of person, even as a kid."

"What does that have to do with a curse, Mr. Diamond?"

He held up a hand. "Be patient. I'm getting to that. The wedding wasn't the end of Isaiah's fun. He charmed that sweet little Bettina until they were married. Then he showed her his true colors.

"Isaiah was a drinker—and a mean drunk, to boot. Nearly every night he'd go out to the local tavern and come home with a snootful. He'd wake his poor wife out of a sound sleep and make her wait on him. Poor thing was terrified. She'd try to follow his orders, but sooner or later she'd slip up. Isaiah made sure of that. And then there were the beatings."

"That's horrible."

"That wasn't the worst of it. Bettina was not the healthiest person, and all this aggravation with Isaiah only made her sicker. To make matters even worse, Isaiah insisted on her having another baby every year. Made him feel like a big man, I suppose. You know the type.

"The doctor warned Bettina she was taking her life in her hands by having so many babies, but she was too afraid of Isaiah to cross him. She kept getting weaker and weaker until she could hardly drag herself out of bed."

"That revolting creep," I said, feeling furious on behalf of this frail stranger in history.

He sucked in a chestful of humid air. "That isn't the end of it. The more Bettina suffered, the happier he was. The games got meaner. He took to bringing home other women: whores. And he'd force Bettina to watch while he carried on with them. Isaiah beat that sweet woman right into the ground. Got so she gave up trying after a while. Just lay there, waiting for her humiliation to end somehow."

"How could they name a university after a disgusting creature like that? It seems impossible."

Diamond scratched behind his ear. "Money? Power? Who knows? His real character has been pretty well rewritten by the university's public relations people. It's hard to imagine how some people can be so rotten. But you and I know there's no limit, don't we?"

"No, I guess there isn't."

"Well, there was certainly no limit for Isaiah Cromwell. None at all. One night, when Bettina was lying in bed suffering from the misery of flu on top of everything else, he came in stinko and decided it would be great fun to watch his wife dance. Gypsy style, you know—wiggles and veils—the works. So he drags the poor thing out of bed and starts clapping and whistling and ordering her to strut her stuff. She was too afraid to refuse.''

"God."

Diamond nodded. "He made her go on and on, half naked in the cold night air. Bastard wouldn't light the stove, nothing. She danced until she dropped—and died.

"No one might have known what really happened to her, but a few months later Isaiah bragged about it during a drunk. That's how the real story got out."

"That's terrible, a terrible story. But what does all that have to do with a curse?"

Diamond squinted at the book and flipped through the brittle, yellowed pages. "Look at this." He handed the volume to me.

I could not make sense of the scratchy handwriting and the stilted language. "It looks like some old holographic will," I said. "That was common in those days. A person made up his own will, wrote it out by hand and signed it with no witnesses—nothing. Most states don't recognize them anymore."

"Look at paragraph fifteen, Sarah Spooner."

I flipped through several more pages until I came to the section marked XV. I struggled to make out the words:

*   *   *

Be it fully known and feared from now and for all posterity until the day of eternal judgment that the issue of Isaiah Cromwell and his heirs and assigns will reap the black harvest of his bitter deeds. And so it shall be for he who stands in the way of this noble justice by innocent knowledge or by design. And know ye that hence one year and one century from this very day, the black harvest will grow to consume the fruits of his labors in a final fire of retribution.

"Weird," I said. "What does it mean?"

Diamond clicked his tongue, and his chest heaved with emotion. "That's it. That's the curse. It means that everything Isaiah Cromwell built will begin to crumble after a hundred and one years. Everything. That means the university and everyone connected with it. And this is the year.

"The original copy was found on Isaiah Cromwell's body when he was laid out in his coffin in the family parlor. The pages were spattered with blood and draped over him like a shroud. No one knew how they got there. There was a crowd of people around almost every minute."

"Was he murdered?"

"Not according to the book. It says Cromwell lived to be eighty something. His mind was gone by then, didn't know who he was, couldn't take care of himself. Nothing. Turned back into a helpless infant.

"For the last few years of his life he was convinced there was someone watching him all the time. Slept with all the lights on, refused to be alone in his house for a minute. He used to have these screaming fits in the middle of the night that all but woke the whole town. 'Get away,' he'd say over and over. 'Don't touch me.' There was talk of putting him in a booby hatch, but the Cromwells had too much power and influence to put up with that. Finally his motor just ran down, or he scared himself to death."

"Or someone else did."

Diamond shrugged. "Nothing would surprise me."

"Well, almost nothing would surprise me, Mr. Diamond. But I must say, it does surprise me that you believe in this curse business."

"I didn't. For a long time I thought it was just a bunch of hogwash. But no more. Now I know better. I know it."

"What changed your mind?"

He caught his lower lip between his teeth and stared out over the campus. "You know enough already, Sarah Spooner. Too much."

"Be reasonable, Diamond. You said it yourself, in for a penny . . ."

His words were a chill breeze. "I know the curse is real. I was shown."

"How? What happened?"

He spun toward me and locked my arms in a vise grip. "Stop it. You have to stop asking all these questions! It's dangerous. Crazy dangerous. Why can't you just believe me? Why won't you listen? Get away from here! Get out of Cromwell before it's too late!''

I kept my tone lilting, sane and even. Chief Dexter's words echoed in my mind. Old Al off the deep end, snapping like a twig. ''Please, Diamond. If something has happened to frighten you, tell me about it. Maybe I can help.''

A sloppy trail of tears slithered down his cheek, and his chest pulsed with anguish. ''There is no help. All you can do is get away. Don't you see?''

''I wish I did.''

Diamond seemed to shrink. ''I don't know what else to say. Please believe me, Sarah Spooner. It's the only way.''

I looked over the paragraph about the curse again and noticed the signature. ''Who was P. Roger Morgan, anyway?''

''That was Parrish Morgan, son of Samuel Parrish. Bettina was his illegitimate daughter.'' He took a deep breath and leaned against the railing. ''The curse was his way of avenging his daughter's death. He vowed to make the Cromwells pay. And now it's happening.''

''Be reasonable, Mr. Diamond. Please. These are just words. You don't really believe all that foolish superstition.''

''Yes, I do. And you'd better believe it, too, before it's—''

With a jarring hiss the clock advanced to the half hour, and the carillons began to chime a deafening roar of boomed melody. I held my ears in a vain attempt to mute the thunderous gongs. Diamond was unfazed. He made a vague effort to be heard, then went back to his aimless staring and waited for the cacophony to end.

After the chimes were still, he waited a few minutes more for the echoes to clear from my mind. He pointed to his ear and moved his lips in broad parody. "Sorry about the noise. Can you hear now?"

"I may never hear again." My voice was tinny and far away. "What were you trying to say?"

He shrugged. "Doesn't matter. It's probably too late already."

"Mr. Diamond, get hold of yourself. Please don't worry about me. Nothing is going to happen. I'll be fine."

"Only if you get out. That's the only way. Stay here and it'll get you sooner or later. All of them were on to it somehow. I'm sure of it. All of them."

"All of whom? What are you talking about?"

"The suicides. The deaths. It's all connected to the curse. I'm sure of it. They all found out about it somehow, and now they're gone. I'm next, Sarah Spooner. I'm right up there at the top of the list. Nothing I can do anymore. But you can still save yourself."

"Please, calm down. You're upset. That's all."

"Look over there . . . look." I followed the path his finger traced over the range of Cromwell's land. "You see?"

''What am I supposed to be looking for?''

''Read this.''

I took the open book again and read the paragraph he chose. The curse was cast in the land, it said. You could see the mark of it charred in the face of the flats and gorges. I was beginning to see a little padded booby hatch in Diamond's future. Sad. ''I don't get it.''

''Look at the gorges there.'' He pointed off to the right where the Sachem Gorge formed a gentle arc that intersected with the straight, bold slash of the Mahkeenac. ''You see how it forms a capital *C*?''

''Yes. A capital *C* with a line through it.''

''Exactly, Sarah Spooner. The *C* is for Cromwell, and the line means Cromwell is crossed out. Eliminated. Can you read upside down?''

I looked at the ragged form again, picturing how it would appear from the other side. ''I guess it would be a *P* that way.''

''P . . . for Parrish.''

''That's clever, Mr. Diamond. But not exactly hard evidence.''

''You have to believe me. You have to leave before it's too late. It'll get you too. I know it will. Go now, today. While you have a chance. Run while you still have legs.''

I placed a hand on his shoulder. ''Please, get hold of yourself. Nothing's going to happen to me or to you. Anyway, if you're so worried, why don't you leave Cromwell? Nothing's stopping you. Be sensible.''

He was caught in a staccato whimper. "I . . . can't. I had a chance but I blew it. I can't explain. You'd only get in deeper than you already are. You go. Now. Go before it's too late for you too. There's nothing in this place but trouble."

"I'll be all right. I promise. Think about it, Mr. Diamond. You're upset and you're not thinking straight. It's no wonder after all you've been through."

His eyes were large with fright, and he shuddered.

"Come on, Mr. Diamond. Let's go. It's cold up here." I took his hand and led him in through the sliver of an archway, catching my breath until he made it safely through the narrow passage. Leading the way down the dizzy circle of stairs, I kept an eye on him, certain he would topple and fall with the slightest breeze of bad luck. "Easy, Mr. Diamond. Be careful. Good. That's good." My muscles ached with the tension of moving my mind through his every step and the strain of fixing his hand to the rail with the full power of my determination.

Finally we were back in the base of the clock tower, trudging through the carpet of bird droppings. Diamond followed me back into the windy haze and across the broad lawn to the car.

I turned the radio to loud, mindless music and drove back toward the Barrington Arms. Beside me, Diamond fell into an instant, dead sleep. Poor man had tormented himself to the point of total exhaustion. Curses, sacrifices, bloody black spirits from the underbelly of the universe. The mind could invent an endless supply of inexplicable evils to account for the raw truths it could not otherwise accept.

Or the mind could shatter in small, useless fragments.

-18-

The lobby was littered with clusters of matched luggage and impatient guests waiting to check out. During the three-day hiatus until the start of reunion, there was little reason for any right-minded individual to be in Cromwell.

The gum-snapping blonde was extracting billing records from a jammed wooden file and tapping numbers into the computer in maddening slow motion. She used the tip of a pencil eraser to avoid injury to her blood-red talons, depressing each key with great dramatic care and squinting at the video display before moving on to the next entry. When the printer disgorged the final tally, she took yet another eternity to fill out the charge slip and tear the precious carbons to minuscule fragments. The mumbles and groans of displeasure grew to a steady, mutinous buzz.

Winston Lawrence ducked in through the rear door. His hair was drenched with perspiration, and the starched white shirt had melted against his back. Mopping his florid cheeks with a plaid handkerchief, he began jabbering in impotent bursts of frustration.

"Oh, my, my. This will never do. Now, Lisa, we mustn't keep all these people waiting, must we? Can't you work a bit faster on the machine, dear? Computers are for speed, you know. Efficiency. And you did claim you had excellent skills, my dear. This is really not satisfactory. Not satisfactory at all."

She stuck a contemptuous hand on her square hip and snapped her wad of Double Bubble in his face. "I'm doing the best I can, you know. You think you can do better, be my guest. I got plenty of better ways to spend my time."

Diamond slogged down the stairs. He was wedged into an enormous Hawaiian shirt and flag-sized jeans. The purple troughs under his eyes had spread into giant wells of weariness, and there was a chalky cast to his complexion. Brushing past the crowd, he turned down the hall leading to the dining rooms.

Half a night of gentle reason had not made a dent in his madness, but I felt compelled to try once more. I walked out onto the terrace and found him seated at a small, round table facing the municipal golf course. Perched on a graceful little wrought-iron chair, he looked like a giant hot-air balloon tethered to the earth by an optimistic thread. I pulled up a chair and sat beside him. He blinked at me and looked away.

A foursome was hitting off the twelfth tee. I watched as a woman with cotton-candy hair and a yolk-yellow pantsuit took her place between a pair of red markers, swayed into an awkward stance, and clubbed the ball with the pink-painted head of her driver. It rose in a jerky arc, swished through the leafy crown of a swamp maple, and came to rest in a sand trap.

"She should be somewhere else," he said. "Like you, Sarah Spooner."

Next at the tee, an elderly man with jug ears and black-rimmed bifocals took a careful swing and a small, satisfied bow as his ball flew a certain track to the distant center of the fairway.

"I'm going to leave soon. I told you that. But I still have a few things to clear up in Cromwell, Mr. Diamond. Like the matter of Nick's missing papers. In fact, I finally reached Professor Goldenberg, and he's agreed to see me later this morning. Don't worry, I'll be fine."

He carved his jelly omelet and sprinkled each triangle with a dunce cap of powdered sugar. His eating was lifeless, mechanical. So was his voice. "Go away. Run while you still have legs."

I sipped at a ceramic mug of black coffee. Rising tendrils of fragrant steam eased the pressure squeezing at my temples. A young woman in a blinding hot-pink ensemble hacked at the grass, fronting her ball until it dribbled off the tee and rolled a few lurching feet along the ground.

I could feel Diamond slipping away, drowning in his fears and superstitions. "I'll be fine. You'll see."

He answered with a shrug, his repertoire spent. All night he had spewed his warnings: "Fly while you still have wings." "Bolt before they nail you."

"There is no curse, Mr. Diamond. I don't believe in curses. Where is the evidence? Where is the logic?" My protests were lost in the murky distance in his eyes and the terror behind the mist.

The fourth golfer approached the tee. His driver's cap hung off to one side, and pale, ropy legs protruded from his plaid Bermudas. He swung without ceremony and returned to the waiting cart. All four climbed in and drove off on their jolting way toward the green.

"I'll be fine," I said again, and felt a sinking sense of loss.

"You don't listen. Listen while you still have ears."

"Please, Mr. Diamond. Don't do this to yourself."

He tugged at me with his pleading expression. "Things have happened. Things I can't repeat. If you won't take my word, that's that. I can't do any more. I've done all I can. Time is running out." He pulled his battered copy of *A Concise History of Cromwell* from his back pocket and ruffled through to the page he sought. "When June turns ten, begins the end." He stood and moved away in a trancelike glide. At the end of the terrace he stopped for a spare second and turned to fix me with an odd, twisted smile. "Good-bye, Sarah Spooner. Good . . . bye."

"I'll be back by two, three at the latest. I'll see you then."

"Good-bye," he mouthed. And he walked slowly away until he was swallowed by the shadows of the hotel.

I left the Barrington and followed the convoluted directions Professor Gerard Goldenberg had recited in his gentle singsong over the phone. Walking through an outlying section of Cromwell known as the Pinnacle, I passed clapboard row houses and garden apartments fronted by plastic wading pools, rusted swing sets, and webbed lawn furniture. This was the area favored by up-and-coming academics and their hyperintelligent offspring. Here they had their book clubs and bridge tournaments and passed their leisure time looking down their noses at the less intellectually fortunate.

A few older professors, such as Goldenberg, stayed on in the neighborhood, expanding their modest starter houses with a room here, a wing there, until they lost all semblance of architectural sense.

The GOLDENBERG sign protruded from one such monstrosity, a giant yellow patchwork of jogs and angles with a fudge-brown roof and lemon shutters. A vintage black sedan was parked in the driveway casting a bubble of shade over a fat, sleeping beagle. As I climbed the crooked cement steps to the front porch, the dog cracked a bloodshot eye and flapped his stubby tail in greeting.

The doorbell gonged a double chorus of "How Dry I Am" and was still. I heard the slow progress of footsteps thumping down the stairs and across the foyer. Eyes burned through the peephole. "You Spooner?"

"Yes." I heard locks twisting and chains sliding on their tracks. Finally the door swung open, and Professor Goldenberg appeared, a wizened old man with a look of perpetual surprise and the bonus of a twinkle in his soft gray eyes. "Come in, come in."

The foyer floor was painted blue and border-stenciled with trellised flowers. There was a riot of plants everywhere: orchids blooming on delicate spikes; luxuriant greens spilling from ceramic pots and porcelain tubs. Ferns hung from the ceiling by trails of braided rope, and odd green pigtails cascaded from a line of small plastic pails. My head filled with the rich scent of earth and humidity.

Goldenberg walked slowly through the jungle, pausing to pinch and pluck, shooting a smelly mist of vitamin spray through a glass atomizer. "My children," he said as he dusted the broad leaf of a rubber plant with the cuff of his worn blue shirt.

Plants lined the floor of his study and climbed to perch on the brick-and-board shelves and windowsills. On the dull wood surface of his desk there were water marks beside a pair of soiled canvas gloves and a profusion of exotic seed catalogs. He slipped on the gloves and took a dirt-caked trowel and wood-handled pruning shears from his desk drawer. "Mind talking in the greenhouse?"

We crossed a picture-perfect lawn to the metal-frame glass building. Inside, the sunbaked air was circulated by a pair of noisy fans. An overhead vent was propped open, and the ceiling was splashed with cooling white paint. Still, I felt like a raw biscuit set in a red-hot oven. Goldenberg watered and sprayed while I followed behind, melting slowly in his wake.

"Your boy, Nicholas, was the most interesting young man. Unpredictable. Do you know what I mean?"

"Not exactly."

He stroked the crown of an ailing geranium and painted the leaves with a strong-smelling salve. "He was never the same from day to day. It's hard to explain. And there were flashes of real brilliance, though he tried his best to keep his brains a secret."

I was not in the market for more amateur analysis. I told Goldenberg about the missing papers and my meetings with the other English professors. Worry clouded his face.

He patted the broad-leafed head of a caladium and pinched the dead brown blossoms from a clump of button mums. "This is not the first I've heard of missing papers. There have been wicked whispers all year. That dirtiest of English words has been bouncing around the department like a rubber ball: *plagiarism.* There were so many rumors and accusations, you had to duck in the halls to avoid injury. A plagiarism panic is an occupational hazard in any English department. Cromwell has had more than its fair share. I suppose it's natural, given our size and stature."

With a length of heavy green twine he tied the thick offshoots of a barrel cactus to a wooden support.

"I don't want to get into department gossip or office politics, Professor. I just want to find those papers. They may help me understand what happened to Nicky."

The professor finished his rounds and stepped outside. The day felt crisp and invigorating compared to the stifling greenhouse heat. A swell of dizzy relief overtook me.

"I know you're not interested in our little family squabbles, Mrs. Spooner, but you may not be able to avoid diving into the dirty laundry if you want to find those papers. Of course, that's just my opinion."

A large, dour woman stuck her head out through an upstairs window. "It's hot as hell out there, Goldy. You trying to get yourself a nice new heart attack or what?"

"I'm fine, Midgie. You know I don't mind the heat." His smile was strained. "My wife," he whispered. "General Goldenberg."

"I heard that, Gerard. I heard every word. That's not funny."

"Only kidding, sweetheart. This is Sarah Spooner, Midgie. One of the Cromwell parents."

"Hah. Look, my friend, you want to spend next spring pushing up daisies, that's your affair. You just be sure the next one kills you off. I am not interested in taking care of a sick, stubborn mule."

"I'll be fine, Midgie. Just fine."

"I'm warning you, Goldy. I will not spoon mush into your stubborn mouth or clean up your drool. You turn yourself into a helpless invalid, you're on your own.

You'll change your own Pampers, Goldy. I swear it.''

"Yes, dear. I understand."

She twisted her face in disgust, pulled her head in like a giant tortoise, and drew the curtains. Goldenberg's shoulders hitched in an embarrassed shrug, and he held up his empty palms. "I have a heart condition, and it worries her to death. We go back a long way, Midgie and me."

"You were talking about the papers."

"Oh, yes, right. I have been on the Cromwell faculty for over forty-seven years. Hard to believe how the time goes. Forty-seven years . . . You learn a few things in all that time—like how to keep your mouth closed. How to listen and find out what's really going on between the lines. The rumors died down, but there may have been something to them."

On the way into the house he stopped several times to bend in a creaky arc from his waist and tug at an errant weed. He carried his harvest of clover and crab-grass inside and deposited it in the metal wastebasket under his desk. "You want a cold drink? A beer, maybe? Nothing like a cold beer on a hot day."

"No, nothing thanks. Just to hear about the papers."

He stuck the tip of his finger in the soil of a Boston fern and frowned. "Air pockets." Tamping with the heel of his hand, he hummed a soothing melody at the plant. "They like music."

Impatience was taking me over. "You said you thought there was something to the rumors?"

Wiping his hands on his baggy corduroys, he retrieved a large scrapbook from its place beneath a row of potted herbs. Damp, rusty stains adorned the cover. "Look." The book was full of clippings, some crackling dry and yellowed with age, others recently torn from the pages of a local paper or some obscure literary journal. All reported some feat of creation or criticism by a member of the Cromwell English faculty.

"Publish or perish," Goldenberg said. "Faculty members are expected to keep their names in print or else." He drew an invisible knife across his throat.

"You do think someone may have stolen Nick's papers?"

Goldenberg's face softened as he hummed a creaky chorus of "Stardust" to a dissipated fern. "Let's say there is an interesting coincidence here. Papers disappear, papers are produced. Poof! Magic. Look at the last few pages."

I flipped through to the end of the book. There were several recent entries about a much-heralded new light in the literary constellation: sensitive personal reflections, humorous essays, brilliant short stories. "Sparks of talent in an otherwise bleak landscape of literary promise," one read. All the articles were about an associate professor at Cromwell University—one Hardy Steppington Miles.

"You suspect Miles?"

"Suspect? Me? I'm too smart for such things, my friend. I have been collecting Hardy's clippings just to have them—in case anyone might be interested.''

"But why would an English professor need to steal writing from students?"

He dipped a thermometer into the soil of an ailing lemon tree and marked the progress of his watch. "Why is a good question. You want to know the possibilities? Laziness. Greed. Panic. Stupidity. No talent. All of the above. Who knows? Desperate men can be pushed to commit desperate acts. When they get on your case to publish, it can feel like frying under a sunlamp. They can make it hard to act rationally. I know. I remember when I was in a spot like that. I would sit until my behind fell asleep staring at the blank pages. Nothing would come. Nothing. I remember tugging at my hair— I had some then—hoping to pull out the ideas. Thank God for my Midgie. 'Goldie,' she told me. 'Cut the crap and put something down on that paper. I don't care if it's roses are red. . . .' She stood glaring at me with her arms folded until I got started. Without her . . ." He read the thermometer and shook it down. Closing the album, he seemed to sink in his chair. His face paled, and he took a deep, hesitant breath. "I'm okay," he mouthed. "I just have to give up the nightlife. Or maybe the day life. Or both."

"What can I do, Professor? How can I find out if Dr. Miles has Nick's papers?"

He fanned himself with a Holland tulip catalog, and the color inched back into his complexion. "I don't know. I'll be honest. If Hardy Miles has been poaching, you may never be able to prove it. Unless you had the originals in your son's name to compare, how can you make any accusations? I doubt he'd be dumb enough to keep originals, though . . .''

"Yes?"

He folded his hands and lowered his voice to a whisper. "It's a long shot, but Miles is known for his filing system. He keeps articles, tests, you name it. Scraps of things you'd never expect. Maybe out of habit . . .''

Maybe. "I guess that's my only hope." My mouth was chalk-dry and a sick fear inched up my legs. "I'll find out."

Goldenberg led me out through the flowered foyer and walked beside me to the edge of the drive. I felt his wife's eyes on the back of my head. He looked up at her and set his mouth in a tight smile. "I'll be right in, Midgie. How about we take a nice nap—together."

"So now you're a frisky stallion, are you? You just better keep up your insurance payments. That's all I'll say. I don't expect to be one of those weeping widows with holes in her shoes while you're off laying in a nice, deluxe coffin in Mount Carmel. I expect to replace you as soon as I can, Goldy. I'll bring a date to the memorial service if I can get one. I swear it. And it takes money to compete in today's marriage market. I'll need new clothes, a face-lift, maybe a perm."

He waited for the shutters to close and took my hand between his. "You be careful, Mrs. Spooner. Let good sense guide you."

"I will."

An odd, knowing sorrow filled his eyes. "If only I could help you . . ."

"That's okay."

"It would be fun. I could use a little excitement, believe me. There's living and then there's . . . living. This is . . . I don't know what you'd call it. Anyway, good luck. Be careful," he said, and went inside.

The beagle cocked his head as I passed on my way to the road and growled a halfhearted threat. I offered a playful snarl in answer, and he sank back between his paws, as if I were not worth the trouble.

Or maybe he somehow knew I would be taken care of soon enough.

-19-

I entered the English building through a rear door and stole through the empty corridors toward Miles's office. A strong ammonia smell made my eyes water, and I heard a janitor singing down the hall and the relentless slap-slosh of his string mop.

The office door was locked. Feeling like a refugee from a B-movie, I slipped one of my charge cards out of its plastic holder and wiggled the edge against the sliding bolt. The lock yielded, and I ducked inside as I heard the approach of mop and footsteps.

With the shades drawn, the office was blanketed by dense stripes of shadow. I picked my way through the clutter, leading with outstretched hands and a tentative toe, until I stood in front of the bank of files.

Outside the door, the janitor swished and hummed. My heart lurched as his mop handle rapped against the glass door panel like the determined fist of an angry intruder. His inky form was framed against the glass, and my imagination drew suspicious, slitted eyes working to slice through my slim shelter of darkness. Frozen in place, I waited for the silhouette to turn away and for the rhythmic sounds of his labors to resume.

He left at last, and I waited a further eternity until sounds placed him at a safe distance down the hall. With great care I slipped the first drawer open and peered into a black void.

Stupid. I was completely unprepared for a well-executed burglary. I thought of all the equipment I should have—a flashlight, lock picks, camouflage gear. But I had come here directly from Goldenberg's without a proper plan, certain only that this must be done quickly, before I misplaced the spare remnants of my nerve.

Staring until my eyes burned with effort, I was able to make out the black alphabet tabs separating the banks of files. The *A*'s and *B*'s were in front, the *C*'s through *F*'s wedged in the back of the jammed drawer.

I slipped out the bottom drawer and found the end of the alphabet. The *S*'s were a deep, discouraging stack of files toward the rear of the drawer at knee level. Now what?

With an experimental tug I was able to disengage a single folder. I propped up the one behind to keep my place and walked toward the window. The janitor was well away, but I could not chance putting on the light. He might notice a sudden change in the look of the office.

Holding the tab end of the file at a careful angle, I was able to make out the heading: "Swift's letters." Snippets of paper fluttered from the stuffed folder as I pushed it back in place. Groping along the gritty floor, I found several paper scraps and tucked them in my pocket.

By a long, labored process, I finally located a folder marked "Spooner" between "Spoon River Anthology—Notes" and "Spoons—References." My hands shook with a harsh tremor as I lifted the first typed sheet and held it up to the sliver of light.

Nicky's familiar handwriting. His odd slant and bold slashes. My heart strained against my chest like a trapped animal. I slipped the folder into my purse and pushed the drawer shut.

Inching the door open, I peered out into the corridor. The janitor had traded his mop for a smoke and a small brown bagful of some liquid refreshment. He leaned back against the wall, his head bobbing to the beat of an imaginary melody.

Trapped, I left the door open a crack and waited for him to move along. He puffed and sipped and tapped his foot against the floor, keeping his private beat. Several minutes passed, and I peered out again, hoping to spur him to action by the sheer force of my will. He seemed anchored to his spot, the rounded crest of his bony shoulders held fast to the wall by lazy glue. His eyes were vague and heavy-lidded. "Go away," I mouthed. "Please go."

Finally he began to move, slow as a sailboat in a stingy breeze. He crushed the smoke under the well-worn toe of his work boot and slipped the pint into the back pocket of his baggy pants. Go . . . Go . . .

His pace quickened and I almost cheered in response. Then I heard it, too, the noise that had moved him. Firm footsteps clacking on the stairs, coming toward us. The man sloshed his mop in the bucket and squeezed it out.

Closer. Too late to run. Too late. Don't let it be him.

The voice. "Hello, Jimmy. How goes it?" Unmistakable. It was Miles. My luck, I thought through the thunder of horror pounding in my ears. My luck.

He approached the office and paused with his hand on the knob. In a clutch of panic I squeezed in the tiny space between the files and the wall and crouched out of sight.

"You must enjoy this solitude, James. I imagine it's rare for the building to be this calm and quiet."

"You know it is, Dr. Miles. You said a mouthful."

He came in and flipped on the light, drowning the room in a blinding wash of fluorescent glare. My body was caught in a spasm of terror, and I struggled to breathe past the fist of fear in my throat. Miles ambled around the office like a Sunday stroller, clacking his tongue against the roof of his mouth and pausing, every so often, to scribble something on the notepad he carried. Several times his feet came within inches of my head as he passed my hiding place, so close that I felt the tiny current of a breeze from his steps. Don't look down. No!

I heard the squeak of his desk chair as he sat and made a phone call. "Penny? Dr. Miles here. Tell Barton the piece will be on his desk Monday morning. . . . And tell him it is brilliant—if I do say so, heh, heh. That should leave you time to make the deadline for the October issue. . . . Yes, dear. Thank you as well. I look forward to seeing the proofs."

Hanging up, he clasped his hands and addressed an invisible audience. "*The Liberty Review* featuring a brilliant work of short fiction by Dr. Hardy Steppington Miles. Ta da," he said, and bowed from the waist. "Thank you, one and all. Thank you, thank you. The Pulitzer prize, you say? I am speechless. Truly." He raised his voice to a warble. " 'Oh, but Dr. Miles, you certainly deserve it.' Now, now, my dear. You embarrass me. Now, now. Enough applause, really. Thank you, thank you."

He turned to ruffle through the middle file drawer, retrieved several folders, and packed them in his worn brown briefcase. "That's it, then," he mumbled, and crossed to the office door. "Simple. Success the easy way."

With his hand on the knob he took a last, lingering look around. Stiff with fear, I could feel his eyes burning in my direction. My stomach heaved. Goldenberg's words circled in my mind. Desperate men—desperate acts. Don't see me. Don't!

I heard him open and shut the door and twist the key in the lock. "Take care to lock up, will you, Jimmy?" he called. "This door was open. I have valuable papers in there, you know. Wouldn't want anyone walking off with any of them. You know you can't trust anyone these days." Then his footsteps retreated down the hall, fading to an innocent echo.

Slowly I uncoiled and stretched away the stiffness. Prickles of life returned to my legs. And I left the prison of Miles's office feeling as shaky as a recovering invalid.

The corridor was empty, the building dim and silent. Grateful, I tiptoed downstairs and toward the rear exit, clutching Nick's papers against my chest. Here were the answers. I was sure of it. If I could expose Miles as a thief, the rest would fall in place. A desperate man was capable of committing desperate acts—even the most unthinkable.

"Help you, ma'am?"

The janitor stood just inside the door, blocking the way with folded arms and a supercilious smirk. His left eyebrow was tugged up under a flap of dull black hair. Drawing a bellyful of smoke, he looked me over. "Help you, I said?"

"No . . . I'm just leaving."

"Oh, yeah? You all done here?"

"Yes. I mean, I thought I might find Professor Goldenberg here, but I guess he isn't coming in today." My mouth was as dry as chalk and I struggled to keep the shrill of fear out of my voice.

"Oh, yeah?" His smile stretched to reveal a false row of Chiclet teeth and pale, sickly gums. "That why you were hiding in Professor Miles's office? You thought Doc Goldenberg might be in one of Miles's drawers or something?"

The heat rose in my face. "What do you want?"

He rubbed his fingertips together. "Depends on what you want, ma'am. You want me to do my duty and tell Doc Miles you dropped in and went through his stuff, maybe took something, that's free. You want my lips sewn shut, that's an operation. And operations cost."

"How much?"

"How much you got?"

I fumbled with my purse and found two twenties crumpled in the change pocket of my wallet. He accepted them with a satisfied grin, slipped them in his back pocket beside the pint, and began mopping his way down the hall. I slipped out through the back door and into the dull, humid afternoon. I was shaken but satisfied. This was something real, something to take Diamond's tortured mind off curses and dark spirits. Nick's work, his thoughts, his handwriting as it was before. . . .

From the clock tower I heard the hiss and click of the advancing minutes. Looking up, I saw the ornate minute hand approach the hour. There was an expectant tremor and the first gong reverberated through the stillness. I watched as the chimes shifted and began to clang a slow, plaintive melody.

Transfixed, I stood until the chimes fell silent and ponderous echoes filled the summer sky. I held my purse against the tug of a playful breeze and peeked inside at the folder. Nick's handwriting. I would listen to what Diamond saw in those bold strokes and sweeps. At least, I would try to listen. And he would listen to my suspicions about Miles.

A solitary figure was walking across the campus toward me. His head was hunched into the collar of a shabby trench coat, a floppy hat casting his face in shadow. I didn't recognize him as Warren Lawrence until he came within a few feet of where I stood. "Muh-missus Sp-spooner. What a p-pleasant surprise. 'Y-y-your heart's desires be with you!' *As Y-you L-like It,* I, i." Staring at me, he frowned and wove his fingers in a tight ball. "If y-you don't muh-mind my s-s-saying it, Muh-missus Sp-spooner, you look a b-b-bit upset."

I felt myself soften. "A bit is an understatement, Professor Lawrence, if you want to know the truth."

"I was j-just going for a c-c-cup of t-tea at the stuh-student union. W-won't you join me?"

As I hesitated, he took my elbow and steered me toward the large brick building. "Puh-please come. I huh-hate t-to drink alone."

We descended a rear stairway past the level of the student cafeterias and reading rooms and emerged on a floor divided into small offices, club rooms, and, at the end of the hall, the faculty lounge, a homey little parlor furnished with plump couches and tea tables.

Lawrence motioned me to sit and cocked his finger at a bored statue of a man standing in the corner. "T-two teas and a pl-plate of blueberry muffins, Harold." He squished onto the stuffed settee facing mine and fixed me with a kindly smile. "Suh-so, t-tell me, what s-seems t-to be the problem?"

"It's nothing. I just think . . . I may have found out what happened to Nick's missing papers."

His face tensed with interest. "Oh?"

How much was safe to tell him? At first I tiptoed around names and facts, giving him only the spare skeleton of my suspicions. Then, as he sat with a kindly, noncommittal expression on his face, I began filling in the blanks, describing my conversation with Goldenberg, Diamond's obsession with the Cromwell curse, and what I'd found in Hardy Miles's office. I felt a rush of relief, unloading my fears and confusion. Lawrence was a perfect listener. Patient, sympathetic.

When I finished, he let out a long, labored breath and stared through me, ordering his thoughts. He rose and placed a flag-pledging hand over his heart. " 'Oh c-conspiracy! Sham'st thou to show thy dangerous b-brow b-by night, When evils are m-most free? Let's c-carve him as a dish fit for the gods, Not hew him as a c-c-carcass fit for huh-hounds.' II, i, *Julius Caesar*. F-frankly, Missus Spuh-spooner, I g-gave you m-more credit than to think y-you were the t-type to b-believe such r-rubbish. G-goldenberg is j-just j-jealous of Hardy M-miles. 'So f-full of artless jealousy is g-guilt, it spuhspills itself in f-f-fearing to b-be spilt.' Act IV, *H-Hamlet*.''

"But I found Nick's papers in his files. And Professor Goldenberg said—''

He raised an angry fist and his face purpled. '' 'The g-game is up. Slander, whose edge is shuh-sharper than the sword, whose t-t-tongue outvenoms all the worms of N-nile, whose b-breath rides on the posting winds and d-doth belie all c-corners of the world.' *Cymbeline*, III, iii. I w-wouldn't t-take G-goldenberg seriously if I were y-you. H-he's a v-vicious g-gossip. Always was.''

"Then why would Miles have Nick's papers in his office? When I asked him about the missing papers, he said he knew nothing about them.''

"H-hardy is a p-pack r-rat. S-saves everything. Always d-d-did. But he's n-not a thief, I assure y-you. W-with all the j-j-junk he k-keeps, you c-can hardly expect him t-to r-remember everything. J-jerry G-goldenberg is a d-dangerous m-man, M-missus Spooner. D-don't listen to h-him. He's t-tried this b-before with other p-people in the d-department. If they d-didn't feel sorry for the old m-m-man, they would p-put him out to p-pasture. B-but he has a b-bad heart and all. I s-suppose they're willing to wait until he g-goes out on his own.''

I had an image of the old professor stroking and serenading his precious plants. "It's hard to think of Goldenberg as dangerous, Professor Lawrence. Anyway, why would he make up such a story? It doesn't make sense.''

'' 'B-but jealous souls will not b-be answered so; They are n-not ever jealous for the c-cause, b-but jealous for they are jealous; t-tis a m-monster b-begot upon itself, b-born upon itself.' *Othello*, Act III, S-scene iv. I c-can't t-tell you why. I c-can only advise you to t-turn a d-deaf ear. 'It is a t-tale t-told by an idiot, full of s-sound and f-fury, signifying n-n-nothing.' Act V, *Macbeth*. Join the wise m-masses who ignore that w-wicked old m-man.''

Nothing was simple, nothing clear. To myself I had to admit that it was peculiar for Goldenberg to keep an album of other faculty members' clippings, especially when he said he kept the clippings ''in case,'' as if he were trying to build evidence against his colleagues. Odd. But . . .

''B-believe me. There's n-nothing to what G-goldenberg says. F-forget about it. F-fill your m-mind with l-loftier notions.''

I sipped my tea and tried to sort through the muddle of my thoughts. Professor Lawrence's belief in Hardy Miles's innocence was as firm as Goldenberg's belief in his guilt. I knew there was one sure way to find out who was right. ''Please excuse me, Professor Lawrence, I have to get back to my hotel.''

He stood as I did, and an edge of desperation crept into his tone. ''I h-hope I've c-convinced you, M-missus Spuh-spooner. There is n-nothing t-to these accusations. N-nothing. I would hate t-to see this g-go any further. Innocent p-p-people could b-be hurt.''

There seemed no reason to continue this discussion. I would know soon enough. ''I'm sure you're right. Thanks for listening, Professor. And thanks for the tea.''

He clasped my hand in his and seemed to unwind. "Oh, y-you're w-welcome. V-very w-welcome indeed."

I left him in the lounge and climbed the back stairs to the main floor. My steps echoed in the cool, empty stairwell, and the sound of my humming bounced back at me in an odd, mournful refrain. After I saw Diamond, I would go back to Professor Goldenberg's house and look at the album again. If any of Hardy Miles's published work matched the papers in Nick's folder, I had all the proof I needed.

The logic that followed sent a chill of fear up my spine. If Miles was desperate enough to steal, maybe he was desperate enough to cover his tracks by arranging a convenient series of "suicides." Seven of the victims were English majors. I wondered how many of the others had taken the popular survey course in British literature from Hardy Steppington Miles.

Walking across the campus, I felt overwhelmed by the awful possibilities. Either Goldenberg was a vicious, pathological liar or Hardy Miles was a plagiarist or worse. Either way I had waded into a deep, difficult mess.

Missing Diamond and his wholesale insights, I quickened my pace and headed through the outlying streets toward the Barrington Arms. All this was too much for me to handle alone.

-20-

"It's happening! I knew it. I knew it all along. Oh, my, my. My good lord!" Winston Lawrence spoke in exclamatory bursts to no one in particular as I passed the desk. His head was bowed over the latest edition of the *Cromwell Courier*. Upside down, I noted the headline: CROMWELL CUT DOWN BY ACCREDITATION BOARD. The giant letters were done in a harlot's crimson. Some perverse member of the paper's art department had designed the banner so it seeped over the lead story like fresh blood pulsing from an open vein.

"Oh, my. I imagine Wallace must be furious. Just beside himself."

"Your brother?"

Lawrence looked up and blinked, as if surprised to see me. "Precisely. He does have a quick temper, I'll admit. And nothing sets him off more quickly than an assault on his precious university. This will have him steaming, to be sure."

His eyes twinkled with mischief, as if nothing could

please him more than his important brother's discomfort.

"What happened? Has the school's accreditation been revoked?" I asked.

He squinted over the story. "Not revoked. Not yet. But not far from it, either, from the sound of things. Oh, my. I can just imagine how he must be fuming."

"That's very serious for the university, isn't it?"

"Oh, my, yes. Very, very serious. They would have to shut their doors at once. The very Cromwell name, so long a prestigious one in the academic realm, would be mired in mud. Loss of accreditation is the worst disaster that can befall a university. But then, what can they expect? They were given ample warnings. I personally warned my dear brother months ago."

"You did?"

"Oh, my, yes. I admonished him to take all possible steps to stop the suicides before public outcry led to drastic problems for Cromwell, but he was his usual, bullheaded self. 'We have to expect a certain number of these unfortunate incidents every year, Winnie,' he told me. 'The school can hardly be held responsible.' Wallace has always been a person prone to bullish unreason. Now his stubbornness will have serious, disastrous consequences."

I felt a fleeting rush of pleasure at the thought of Wallace Lawrence squirming at the edge of destruction like a hooked fish. "He did seem a bit . . . hard-nosed . . . the two times I heard him speak."

Lawrence nodded in enthusiastic agreement. "You needn't mince words for my sake, Mrs. Spooner. My brother can be a bullheaded ass, if you'll pardon the vernacular. Simple as that. Always has had that tendency. And now he's about to get his comeuppance. It is a pity for the university, but I can't say it isn't long overdue."

The divine joy of sibling retribution. "I suppose something drastic has to happen to stop all these deaths."

His voice dropped to a hush. "The suicides are far from the only flaws at Cromwell, Mrs. Spooner. When I think of all the rest . . ."

"Like?"

"Oh, my. I really can't. I shouldn't. Suffice it to say, there are other unsavory goings-on in the hallowed halls of dear old Cromwell. When you have been about as long as I have, you learn things. . . . Then, I suppose all of it will come out now. The accreditation board plans to conduct a full investigation—department by department. The school will surely be turned on its ear. Dear Wallace had best secure his flanks, but far be it from me to warn him. Not that he would listen, in any event."

I left him to the pleasure of his revenge and went upstairs. A do-not-disturb sign was suspended from the door of the suite. Gently, I jiggled the knob. Locked.

Unusual for Diamond. Then, thinking back to his string of restless nights, I knew he must be exhausted. A nap would do him good.

I tiptoed away from the suite, down the carpeted corridor, and slipped out of the Barrington through a side door. Emerging from the air-cooled lobby, I walked into a wall of oppressive heat. Through Parrish Common I measured my breaths and moved at an easy stride until the air seemed to lighten. Then I began a tentative jog, arms pumping, legs churning in easy rhythm. A precious morsel of a breeze ruffled my hair.

At the corner I turned away from the main campus, heading instead toward the plantation area Diamond had driven me through on my first day in Cromwell. Less than a week had passed, but it seemed forever since that odd tour through Cromwell's lesser-known nooks and legends. Since then, crazed invisible giants had trampled the landscape of my life until I barely knew my way around.

The campus was quiet. As I ran, an occasional car, jammed with the last of the student stragglers, whizzed by with a jubilant honk. A pickup truck backed toward the service entrance of the vet school, and as I watched, a stone-faced orderly began tossing out the dismembered carcasses of subjects from the anatomy lab.

Noticing me, he managed an off-key wolf whistle and waved a bloody dog's leg in greeting.

Fighting back a swell of nausea, I ran on, past the plant nutrition building and the pomology lab. A sick-sweet scent emanated from the area Diamond had referred to as the rain forest. The dense broad-leafed palms and thick grasses shimmered in the blinding sun and rustled in random places as unseen creatures slithered along the shaded ground.

I tried to outdistance the worries crowding my mind. Cromwell, with all its dark spots and whispered secrets, was drawing me into an ever-widening maze of troubling questions, questions whose answers might be better left alone.

But Cromwell was only part of the problem. Ben and I had pulled so far apart, stretched like a rubber band to the critical point where another inch of distance might mean permanent rupture. I could hardly remember the feel of him, the easy places where our worlds used to mesh and blend.

Then there was Nick, Nick's secrets still teasing at the edges of my understanding. All the unknown fragments of his existence kept coming back to haunt me: Michelle, the psychiatrist, his inscrutable private, sensitive self.

At the edge of the North Campus I looked out over the rolling grounds and somber buildings of the university. The clock tower stood at the center like a watchful parent. Majestic trees cast a bounty of cooling shade. All so still and innocent—so deceptive.

Weary, I plodded back toward the Barrington Arms. Two more auto loads of departing students rumbled past. Everyone was peeling away—Ben, Allison, Pat, and now Diamond was hanging on by a thumbnail. What would I do without Diamond? My rotund rock. If only I could give up and leave this depressing city. But I was still bound to this place where my son had left his life.

In the lobby of the hotel Proprietor Lawrence was hovering over the blond girl, still trying to urge her to a more reasonable pace. "There, now, my dear. Let's move on, shall we? We do need to rearrange our records and prepare for the group arriving for reunion. We will be operating at capacity, you know. I'm certain it will be an enormous help if we can find more efficient ways to keep track of the restaurant charges."

"Lighten up, Lawrence, will you?" the girl snapped. "I hate to break this to you, but restaurant charges are not my life."

Lawrence blinked and pursed his lips.

Nearly an hour had elapsed since I left. If Diamond slept much longer, he was headed for another sleepless night. I went upstairs and knocked. Gently at first. Then harder. "Diamond? Time to get up, Mr. Diamond."

Pressing my ear against the door, I listened for life sounds. Nothing. "Diamond? It's me, Sarah."

Nothing.

I tried again, pounding and calling my loudest, before returning to the desk for an extra key.

"My, my, Mrs. Spooner. Didn't he mention it to you? Mr. Diamond checked out earlier. Then, he did seem in something of a hurry. Perhaps he was called away on some sort of emergency."

"That can't be. He wouldn't take off like that without even saying good-bye." Even as I said it I could see Diamond at the shadowy edge of the terrace, saying it over and over again: "Good-bye, Sarah Spooner. Good-bye." My insides went dead.

"The door to the suite is locked. I didn't take my key."

He turned and scanned the row of mail cubicles. "There you are. Oh, and look. It entirely slipped my mind. Mr. Diamond left you a note. I suppose he simply didn't have time to wait for your return."

I took the folded piece of yellow-lined paper and the spare key and forced myself to go upstairs and face the empty suite.

Diamond's closet was empty, and the desk was cleared and polished clean. His broad stacks of files had been replaced by a fresh supply of ivory-toned, linen-textured Barrington Arms writing paper and a matching mock quill pen. The crumpled candy wrappers were gone from the ashtray and trash basket. Pulling open drawer after drawer in the desk and dresser, I kept hoping to find something, some hope that he wasn't really gone.

Nothing.

As a final possibility, I lifted the carefully laid spread and felt around. There was a single Chunky bar wedged between the bed frame and mattress, and Diamond's prized copy of *A Concise History of Cromwell*. For a second, I was bolstered by the thought that he might come back for his precious book. But no, he wouldn't need it anymore.

With a rush of sadness I stuck the book and the candy in my night table.

Sitting in the floral-print easy chair next to my bed, I opened the note: "Dear Mrs. Spooner, I had to leave. Forgive me for not waiting until you got back, but it was important. I wish you every good luck with your business here. Aldo Diamond."

I was struck by the coldness, the distance. It was a note from a stranger. Then, I reminded myself, Diamond was in fact a stranger. No matter how I had come to enjoy him, we were accidental partners, roommates of convenience. No more.

At least, I was no more than that to him. That was clear. I read the note again, seeking a tiny breath of warmth. A hint of regret. But there was nothing. Business as usual. On to the next adventure.

I sat for a long time, staring at the note until the writing ran together in a meaningless smudge. I tried to imagine what stark bits of knowledge Diamond might be able to glean from his own handwriting, the long, loping ascenders, the slashed downstrokes with the fishhook endings, the round flourish on the capital *D*. Who was Aldo Diamond, anyway?

Here I thought I knew him. But with all the teary confessions, all the wrenching displays of fear and anguish, I didn't really know him at all. All he allowed me to see were certain facts, a concise history of Diamond, edited and abridged.

So what else is new? That's all I had of Ben, of Nicky. People, even the closest people, tended to keep their real selves locked away for safekeeping. Allison was the only one I really knew, and most of that knowledge came from what I knew of myself. We were alike in several fundamental ways. Or were we? How could I pretend to be sure of anything anymore?

There was a timid knock on the door. Winston Lawrence stood outside bearing a tray laden with fruit, cheese wedges, crackers, and a split of chilled white wine.

"Forgive my presumptuousness, Mrs. Spooner, but you did look disturbed by Mr. Diamond's sudden departure. I thought a bit of light refreshment might be welcome."

"Thanks. That's very nice."

"I'll be going, then."

I felt a sudden swell of loneliness. "Maybe you'd like to join me, Mr. Lawrence."

He flushed. "Oh, my. How very gracious of you. I don't wish to be any bother."

"You're not. Honestly you're not. Come in."

Lawrence set the tray down on a folding stand in the front room and perched at the edge of a chair opposite mine. "There, now. Will this do or would you prefer . . ."

"This is fine."

He nibbled on a green grape and seemed to be examining the tray. "I hope I'm not speaking out of turn, Mrs. Spooner, but if you'll forgive me, I feel somewhat concerned about you."

Sweet little mouse. "Don't be. I'm just fine. I admit I was a little surprised that Mr. Diamond took off like that, but it's probably for the best. He needs a good rest, poor man. He's been under a terrible strain."

"Oh?"

"It's a long story, Mr. Lawrence. He had a tragedy in his family, and I think it left him a little . . . unsettled. His imagination was getting the better of him here, I'm afraid. He started to believe all the local myths and legends."

"Like?"

I took a self-conscious sip of the wine. "I've gone on long enough. Thanks for your concern, Mr. Lawrence. And for the tray."

"Oh, my. It was nothing, nothing at all. I must confess, Mrs. Spooner, I feel a particular attachment to my guests at the inn. For the length of your stay, think of me as family, if I may be so bold. The Barrington Arms is my home and, for the time being, yours. Anything I can do to make your stay comfortable and pleasant will be my pleasure."

"I appreciate that." I rose to walk him to the door. "Thanks again—for everything."

Half out in the hallway, he caught my hand in a stilted handshake and fixed me with a stiff, apologetic smile. "Feel free to call on me anytime, Mrs. Spooner. Night or day. I'll be at your disposal."

"Thank you, Mr. Lawrence. I'll keep that in mind."

When the door closed behind him, I felt the first stir-rings of anger penetrate the sense of shock and loss. Why, Diamond? Why now? How could you take off like that without a word? And how in hell am I supposed to get through the rest of this alone?

With a deep, encouraging breath I considered the mea-ger remains of my options. At some point I would have to go to the authorities with what I had uncovered about Hardy Miles's plagiarism and Nicky's missing papers. Now seemed as good a time as any to enlist the help of Chief Dexter and the Cromwell police force, such as it was. I was confident I had enough to interest them, enough to get them to reopen their investigation of the so-called suicides. I found Dexter's card in my purse and dialed.

After a dozen rings I tried the front desk. The clerk fell silent when I asked for the chief.

"Chief Dexter, please," I repeated.

"May I ask who's calling?"

"This is Sarah Spooner. Is Chief Dexter there?"

I was placed on hold, forced to listen to a cloying medley of old Glen Campbell songs played by a pair of dyspeptic violins. I was about to hang up and try again when a crackly voice broke in: "Lieutenant McDowell here, can I help you?"

"My name is Sarah Spooner, Lieutenant. I'm looking for Chief Dexter. It's urgent."

"The chief is unavailable at this time. Why don't you tell me about it and I'll see what I can do to help you."

"I'd really rather speak directly to the chief. You must know where he can be reached."

"Sorry, ma'am. As I told you, he's just unavailable."

"Look, Lieutenant. I'm an assistant D.A. with the New York office. You can't tell me that a police chief is unreachable in case of an emergency. This is an urgent matter that I happen to know is of critical interest to the chief."

"I'm sure it is, but . . . I'm sorry, ma'am. There's nothing I can do."

"Fine. No problem. I'll call D.A. Hodges. I bet there's something he can do." In all my years in the department I couldn't remember invoking Hodges's name once. But, as my mother liked to say, "Strings are for pulling, darling."

The certainty dropped out of McDowell's voice. "Look, I'll see what I can do, ma'am. This isn't my idea. I'll be honest. But I'm on the payroll here. I have a wife and three little kids to take care of. I do what I'm told."

"I don't understand."

"Sometimes the chief decides he doesn't want to talk to a person for some reason. I don't have to agree with him, ma'am, but he is the boss."

A sick feeling was creeping up my legs. "I have to speak to him. You tell him it's a matter of life and death. And tell him D.A. Hodges has a long memory."

"Sure, ma'am. I'll tell him. I'll do my best."

"Please do. It's urgent."

He took my number. "Urgent, right. I'll tell him as soon as I can get in to see him. Meantime, if I can help with that 'urgent' matter . . . I'm always glad to do what I can for a D.A."

"Thanks, but I want to deal with Chief Dexter directly."

Dexter and Diamond went back a long way. I wasn't willing to trust just anyone with what I had found. Too much was at stake. This was no time for him to duck my phone calls.

I could picture big-deal Dexter hiding behind his subordinates like a silly child. I thought about his self-assurance and the way he dismissed Diamond's worries and superstitions. What might his precious computers have to say about his own little quirks and eccentricities? They certainly seemed to know it all when it came to other people and their inexplicable actions.

Inexplicable actions like my son's alleged suicide. I still couldn't wrap my mind around the word or the possibility. Nicky was so much his normal self the last time I saw him. He was home on one of his famous Pony Express runs, when the mails could not get the emergency funds to him fast enough and he decided to come beg in person. I was half lying on the convertible sofa in the den, reviewing the witness list for the Harper case, when the doorbell rang. Through the peephole I saw his measured frown and the calculated hunch of his back. His hand was bent and set atremble, and he held forth a Styrofoam cup.

"Alms for the poor, dear lady. Alms for the poor."

"Come in, you pitiful creature. Please come in. I can give you a few morsels of stale bread and some weak broth. Unfortunately we haven't any money to spare. We gave it all to our spendthrift son."

The world seemed so sane and ordered that day. Allison was off stalking her favorite prey—the Coty bird—in his natural habitat, the perilous wilds of the downtown mall. Ben was away on a conference. At the time I hadn't thought to wonder whether this "conference" might be the two-legged kind. I concentrated on being with my son, marveling again at his metamorphosis from smudged, gangly little boy to full-fledged male person with just the right hint of razor stubble and vulnerability.

It was a perfect spring day: gentle breeze, air scented with fresh-cut grass and sweet lilac, silence mixed with bird song and the distant shouts of playing children. We walked to the local pond for my millionth pebble-skipping lesson.

"Now pay attention, Mrs. Spooner. Because today you are finally going to get this thing right. First you get a good, solid stance, like this. Then go through the steps in your mind. We champion pebble-skippers call that imaging. Gets you in the right frame of mind." He closed his eyes for effect, and his long, spidery lashes cast their fine shadows over his high-boned cheeks. "Next, hold the pebble between your fingers. Not a death grip, just enough to keep control. Then, before you let 'er fly, imagine the stone leaving your hand and skipping across the water. Take your time, and when you feel ready, hold your breath and toss it straight out." With a fluid release his stone leapt away to skim the polished surface and execute a crisp series of hops before ducking beneath the water. Perfect circles shimmered for a breathless instant as testament to his feat.

My turn. Valiantly I stepped to the water's edge and planted my feet in the imprints he left in the rain-softened bank. Each movement a precise imitation. Go through the process in my mind. Cock the wrist, stone perched between thumb and fingertips, rear back, hold my breath, and toss it straight out. . . . Then watch it ker-plunk like a fat klutz belly flopping in a shallow pool. "I did everything exactly right, Nicholas. Exactly what you told me. You're leaving something out, I know it. My mother does that with her recipes. She forgets to mention little things like the onions in her onion soup or the flour in her pie crusts. You can't be blamed, my child. Your need to humiliate me is part of a proud family tradition."

He clapped a conciliatory hand on my back. "Now, don't let it get to you. I bet you'll get it the next time, Mom. Have you been practicing the way I told you?"

I raised my right hand. "Every day for at least an hour. Unless it's snowing."

"Well," he said with a shrug, "maybe that's the problem. You're just not dedicated enough." He allowed a patronizing smile. "Don't feel bad, old girl, you have other talents. And this will come. In fact, I want you to have this." He dug into his pocket and pressed a smooth stone into my hand. I recognized it at once as Sophie, the good luck rock Nick had found on a family vacation as a little boy. Back home, he painted a wide-eyed face on the rock's surface, named it Sophie Mophie Molloy, and began toting it around in his pocket.

"I can't take Sophie, Nick. What would she do without you?"

"You'll take good care of her for me, Mother dear. She couldn't be in better hands."

"I'm touched."

We walked back toward the house arm in arm, a rare moment of close, uncomplicated connection. Allison was my picture-book child—clear and predictable. Nearly everything about her had always made perfect sense to me. But not Nick. He was high literary drama, difficult to read, prone to odd turns and twists. He was the child who should have come with a detailed owner's manual, though I suspected that if he had, it would have been written in Sanskrit. I was always misunderstanding him, and he nearly always managed to leave me feeling that my strokes and timing were the slightest bit awry.

But not that day. The sun was snuggling down over the horizon, casting a pink shadow on the fading sky. I sneaked a peek at my child's sculpted profile, noting the sharp angle of his chin, the slope of his nose, the dense shadows that lined the hollows of his cheeks and shaded the swell of his Adam's apple. His eyes were vague.

"Penny for your thoughts, Nicholas Spooner."

His brow peaked, and his lips curled in a devilish grin. "A penny won't quite do it, Mother dear. But every man has his price. How about . . . let's say, two hundred dollars for my thoughts. Make it two-fifty and I'll throw in a few real sizzlers you can use in my biography. . . ."

"I think I'll let you write the story of your own life, thank you very much."

I was still back there with him when the phone rang. "Mrs. Spooner, this is Lieutenant McDowell."

"Yes?"

"Chief Dexter will speak to you now."

Dexter replaced McDowell on the line, his tone sharp with impatience. "If you're calling again about your son's suicide, Mrs. Spooner, I must reiterate that we have conducted a very, very thorough investigation."

"So you said. In fact, I'm not calling about that. Not directly."

Deep sigh. "Look, I'm really tied up today. We had a big drug bust a couple of hours ago. Whatever it is, can't it wait until tomorrow?"

"It could. But I don't think that's wise. What I've found may tie up all the loose ends at Cromwell. You must have a few minutes for that."

"A few minutes? What is it you want, Mrs. Spooner? Shall I just drop everything and run right over to see you? Is that what you want?"

I kept a tight hold on the fury boiling in my gut. "That would be lovely, Chief. But since you are such a very, very busy man, I will come to headquarters and see you.

That is, if you can spare a few precious moments.''

He gargled in disgust. "Look, lady. I've had it up to here with you and all the rest of the amateur detectives. Believe it or not, we do real work here. We cannot sit around all day playing pretend. You have stories, try Hollywood. I don't have time for stories.''

"This is no story. I've found out some very damning things about one of the Cromwell professors.''

"Come on, lady. Give me a break. I know you're a big-shot Assistant D.A. with Hodges, and I'm not anxious to tick him off. But I will not go chasing my tail to satisfy your vivid imagination.''

"But—"

"But nothing, Mrs. Spooner. That's the end of it. And do me a favor, will you? Don't call again unless you have hard evidence to show me. I'm a busy man.''

The line went dead.

Furious, I slammed the dead receiver in the cradle and ripped Byron "Chip" Dexter's business card to satisfying shreds. I searched for an alternate plan, but my mind fought back with a sudden fog of weariness. I kicked off my shoes and lay t ack against the cool comforter.

I was falling, drifting in a curious void. Sinking in a cool, empty sleep. Worries bounced off my numb surface, harmless and unfelt. Nothing could touch me. Nothing. Sweet, safe surrender. . . .

*   *   *

I awoke with a start. The room was inky dark and filled with a dense, expectant silence. But there was something more, something I could feel. Fingers of fear closed around my throat, and my voice was a choked whisper.

"Who's there?"

No response.

"Who is it?"

The light clicked on, flooding the room with a blinding wash of light. My hand flew up in defense, and a sharp scream built inside me as the shadow took the form of a man.

"Who's there?"

"Mrs. Spooner. My, my, I do hope I didn't startle you. I was concerned when you didn't come down for dinner. When I checked and found you sleeping, I thought I would simply wait here in case you needed anything when you awoke."

"Mr. Lawrence?" I measured my breaths and willed my heart to stop its violent thumping. His expression was so meek and apologetic. "That was . . . thoughtful of you. But completely unnecessary. I told you, I'm fine. Really. Just a little worn out."

"Certainly you are, you poor dear. And no wonder. You have been through a terrible personal trial, a difficult week, and now, with Mr. Diamond gone . . . I imagine you won't really feel yourself again until you leave Cromwell and return to the comfort of your loved ones."

"I guess."

ReerE

"Well, then. You rest now. And please, Mrs. Spooner. Don't worry about anything. I will see that you are well taken care of. You may be assured of that."

I wanted to protest as he sat down at the entrance, folded his legs, and resumed his vigil. But my thoughts refused to make a solid connection with my tongue. I was drifting again, floating in a dream-sea of cool distance. Words—odd, formless words chased me. Threats, warnings. The bitter, pathetic ramblings of a sickened mind. I strained to understand, to listen, but it was too far away. Part of a harmless dream, I thought. Or a vicious, unrelenting nightmare.

-21-

It was nearly noon when I forced open my eyes, but I was still overwhelmed with exhaustion. Winston Lawrence was perched on his chair near the door, fingers laced in a prim bundle, legs crossed, face arranged in a careful mask of polite concern.

"There, now, Mrs. Spooner. Awake at last. Are you feeling any better?"

My tongue was a soggy towel, and the edges of the room were smudged and uncertain. "I don't understand why I'm so tired. I feel as if I've been beaten up."

"Yes, you poor dear," he clucked. "You have been under a terrible, terrible strain. Catches up with one after a time. Here, have a sip of tea. That should perk you up."

The tea was too sweet and had a bitter aftertaste, but I drank it down and felt a pleasant easing in my throat. "Thanks."

I tried to sit, but my limbs were half dead and the room began to revolve like the walls of a drunken stupor.

"There, there, my dear. Poor, dear lady. You have had a dreadful shock. You must rest."

"I can't. I have things to do." The words ran together and turned to mush.

He shook his head. "Forgive me for saying so, Mrs. Spooner. But you are clearly in no condition to attend to anything but your own well-being. You mustn't exert yourself. Let me assist you. I would consider it an honor."

A wide, extravagant yawn escaped me. "I wanted to get something from . . ."

"Yes?"

I hesitated, remembering Professor Lawrence's reaction to Goldenberg's accusations. I wanted to see the album, to compare Hardy Miles's published works to Nick's papers, but . . . "Nothing. It can wait."

"It need not wait, Mrs. Spooner, whatever it is. We don't expect any new guests at the inn until late tomorrow. I am at your disposal in the meanwhile."

"I don't know . . ."

"You can trust me, my dear lady. You must believe that. Whatever you ask will be held in strictest confidence. Strictly between the two of us."

It was hard to think with the dense clouds wafting through my mind. "You won't tell anyone?"

"Not a soul. I promise." He held up his hand and met my eyes with a steady, earnest gaze.

"Okay, then. I guess it's all right. I want to take a look at an album Professor Goldenberg has at his house.

His collection of department clippings. Can you . . . ?''

"Certainly. I know Dr. Goldenberg from social occasions at my brother Warren's home. I would be delighted to go to him and bring back the material you seek.'' He offered me a final sip of tea and prepared to leave.

"May I be so presumptuous as to ask the reason you wish to have this album? Dr. Goldenberg may want to know.''

"I . . . I can't explain. It's too complicated. Just tell him I'll only need it for a day or two. I'll take good care of it.''

"Of course, whatever you say, Mrs. Spooner. You relax now. I'll be back shortly.''

After the door closed behind him I struggled to sit. Slowly the room stopped wavering at the edges, and my eyes were able to hold a clear image. I stood and staggered to the bathroom, clutching the furniture for support.

Filling the sink with chill water, I splashed my face several times and then ducked under the surface, blowing bubbles until the cold shocked me alert.

I took the folder of Nick's work and sat in the flowered armchair, trying to shake off the dull remnants of the fog.

At the top of the pile was a story called ''The Revolving Door,'' about a small girl, Leona, whose parents turned to vicious, menacing black bears when she refused to eat her creamed winter squash. Their pleas and exhortations failed to move her and deteriorated, over coffee with heavy cream and a touch of brandy, to snarls and primitive jungle posturing. After a time Ma and Pa Bear lost all control and began chasing little Leona around the apartment until she was able to sneak out to the common hall and hop in an elevator. The chase resumed in the lobby where the senior bears found themselves stuck in a revolving door. The furry elders were finally apprehended and hauled off to the local zoo where Leona visited them religiously—on Thursdays and Sundays. She never failed to bring each of them a nice, big bowl of creamed winter squash.

The next was a fantasy set in a haze-ridden celestial courtroom where a panel of wizened arbitrators met to write their decision in ''The Case of Hetty Breitmeier.''

Hetty was a pious, petulant woman whose immediate past life failed to meet even her modest expectations. During the day Hetty cared for her invalid parents until their respective deaths. At night, when she had to leave for her job as a collar presser in a steamy, rat-infested shirt laundry run by a leering tightwad named Fenster, her rich, beautiful sister would send the chauffeured Mercedes over to drop off the maid to keep an eye on Hetty's parents. While Hetty's parents slept, the maid watched old movies, snoozed on the living room sofa, and snacked on whatever Hetty had planned for the next night's dinner.

Though she bemoaned her difficult life in private, Hetty kept up a strong, cheerful front for her parents.

She saw her service to them as a duty, a duty to which she held fast through her mother's long, difficult death from a series of incapacitating strokes.

Hetty was finally liberated at the age of sixty-four when her father died in his sleep during a summer rerun of a television talk show. A French chef was demonstrating his secrets for a perfect soufflé at the time, and Hetty waited until the egg whites peaked to call the police. After all, her father would be dead for a very long time.

On the way home from the funeral she allowed herself to think about how she would spend the first day she had to herself in over forty years. While she was daydreaming, a drunken teenager in a dilapidated pickup truck crossed the highway center divider and crashed head-on into Hetty's '62 Ford (the one she polished every Sunday after mass and filled with only top-quality motor oil). She was killed instantly.

The arbitrators debated the merits of Hetty's past life and tried to decide how to bring her back. Hetty told her sad story and pleaded for a better future incarnation. The arbitrators finally agreed to have Hetty reborn as her sister's maid.

I found myself smiling. See, I wanted to scream. Look at this, world. These are clever stories meant to poke fun at the too-stern or serious. I could imagine Nick's throaty chuckle as he invented Leona and Hetty and the other characters in these fantasy sandwiches. Hardly the work of a tormented person, I assured myself. Hardly.

Turning to the next page, I was eager to read more. Nick had real talent. Even now he had the power to surprise and delight me.

The poem was typed. I recognized the strikeovers and smudged *O*'s of Nick's old portable Smith-Corona. It was titled "Departures."

> *Enter night.*
> *Darkness drawn in webs of shadow.*
> *Shrouds the ceaseless doom of day.*
> *Blind as pride.*
> *Buried in the crypt of failed dreams.*
> *Rests the endpiece of a sorry tale.*
> *Cold cast in stone.*

There were more poems. Bleak, hopeless images without a trace of irony or humor. I sipped the tepid tea Lawrence had left. This was not the son I knew. Nick was never so dour or melancholy. Never.

My eyes were gaining weight. All the reading, I thought. I could close them for just a second. There were more stories, but my eyes were burning. All I needed was a little while, just a minute to rest. . . .

"Mrs. Spooner?"

I was pulled awake. The day had dimmed, and Winston Lawrence, framed in the doorway, stood holding the dirt-stained album toward me.

"I can't believe I fell asleep again."

My voice was playing at too slow a speed, and so was his. "That's all right, my dear lady. . . . You need your rest. Here is the album you requested. Dr. Goldenberg said you are welcome to keep it as long as you like."

"Thank you, Mr. Lawrence. That's a big help."

His teeth glowed in the dusky room. "My pleasure, I assure you. You rest, Mrs. Spooner. I shall bring you something to eat."

"That's not . . ." I couldn't find the word. I was at the edge of a cliff, falling. . . .

In a jarring blink, the tray was in front of me and I tried to eat. Nothing had any real taste or odor. My mouth was dried rubber. Lawrence stood by with a benign smile. "That's it, Mrs. Spooner. Eat a bit more. You do need your strength."

"Why am I so tired?"

He shrugged and held up a pair of vacant palms. "You have been through so much, Mrs. Spooner. Such emotional strain and turmoil. A person has limits. . . ."

I forced myself to chew and swallow. There was no time for a nervous collapse today.

"There, that's better." Lawrence had the steady, encouraging manner of a patient parent.

I was beginning to feel better, lighter. I managed a few more bites and stood on shaky legs. "The food did help. Thank you, Mr. Lawrence. You have been very kind."

"No more than anyone would do, I'm sure, Mrs. Spooner." He poured a cup of steaming coffee from a ceramic pot. "There. Do drink that. I believe you can use a bit of a bracer. If there is nothing further you wish at the moment, I'll be going." He backed out of the room, carrying the remains of my food.

I waited for the sound of his retreating steps on the staircase, pushed the coffee aside, and placed Goldenberg's album beside Nick's papers on the bed. One by one I went through the writings, comparing line by line. Page after page.

Nothing. Not one of Miles's articles was taken from anything of Nick's, not even a stray idea.

So much for Goldenberg's theory. Unless . . .

I could still hear Hardy Miles talking to himself in his office: "Success the simple way . . . a brilliant work of short fiction." One last possibility. I called *The Liberty Review*. Glancing at the clock, I hoped the editorial offices hadn't closed for the day. Two rings, three.

"Articles."

I hoped no one would notice the static in my voice. "This is Dr. Hardy Miles's secretary. Dr. Miles thinks he may have sent you the wrong version of the last page of his manuscript. Would it be possible for someone to read me the one you have to make sure?"

I was put on hold. My head pounded in the silence. The final pages of Nick's stories were laid out on the bed in front of me. Endings.

At last an officious voice crackled on the line. "Hello? This is Penny McCardle. I have the last page of the Miles piece. You ready?"

"Ready."

She read in a lifeless monotone. I looked frantically from page to page, trying to keep up with her. My mind was still sluggish, my eyes staggering over the words. The thunderous pounding in my head made her hard to hear. Slower! I wanted to scream. But I could only struggle to find a match.

Not the first, the second. Not that in the corner. She read on and on in her maddening, mechanical voice. I tried to remember the words, but they kept slipping away.

> *Jeremy saw the tiny light beneath the curtain. Leonard was home. "Len," he called in a pinch of a voice. "Lenny."*
>
> *No one answered. There was never enough force behind the words. The hope was stuck in a prison of . . .*

My eye caught the place. I felt a smile tugging at my lips as I read silently along.

> *. . . a prison of his own making. A prison with walls of stiff feeling and an impassable fence made of the barbed wire of his own dishonesty.*
>
> *"Len," he said again, and began to weep softly in the darkness.*
>
> *Len pulled the cranky shutters and fastened the lock. Picking up his frayed copy of* The Adventures

of an Adventurous Man, *he tipped the light just so. Damon was back in the Badlands, playing politics with a cranky rattlesnake. For a minute he hesitated, then shrugged and allowed a dry chuckle. "'Night, Jeremy," he said, and started the next chapter.*

"So?"

Penny, the officious monotone on the other end, cleared her throat and rephrased her question. "So is it the right ending? We're almost on deadline, you know."

"Yes, it's the right one. Thank you."

My mind snapped to attention. Hardy Miles had stolen Nicky's work. And who knows how many others? If desperation pushed him to steal, desperation may have pushed him to cover his tracks no matter what the cost. Hardy Steppington Miles might well be responsible for the rash of "suicides" that threatened to cause the untimely demise of Cromwell University.

What next? It was a huge leap from locating stolen papers to proving a series of cold-blooded, calculated murders. Too big a leap for me to take alone. I remembered Chief Dexter's warning to stay away until I had evidence. Here it was—hard evidence. Much as I would have liked never to speak to the abrasive Chief Dexter again, I needed his help to solve this thing once and for all.

Again I had to thread my way through a maze of obedient subordinates. When I told Lieutenant McDowell what I had found, he was sure Dexter would be interested.

The call back came in under five minutes. Dexter's voice was stiff with impatience, but I was certain he would come around when he heard about Professor Hardy Steppington Miles and the exact match between Nick's story and the piece Miles submitted to *The Liberty Review*. Without a pause I related the entire story, including my visit to Miles's office and my run-in with the extortionist janitor. There was no response but the even sound of his breathing.

"Professor Goldenberg was right, Chief. He said desperate men were capable of desperate acts. Think about it. Hardy Miles would have lost everything—his job, his professional reputation—if he was found out. There might have been civil suits and worse if one of the students he stole from blew the whistle on him. My theory is that he saw no choice but to get rid of them. He rigged the murders to look like suicides so no one would find out about the stolen papers."

Dexter's tone dripped with sarcasm. "So that's your theory, is it, Mrs. Spooner? As they say on *Romper Room* and in Southern California, thank you for sharing that with me."

"I'm afraid I don't think this is a joking matter, Chief Dexter. We are talking about murder here. Mass murder."

"Forgive me for disagreeing with you, Mrs. Spooner. What we are talking about is not murder at all. We are talking about a wild, unsubstantiated theory by a self-appointed vigilante with a vivid imagination. Next thing you'll tell me Jesse James was driven to murder and mayhem by a drawer full of unpaid parking tickets. If Professor Miles, or whoever, was pilfering his students' essays, that's university business. You want to accuse him of lifting your son's English papers, discuss it with the English department or the college administration. Taking words does not make a man a murderer, Mrs. Spooner.''

''But seven of the dead students were English majors. You said so yourself.''

''And four of them were wearing toenail polish. Maybe we should arrest someone from Maybelline. Come on, Mrs. Spooner. Give it up. Go home where you have close relatives to annoy.''

''Can't you at least check and see if the other victims took one of Miles's courses? Wouldn't that convince you?''

''No, Mrs. Spooner. But I have my regular appointment with my gypsy soothsayer this afternoon. Maybe I'll run your theory by her. If she buys it, I'll get right back to you. In fact, I'll even ask her if she's interested in hiring part-time help. Tell me, do you have your own tea leaves and tarot cards, or would you want her to provide them?''

''Can't you at least consider the possibility that I may be on to something?''

"I'll consider that you may be on something, lady. That's about it."

The phone was slammed in its cradle, and I heard the expectant hush of a dead line.

Now what?

I felt a sudden ache of loneliness. I willed good old Diamond to amble through the door, porky hand stuffed in a paper tub of peanut brittle. My wish came fully furnished with the curious peak of his eyebrow and the sober thoughts that squeezed through the stuffed sanctum of his mouth. "Don't say I didn't warn you, Sarah Spooner. You're in it up to the old eyeballs now, aren't you?"

So it seemed. But I wasn't about to give up. Bullhead Dexter was not going to defeat me. In fact, the chief had been far more helpful than he intended. His suggestion was perfect. The university administration was just the ally I needed. Who had a bigger stake in Professor Hardy Steppington Miles, missing student papers, and their possible link to the "suicides"?

Delighted with the fresh possibilities, I called the main university number and asked to speak with Chairman Wallace Lawrence. "Personal and urgent," I told the operator.

I could hardly believe my good fortune when, after two rings, Lawrence himself came on the line. "Hello, this is Wallace Lawrence."

"Chairman Lawrence, my name is Sarah Spooner. My son Nicholas was—"

"I shall be unavailable until the start of reunion on Thursday, but if you leave your name and a brief message . . ."

A recording.

Thursday, June tenth. Two days from now. How was I going to wait two more days? My impatience would push me over the edge by then.

June tenth. What was it about that date? I searched the dim corners of my memory. No use. Probably the birthday of some long-misplaced friend or the anniversary of a best-forgotten event.

Two days to wait and worry.

Why not take Winston Lawrence up on his offer of help? If I explained everything to him, maybe he could get his brother to see me at once. Chairman Lawrence was probably hiding from the press and the threat of the accreditation board. But he would want to hear what I had to say. I might even be able to offer him the hope of salvation for his precious university.

I showered and dressed in a hurry, taking care to look sane and convincing: wild tangle of hair tamed with an elastic band, crisp blue linen suit, sensible navy pumps, professional posture, steady gaze, a splash of power cologne.

Satisfied with the image, I went downstairs to find Winston Lawrence. But the lobby was deserted, and a note tacked to his office door explained that he would not be back for several hours.

Disgusted, I went out on the terrace and sat staring out over the golf course. A trio of middle-aged men in knit pastel berets and droopy madras Bermudas were approaching the adjacent tee. The tallest man, a faded redhead with a chip-toothed smile and the voice of a bullhorn, plucked his four iron from a giant red bag and began posturing for his companions. "Watch this closely now, boys. You might pick up a few pointers."

"Here's a pointer for you, Marty. Stick it where the sun don't shine."

The two dissolved in a chorus of childish giggles. How could they be so carefree? Especially here. Two days ago I sat here with Diamond, watching the fear in his eyes, listening to his odd warnings. I could still hear the words: "It's too late for me, Sarah Spooner. Run while you still have legs."

Why didn't I take him more seriously then? Maybe I could have found out what hidden horrors he carried away with him when he ran. But I assumed he was just a little unbalanced, thrown off by what had happened to his wife and son, that he would come to his senses after a while. "Listen while you still have ears. Good-bye, Sarah Spooner. Good-bye. When June turns ten, begins the end."

When June turns ten. That's where I heard about June tenth. Diamond said something about that date. In fact, he read that strange line in his book about Cromwell's history.

What or whose end was prophesied for June tenth?
shivered, realizing how many of Diamond's dire predic
tions had come true.

When June turns ten. Odd that Wallace Lawrence
would be "unavailable" until that particular date. Odd
that the reunion, when Cromwell's most important con
tributors and supporters visited the campus, would begin
that day.

Two days from now. Maybe it was all a curious co
incidence, but I was not about to take that chance. Bolt
before they nail you, Sarah Spooner.

I could picture Diamond's world-weary eyes, dripping
sorrow. "It's too late for me, Sarah Spooner. Go home
Get away from here."

"Soon," I whispered. The trio clattered away in their
golf cart, laughing and trading insults. They climbed a
gentle rise in the fairway and were lost from sight.

The sun dipped behind a mass of charcoal cloud, and
a guttural roar of thunder pierced the stillness. Rude rain
plunked on the wrought-iron table and freckled my linen
suit.

I went inside, walking the same path Diamond had
taken two days ago. Two days. I had no time to waste,
or it might be too late for a number of things.

-22-

"Going somewhere, Mrs. Spooner?"

I suppressed a swell of anger as Winston Lawrence materialized from a shadowy corner of the front lobby, startling me. His face was wide with innocence, his head cocked at a calculated angle like a curious dog.

"Actually, I was waiting for you. I need to meet with your brother, Wallace. I have some information about the deaths at Cromwell that may change everything. In fact, I was hoping you might be able to get him to see me right now—today."

"Oh, my. I don't know if that's possible, Mrs. Spooner. Wallace is always on a very rigid schedule, and now, with all the furor at the university and the reunion about to begin in a matter of days, he is nearly impossible to reach, even for me."

"But it's an emergency. Please, Mr. Lawrence, you have to believe me. I must see him right away."

"There, there, Mrs. Spooner. Try not to upset yourself any further." He steered me to the rose velvet banquette beside the slatted bird cage and urged me to sit. "Why don't you tell me what you have learned? Perhaps I can arrange something."

He pulled up a carved side chair and sat opposite me, waiting. I studied the face—benign, timid. This birdlike, little man was my last hope, my only chance.

Taking care to sound calm and reasonable, I told him everything: my suspicions about the "suicides"; what I had discovered about Hardy Miles and Nick's stolen papers. And the rest, all of it: the Cromwell curse, Chief Dexter's refusal to recognize the frightening possibilities. Finally I pulled Diamond's dog-eared copy of *A Concise History of Cromwell* from my purse, where I had placed it in hopeful preparation for a meeting with Chairman Lawrence. "Read this."

I handed him the book, open to the passage Diamond had quoted. "When June turns ten, begins the end." I had managed to locate that odd beginning. It was followed by a detailed prophesy of the demise of Cromwell University in a "hail of shame and retribution" on that particular date.

Winston Lawrence read slowly, tasting the words. Finished, he turned the book over in his hands and placed it open across his lap. Looking up at me, he frowned and scratched between his eyes. "My, my, this is most disturbing indeed. I'm sure you're correct. Wallace will want to hear of this at once—immediately. You wait right here, Mrs. Spooner. I shall make certain my brother is fully informed."

I felt a rush of relief. "Will you ask him to meet with me, Mr. Lawrence? This has to be handled exactly right if we're going to apprehend Miles and link him to the deaths."

"Certainly. I understand. An immediate meeting. You wait right here. I shall see to everything."

He disappeared down the back hall to his office and closed the door. I heard bursts of muffled conversation and the nervous tapping of his foot against the bare wood floor. Chairman Lawrence had to believe my story—he had to.

Breath held, I heard the office door open and the footsteps padding in my direction. As he crossed the lobby I searched Winston Lawrence's face for a sign. Nothing.

"What did he say, Mr. Lawrence? Will he meet with me? Did you explain how urgent this is?"

Holding up a hand, he managed a tentative smile. "Now, now, Mrs. Spooner. I understand how critical a matter this is. And so does Wallace, naturally. My brother may have his shortcomings, but he is a brilliant man, a man of action. He took immediate charge of the situation as usual. Rest assured, you shall have a full opportunity to express your concerns and tell Wallace everything you have learned."

"Thank you, Mr. Lawrence. Thank you so much. When can I see him? Does he want me to come to his office?"

"No, not at all. Wallace agreed to a meeting here, at the inn. Our facilities are far more comfortable and private than any the university can provide. He assured me all the principals will be here by late this afternoon: Chief Dexter, my brother, Professor Miles—"

"Miles? No, he can't do that. You don't understand."

"There, there, Mrs. Spooner. Please calm yourself. My, my. All will be well, believe me. Wallace is experienced in dealing with the most delicate, difficult matters. Confrontation, careful confrontation, has proven most effective for him in the past. Trust in his judgment, Mrs. Spooner. Please."

I shuddered at the thought of a face-to-face encounter with Hardy Miles. But Chairman Lawrence might be right, it might be the only way to force his hand. Otherwise, with Nicky and the others gone, Miles could be able to bluff his way out of the plagiarism charges. It would be his word against the strength of a few documents. Not a strong case at best. If he talked his way out of the stolen paper issue, nothing would be left to link him to the "suicides." Nothing.

"All right, Mr. Lawrence. If your brother is convinced it's necessary."

"Oh, my, yes. Wallace was very definite on that point. A direct confrontation is the only sensible course. What with the element of surprise and all, Dr. Miles might well be moved to confess everything. That would restore Cromwell's good name and insure the deserved future of a fine university."

"I suppose . . ."

"Have faith, Mrs. Spooner. You have done the right thing, bringing these disturbing matters to my attention. Now they shall be properly disposed."

Winston Lawrence fussed over me like a fawning parent, insisting I let him serve me lunch in the deserted dining room, watching while I did my best to choke down a crustless chicken salad sandwich and a tall, frosted glass of cloying lemonade. Several times he checked his watch, as if awaiting the first arrivals at a party.

"When do you think they'll be here?"

"Oh, several hours at the very least, Mrs. Spooner. My brother had to locate the central parties and make all the necessary arrangements."

"Arrangements?"

"Why, certainly. He wishes to have a stenographer present, recording equipment. Whatever is necessary to ensure that Miles's statements are properly documented."

"Yes, that's important." The knots of tension were beginning to loosen. Chairman Lawrence seemed to know what he was doing. Catching Hardy Miles was not enough. He had to be made to pay for what he did.

"Well, then. Why don't you rest awhile, Mrs. Spooner. I'll call for you as soon as anyone arrives. You do look exhausted."

I felt another wash of fatigue; my eyes were wavering out of focus. "Sounds like a good idea. Please excuse me, Mr. Lawrence. I guess you're right. All the horror of the past month has caught up with me.''

I plodded across the lobby to the staircase. Dour young faces stared back at me from the sketches on the wall. The three-headed monster jittered in its frame. ''I'm so tired.''

''That's fine, Mrs. Spooner. Not to worry. All is under control. Wallace has seen to everything, all the details. You need only rest and regain your strength.''

Back in my room, I fell on the bed in a dead heap. In an instant I was dragged from consciousness and into a terrifying paralysis of sleep. Something was holding me down—a thick, evil presence with sour breath and in-human strength.

Struggling to escape, I forced my way to the dull edge of consciousness. Strange sounds echoed in the empty room, and there was the sick scent of fear and hope-lessness. ''What is it? What's happening?'' But the im-ages swirled beyond my reach or reason.

''Please''—my tone was desperate, weak—''who's there?''

I saw the blade first, the sharp glimmer of a polished point. Coming at me. Aiming at my chest. ''No! No, please!''

Hands tearing, pulling me up and away. Dragging me half dead through the room. Iced feet on the bathroom floor, the rush of water, drowning me.

Sputtering, I came awake and stared into the squinting eyes of Hardy Steppington Miles.

"Mrs. Spooner? Wake up! Mrs. Spooner, can you hear me?"

Terror squeezed at my neck, but I managed to keep my tone controlled. "What are you doing here?"

"I heard you screaming as soon as I walked in the front door." A wicked grin twisted his lips. "You sounded like something out of a Hitchcock movie."

"I must have been dreaming. I'm fine now. Please go, Dr. Miles. I'll be down for the meeting in a few minutes."

"So you will." He made no move to leave. His face curled in a satisfied sneer. "I must say you were out cold. If one didn't know better, one might suspect you were indulging in some narcotic, Mrs. Spooner. Perhaps that explains your vicious delusions."

His expression was cold, bloodless. "I'm sure Mr. Lawrence is waiting for you downstairs, Dr. Miles."

"Well, he'll just have to wait a little longer. First we have to talk."

I stood and started inching toward the door. "We have nothing to talk about, Dr. Miles. Anything you have to say to me can wait for the meeting."

I was almost past him. A few steps and I could make a run for the stairs. Almost there.

Iron fingers caught my wrist and held it in a death grip. "This is between you and me, Mrs. Spooner. Sit."

He pushed me down on the bed. My mind was racing, trying to outdistance the fear. "Mr. Lawrence will come up to get me . . . any minute. You can't get away with this.''

''You are an impossible woman, Mrs. Spooner. Always nosing around, looking for trouble. Well, this time you've gone too far. Too far!'' He leaned over me, lips pulled taut, eyes blazing fury. ''You won't get away with this, lady. You'll see.''

My voice was a pleading whimper. ''I . . . don't know what you're talking about, Dr. Miles. Please. Leave me alone. I haven't done anything to you.'' I was caught in a spasm of terror, trying to find some way to escape. A way out.

Standing, he gave me a contemptuous look and issued a dry chuckle. ''I plan to take care of you in my own way. Soon enough. But for now, just know you are treading on a very narrow ledge. Very, very narrow. You keep your mouth shut at this meeting if you know what's good for you. You don't say a word.''

Mute with horror, I watched him back away and out the door.

I fought back a strong urge to run. This meeting would put Hardy Miles where he belonged, where he was no longer a threat to anyone.

I did my best to put myself back together and went downstairs. Miles was chatting with Winston Lawrence in the lobby, acting as if nothing had happened. I caught his eye in a meaningful exchange. *We'll see about who knows what's good for who, Dr. Miles. We'll see sooner than you can imagine.*

Spotting me, Proprietor Lawrence stood and instructed us to follow.

He led us through a small door opposite the front entrance and down a dim stairway. At the bottom he turned into a musty tunnel, lit at intervals by bare bulbs that wavered as we walked. Our steps clattered against the damp, cement floor, and we moved through the narrow corridor in single file, a piteous parade of the furious and fearful.

The tunnel continued through a series of turns and angles until I was lost in confusion. "Where are we going?" I asked again, and was answered once more by the flag of Winston Lawrence's index finger, urging my patience.

No one spoke until we came to a heavy metal door at the tunnel's end. Winston Lawrence pulled a ring of keys from the pocket of his baggy brown trousers and worked the dead bolt.

Inside, we mounted a plush blue-carpeted stair. At the top we found ourselves in a spacious living room done in peach tones and soft, soothing blues. There were cozy arrangements of sofas and settees, a marble fireplace with brass fittings, and a mantelpiece lined with graceful porcelain figurines. Along one wall was a polished pecan table ringed with graceful Victorian chairs. Heavy, lined blue drapery hid a wall of windows.

"Where are we?"

Winston Lawrence took in the room with a sweeping, proprietary gesture. "My special retreat, Mrs. Spooner.

A place I keep for only the most important people and occasions. We can meet here without fear of interruption.''

"What about the rest of the party?" Miles snarled. "Did you leave them a treasure map?"

I had to admire Lawrence's unwavering calm. "They know where to find us, of course, Dr. Miles. The others will join us shortly."

"Hooray," Miles said. "I can hardly wait."

Winston Lawrence bustled about the room, plumping throw pillows, straightening the oversize art books on the polished coffee table, placing the peach settee at a perfect right angle to the flowered blue sofa. Finally he stood back and scrutinized his efforts. "There." He clapped his hands together. "Now, why don't you two take seats at the table. I think that would be the best arrangement, don't you? Mrs. Spooner, you sit there, at that end. And Dr. Miles can sit opposite you. We'll leave places for Chief Dexter and my dear brother in the center. That should work out well, don't you think?''

I sat stiffly at the foot of the table and Miles loped over to the tapestried chair at the head and took his place.

"Now what, folks? A nice game of pin-the-tail-on-the-professor? It's a rare privilege to be summoned to an emergency meeting by our esteemed chairman. A rare privilege I can do without very nicely."

Lawrence checked his watch. "I'm certain the others will arrive momentarily. Why don't you allow me to get you some refreshments in the meantime. What is your pleasure, Mrs. Spooner? Dr. Miles?"

"Anything," Miles said. "And make it a double."

"Nothing for me," I said. A lump of fear was stuck in my throat. I couldn't tear my mind away from what Miles had done, what he was capable of doing. How could Lawrence be so calm and normal? He probably didn't believe Miles was guilty. How was I going to convince him? And the others?

"Now, now, Mrs. Spooner. That will never do. You must allow me to get you something. Iced tea, perhaps? Or something a bit stronger? And some nice pastries, of course. I do think it's uncivilized to hold a meeting without proper refreshments."

"All right, iced tea will be fine." The last thing I needed was anything stronger. Seeing Hardy Miles, being around him, had chilled me awake. And I didn't want my guard lowered an inch until this meeting was safely over.

"I'll be back in a moment." Before I could protest, Lawrence slipped out through the back of the room and was gone.

Alone, Miles's angry eyes burned at me. "Mouth shut, Mrs. Spooner. You remember that. Or you'll be sorry."

"I . . . don't know what you're talking about, Dr. Miles."

"You know exactly what I'm talking about, lady. I'm talking about accusations, slander. You will be sorry. Sorrier than you can imagine."

Fury was displacing the fear. "You're the one who's going to be sorry. I know all about you. Everything. Soon everyone will."

He stood and sent his chair clattering against the wall. I shivered as he approached me, scarlet with rage. "You've gone far enough. Far enough! I'll show you." He was coming toward me, menacing.

"Leave me alone!"

The door clattered open, and Winston Lawrence came in carrying a white enameled tray set with drinks, a plate of delicate lace cookies and filled pastries, and a single sweetheart rose in a silver bud vase. "Well, well. Here we are." He flashed a quizzical look at Miles. "Please sit down, Dr. Miles."

Miles backed off and sat. He downed the double Lawrence had brought and poured himself another from the crystal decanter. The flush of color began to recede from his face.

I ordered my galloping pulse to resume a normal rhythm. Soon Chief Dexter would be here, and Chairman Lawrence. They would know how to deal with Miles.

His voice softened from the liquor. "How much longer till the inquisition, Mr. Lawrence? I don't like waiting for my tar and feathers."

"I'm sure the others will be right along. We really can't begin the meeting without them." He frowned. "You're not drinking your tea, Mrs. Spooner. I hope there's nothing wrong with it. I made it especially for you."

I took a tiny sip. Too sweet. Lawrence had a heavy hand with the sugar. I took another sip and held the cool glass to my lips, pretending to drink. After all of Lawrence's concern and cooperation, I didn't want to insult him.

I turned away from Hardy Miles, but I felt his eyes on me, hot coals of fury trying to pierce the shaky armor of my self-control. "Where are the others, Mr. Lawrence? Shouldn't they be here by now?"

"Shortly, Mrs. Spooner. Relax and drink your tea now."

I took another sip.

"I'd think they'd run right over to hear all about the lies you've been dishing out, lady."

I met his eyes. "They are not lies, Dr. Miles. Every bit of it is true and you know it."

He stood and spat his words in a drunken rage. "Pure, unmitigated crap, Mrs. Spooner. You'd better be able to prove everything . . . every word!"

"I will. I have all the proof I need. The paper you turned in to *The Liberty Review* was lifted word for word from one of my son's stories. I have his original."

Miles's eyes widened, and he started to laugh—an insane, hysterical cackle.

"Where the hell is Chief Dexter, Mr. Lawrence? I want protection from that woman."

Miles gasped and sputtered until the laughter was played out. He held up a hand. His words were losing form, running together as the liquor claimed his tongue. "Is that it? That's your so-called evidence?" He held the chair back for support. "Did it ever occur to you that my work was the original and your son's was the copy? Did it?"

"What are you talking about?"

"I had all my students do a redraft of that story, Mrs. Spooner. The assignment was for them to copy the piece over and make punctuation changes to match the style of a British novelist. I used it to teach them about punctuation style, Mrs. Spooner. I gave that assignment to my last three classes in British literature. You can ask any one of the seven hundred students in those classes."

"But . . . Professor Goldenberg said—"

He was rocking like a boat in a storm, clutching the chair. "Jerry Goldenberg is a damned old fool. He's been dying of jealousy since I started getting things accepted by the major literary journals. He never liked me. Not since I edged him out for the department chair ten years ago. Ever since, he's been trying to discredit me, pointing the finger at me. Making groundless accusations. There was nothing to any of them. Not a shred of truth. Whoooo." He slumped down in his chair. "What the hell was in that drink?"

A dissonant pulse was stabbing at my head. "Then why did you tell me you didn't know anything about Nick's papers, Dr. Miles? All his work was in your files."

"I . . . keep . . . everything. Forget . . . what I . . . have. My . . . wife . . . always . . . says."

"You really didn't know? Dr. Miles, are you all right?"

I watched in horror as his eyes rolled back in his head, exposing blood-smeared whites, and his lids fluttered closed. Something was rattling in his throat.

"Dr. Miles?" I raced over to him and pressed my fingers to his neck. His pulse was thready, barely there. "Something's wrong with him. Call for help, Mr. Lawrence. Hurry!

"Dr. Miles!" I held his nose and breathed into his mouth. But even as I did, I could feel the last pulses of his life seeping away. "Call someone!"

Lawrence settled himself daintily on the side chair and watched. His face was set and serene. He issued a vague sigh. "There is nothing anyone can do, I'm afraid, Mrs. Spooner. Poor dear Dr. Miles seems to be well beyond human help."

"Hurry up. He's stopped breathing. I can't get a pulse!"

"Dead, is he?" Winston Lawrence rose and came around the table to where Miles was sprawled—lifeless. He extended a finger and poked the professor playfully on the chest. "Dead, indeed. He certainly is. Farewell,

Dr. Miles. Happy landings.''

"Oh, my God. Call the police. Please, Mr. Lawrence. Hurry!''

He patted my cheek. "There, there, my dear. No need for hurry any longer, is there? Dr. Miles has gone to his proper reward.'' He took a lace cookie from the tray and nibbled a chocolate coated edge.

"No, you don't understand. I was wrong about him. He didn't steal Nick's work. Didn't you hear? Didn't you?''

In a stupor of shock I watched as Winston Lawrence lifted Miles's body like a sack of potatoes and set it on the flowered sofa. He folded Miles's limp hands across his chest and pressed his eyelids closed. For a few minutes he fussed over the corpse as if it were a display mannequin, buttoning the dark blue sport coat, posing the legs at perfect parallels, smoothing the creases from the gray flannel pants. "Much better,'' he said at last, satisfied smile spreading across his face. "I cannot abide untidiness.''

He plumped the pillows surrounding the body and moved the coffee table a fraction to the left. "There now, Mrs. Spooner. One problem solved and onto the next. Tsk, tsk, you haven't drunk nearly enough of your tea, my dear lady.''

The drink. Miles's words echoed through the thunder in my head: "If one didn't know better, one would think you were taking some narcotic . . .'' That's why I was so exhausted. Tired as death.

"You killed him." I was cornered. Trapped.

Lawrence blinked and curled a corner of his mouth. "Why, yes. I suppose I did. Though, to be precise, it was the poison that killed him. In a reasonable dosage Professor Miles might have suffered no more than a long, lingering sleep. But the man was so thirsty. Greed can be a dangerous, dangerous vice."

Poisoned sleep. All of it came rushing back to me. The lost days, the numbing paralysis. Winston Lawrence was a lunatic. If only I could keep him talking until the others arrived.

"It's okay, Mr. Lawrence. You thought he was a dangerous man. You were only trying to protect yourself. Self-defense. Everyone will understand."

He squinted at me. "Oh, my, no, Mrs. Spooner. That is not correct. Not at all. I do not commit crimes of passion. All my actions are planned. Calculated. Hardy Steppington Miles was in the way of my noble ambition. You placed him there."

"What are you saying? I don't understand."

"No, it seems you do not. Perhaps if I explain, Mrs. Spooner. Yes, yes, you do deserve a suitable explanation before you follow Dr. Miles to the place beyond harm."

Miles's body twitched in a death spasm. My stomach heaved in terror. "Please, Mr. Lawrence . . ."

"Oh, my, my. Do I frighten you, Mrs. Spooner? You do look terribly frightened. Too bad. But a necessary evil, I'm afraid. Fear is a by-product of my mission. But

the mission comes first. You can understand that, can't
you?''

"Let me go. I won't say anything. I'll forget I was
ever here.''

He giggled. ''My dear, dear Mrs. Spooner. You are
the most amusing woman. Of course you'll forget. I'll
make certain of that. Death is an excellent eraser of
memory, don't you think?''

I pushed back the fear crowding my mind. Chief Dexter and Chairman Lawrence would be here soon, any
minute. They would deal with this lunatic. All I had to
do was stall for time.

"Why all this, Mr. Lawrence? You said you'd explain.''

"So I did, did I not? Well, then, I shall tell you everything, Mrs. Spooner. And then you shall carry my most
prized secrets to your grave.''

-23-

Winston Lawrence took Hardy Miles's place opposite me at the table. His eyes were glazed, his lips working over some private question. "Let me see, how to begin . . . such a lengthy, complicated tale, Mrs. Spooner. I must tell it correctly, in all necessary detail.

"It began, as you may already know, in history. My family has long been at odds with the reigning powers. More's the pity, but that is often the case. Power corrupts and corruption alienates."

My thoughts wandered. He was talking nonsense. Leading me along some meandering path to nowhere.

"So comes the time when all scores must be settled. My, my, these are a long, long time coming. A century or more. Patience can only be stretched so far, you know. Then it snaps in a furious gesture of release."

Bubbles of saliva spilled over onto his lower lip. He prattled on, oblivious.

"So it has come to this. Fires of final retribution. All kindled by a century of greedy corruption."

His rambling had a numbing effect on me. I tried to focus, to make sense of what he was saying.

"My, my, I never imagined the pure joy of it, the sense of release. Lovely."

I suppressed a yawn.

"Bored, Mrs. Spooner? Perhaps I can make things livelier for you."

"No, please. I was just wondering when the others will get here. I'm sure they'd like to hear your story too."

His eyes widened to circles of wonderment. "The others? I'll be honest, Mrs. Spooner. Something tells me Chief Dexter will not be attending our little meeting. I fear I am growing forgetful. It simply slipped my mind to request his presence. Pity. Heh, heh."

"But your brother?"

"Wallace? Oh, yes, he'll be along. Right along."

I felt a rush of relief.

"In fact, I feel him coming." Lawrence reached in his breast pocket and extracted a brown plastic comb. His face clouded over as he swept his hair back and away from his face until it was slicked in place, exposing a high brow and a stern, steady gaze. Taking a deep breath, he squared his shoulders and shot a steel rod of resolve through his spine. His voice was filled with a thunder of authority.

"Mrs. Spooner? Nicholas Spooner's mother? I detest having to appear the cold, difficult tyrant, Mrs. Spooner, but your son and the others have wrought incalculable

harm on our esteemed university. I cannot in good conscience feel any remorse for them, none at all.''

I was nearly mute with shock. ''Chairman Lawrence?''

He stood and began striding around the room like a
speaker addressing a large audience. ''I will not allow
reckless, foolish youngsters such as yours to destroy
what has taken more than a hundred years to create.
Do you understand me, Mrs. Spooner? I won't have
it.''

How could it be? What did it mean? The numbness
was creeping up my legs. ''This is insane.''

With his head tipped toward an invisible adviser, he
stared through me, heeding some silent voice. ''What's
that you say? . . . Oh, all right. How tiresome. Be heard
if you insist, Warren.''

He raked the comb through his hair again and made
a perfect part down the middle. A smile softened his
face, and his voice moderated. ''D-don't listen t-to them,
M-mrs. Spuh-spooner. M-my brothers t-tend to ramble
off the central t-track. 'For m-me, I am a m-man m-more
sinned against than s-sinning.' That's *Lear*.''

There had to be a way out, an escape. I looked around
the room. The drapes locked out the world. Where were
we? ''Why would your brother kill Hardy Miles, Professor? And what does he mean by a century of greedy
corruption?''

''W-winston is the d-dramatic one, M-mrs. Spooner.
Always m-making a b-b-big d-deal. I'll t-tell you in
p-plain English. The university is ours. It b-belongs t-to

us, always- has. All we want is p-proper recognition. 'And liberty p-plucks j-justice by the n-nose.' *Measure for Measure.*''

The voice thickened, and the hair was raked back with determined fingers. ''Shut up, you damned fool. I'm sick to death of your quotes and alleged wisdoms. The university does not belong to you, Warren. Never will. They gave you a chance, but you were never up to the challenge. Not even close. Imagine you trying to run a major institution of higher learning with that infernal stammer. Bad enough your poor students have to put up with you for an hour, three times a week. They laugh at you behind your back, you foolish buffoon. Do you know they call you La-la Lawrence? Are you truly oblivious to your own humiliation?''

''Now, now.'' A tinny timidity crept into the voice, and Lawrence mussed his hair and slumped in a posture of defeat. ''Will you boys never learn to get along?''

He turned to me and cupped his hands apologetically. ''The story is too long and difficult to tell in any detail, Mrs. Spooner. Suffice it to say that the Parrish name has never received its just due at this institution. Isaiah Cromwell and the generations of his heinous ancestors have kept claim and title to what rightfully belongs to the Parrishes. Now all that will be made right. Come, I'll show you.''

He took me by the elbow and steered me out through the back door, down the carpeted stair, and back into the clammy depths of the underground tunnel. The

nnel dipped and passed a series of darkened sidewalks.
ould I duck into one and escape?

He seemed to read my thoughts. "They are the way
nowhere, Mrs. Spooner. You may take my word for
at. Follow me."

We ascended another carpeted stair and entered what
ight have been a ballroom in a former era of pomp
nd grandeur. Above the center of the polished floor was
Venetian crystal chandelier; delicate spires of light
ripped from pink glass petals and shimmering green
anslucent leaves. A long plank table was set squarely
eneath the bounty of light. It held a profusion of min-
ture buildings and streets rendered in astonishing de-
il.

Lawrence stood beside me in silence, admiring the
odel. "Parrish University, Mrs. Spooner. You see the
ain campus . . . there. The buildings remodeled, of
ourse, modernized. The engineering complex has been
xpanded, as you see. A greater emphasis on the aero-
autical and thermonuclear areas. And the veterinary
ollege has been eliminated to allow expansion of the
opulation ecology program—"

In mid-speech he had turned into Chairman
awrence—stiff, certain.

"What connection are you to the Parrishes?"

His eyes burned into mine. "I am Wallace Lawrence,
on of Lawrence Prescott, great-great-grandson of Sam-
el Parrish. The blood of a proud heritage courses

through my veins and cries for vengeance. Vengeance at long last.''

His eyes rolled crazily in his head as he spoke. "The Cromwell name will be stained with blood and ruin for all eternity. There will be no further tribute to that atrocious man and his dreadful descendants.''

Dizziness washed over me. "The suicides?"

His face changed. " 'All's w-well that ends w-w-well: still the fine's the c-crown; Whate'er the c-course, the end is the renown.' W-we have only d-done what is absolutely n-necessary, M-mrs. Spuh-spooner. Certain sacrifices m-must b-be m-made in the n-name of justice.''

My arms hung like sacks of stone. I was overwhelmed with the words, the horror. My son. "How could you?"

He shook his head and laughed. "Do you think the fate of a fine university can be balanced against a single life, Mrs. Spooner? Or even a number of lives? Oh, my, my. How caught up we get in our personal interests. My dear lady, I didn't know your son, but I'm certain he was a mortal individual whose life and history will fade in a single blink like most others. But a university! A place of growth and learning! The institution always transcends the sum of its parts.''

Even in the meek, reticent guise of Innkeeper Lawrence there was the violent current of madness. "How could you?"

"Come, come, my dear. I'll show you."

He gripped my arm and led me through to an adjoining room. The space was bare except for a single gray

weed armchair set beside a glass table that held crystal
dishes full of candies and mints. A large, luminous
screen was suspended from the ceiling, and the light was
blocked by coal-black shades.

"Sit, my dear. I do want you to enjoy the show."

He slid open a concealed door to reveal a closet full
of ancient camera equipment, box Brownies and clumsy
portrait models with accordian-pleated viewfinders and
fabric screens. There were stands and tripods and countless slide carousels arranged in meticulous rows and
lines of perfect order. On tiptoe, he took a vintage movie
projector from the top shelf and propped it on a folding
stand.

"Sit!"

I sank in the armchair, as heavy as lead. The horror
pushed away all chance of thought or action.

Lawrence fussed over the focus and threaded a reel
of film through the gears and sprockets. Finished, he
flipped off the lights and played the lead through the
dancing beam of the projector. "Relax, my dear. Have
a candy, why don't you? I think you will find this
a most absorbing entertainment. Most absorbing. . . .
And d-don't forget. 'The heavens th-themselves, the
p-planets, and this center observe d-degree, p-priority
and p-place.' The university shall be resurrected, Mrs.
Spooner. Reclaimed in a new, nobler form. And the
deeds of these foul young cowards shall be buried and
forgotten with the Cromwell name."

He was changing with chaotic speed. Soon madness would absorb the final pretense of reason or sanity.

"Are you quite ready, my dear Mrs. Spooner? I would not wish you to miss a single moment."

Numbers flashed on the screen. Ten . . . nine . . . Revulsion bubbled up from my gut. I did not want to see what was coming. After all the risk and determination I did not want this hideous reality shoved down my throat.

Lawrence giggled as the numbers played slowly back to zero. "Ready or n-not, M-mrs. Spooner, here i comes."

-24-

The room was plunged into inky blackness. A dense silence yielded to the insistent whirring of the projector's gears. My breath caught and stuck in my throat like a blade.

Slowly the screen lightened and claimed the image of a young face, blown up to a bizarre balloon of wide-eyed terror. A silent scream stretched the boy's lips, and the cords in his neck bulged to the point of rupture.

His mouth moved in garish slow motion from scream to plea to a final piteous whimper of lost hope. I could read the horror on his lips. "Help! Help me!"

The scene shifted. I was behind the boy, watching the spasms of fear that shook his lean body. Beyond him was the craggy edge of a stone-faced gorge, a dead drop to bloody oblivion.

The hand slipped slowly into view, fingers trembling with a palsy of rage, knuckles bled white with the animal force of a mad fury. The hand dipped and moved with the slow stealth of a predatory snake.

As the fingers slithered toward the boy's back I strained to be there, to help. But as a moan of helplessness slipped through the young lips, the hand reared and struck with lightning speed.

The boy flailed in a comic dance of terror and seemed to catch an inch of safe footing. But the ground gave way, and he was tossed over the edge like a rag doll, hurtling through the emptiness. The camera held tight on his face, warped with horror, the eyes bulging in blind disbelief. He flailed his arms in desperate, groping motions as he plummeted toward the rocky abyss.

As the body neared the bottom the camera shifted into slow motion. For an eternity I watched as the boy hung suspended, inches from the bloody horror of his own destruction. Falling, falling.

Bile rose in my throat, and I turned away. Then punishing steel fingers caught the sides of my face and forced my gaze toward the camera. Holding me so tight, I could not close my eyes. Making me watch.

"No!"

I struggled to look away, but I saw the boy fall. He was smashed against the sharp boulders like a broken egg. Blood spurted everywhere, bright scarlet streaks, angry dashes and smears that cast the gorge in a fire of human anguish. He seemed to explode—dashed to pieces over the silent rocks, the semblance of his humanity torn away.

"God, no."

The camera panned over the ruined form, over the lost life reduced to broken pieces like a well-worn, discarded doll. The limbs splayed at odd, impossible angles. The crushed remnants of the skull, the mouth warped in a garish smile of horror.

"No more . . . please."

Lawrence chuckled and returned to the camera. He rewound the reel and inserted another. The scene played over. A girl this time, really a young woman with the uncertain features of a little girl. She kept looking back at her assailant. Pleading in dramatic bursts. Clinging to some unwavering hope until the hand came sliding across the frame, poised for attack.

I was caught in a spasm of grief and horror. Lawrence held my head, forcing me to watch the fall, the impact, the slow, lazy walk of the camera over a life reduced to bloody debris.

"No more. Please."

He was deaf to me. Humming a gay little tune, he rewound and loaded the projector again. I noticed a small pile of film canisters at his feet, and a hideous thought assailed me. What if Nick's death were there, recorded in all its inhuman horror? How could I bear the sight of Nick's final struggle? I could feel my mind stretched beyond possibility, falling to useless, formless splinters.

Another image played on the screen. The scene was out of focus at first, then wrenched into a surreal close-up. A face broken by the hysteria of fear, laughing madly at a final, impossible joke. I could see the tongue wavering in the boy's mouth, the trail of spittle on his chin as he choked on his own crazed laughter. Tears coursed from his eyes, and his nose was running. The metal fillings in his teeth caught the sunlight.

The hand was playful this time, extended first in a friendly gesture, clapped against a shivering shoulder. Pats of comfort. The boy calming, the laughter gentled. There was a trusting in his eyes that made me want to scream.

Then the push. The body hurtling toward its doom. He looked up as he fell, uncomprehending, and made a small, pathetic waving gesture before he was dashed against the cruel boulders.

A dead calm overcame me as I watched the scene played over and over: the final agonies of stolen lives. I grew more and more distant. Safe. Lawrence's mad giggle was far away. Too far away to touch me where I hid.

"There," he said at last, and flipped the metal switch on the projector. The motor sputtered and was still. "That takes care of the performance, my dear lady. Now to the finale."

Nicky's death was not to be played. I was reduced to a gelatin of relief.

"C-come with m-m-me, M-mrs. Spooner. You shall 'enjoy the honey-heavy dew of slumber.' "

"Haven't you had enough death? Isn't there enough blood on your hands?"

"C-come now. 'C-cowards d-d-die many t-times b-before their d-deaths; the valiant n-never t-taste of d-death but once.' "

He held a full cup in his hand and pressed the rim against my lips. The sick-sweet aroma made my eyes water.

"Drink, M-mrs. Spooner. D-drink, eat, and b-be m-m-merry, for t-tomorrow you die. Heh, heh. M-make that t-today."

I bit my lips together.

"D-do as I say, M-mrs. Spooner." He pressed the cup hard against my teeth, and a splash of poisoned tea wet my chin. "D-d-d-drink!"

The voice changed. "Listen to you, Warren. You sound like a leaky faucet, for heaven's sake. I'll take care of this. Your stubbornness will get you no place, Mrs. Spooner. You may rest assured of that. My patience is nearly spent." Chairman Lawrence leaned so close, his sour breath warmed my cheek. He grasped my nose with his free hand and, when I gasped for breath, forced the liquid back into my throat. I coughed and choked, but he held my jaw closed in the superhuman vise of his grip, and I felt some of the liquid coursing down my throat. Burning.

"There, now, that's much better. Much."

He loosened his grip, and I spat the rest of the poison in his face. Sputtering, he wiped his cheeks, and his mouth curled in a sneer. "Oh, my, my, Mrs. Spooner. That will never do." He crushed my head against his shoulder and forced open my mouth. Holding my nose again until I had to gasp for breath, he poured more of the liquid back and down my throat. Almost at once I felt the numbness creeping up my legs.

Lawrence dropped me back in the chair, and his voice shifted again. "There, now, my dear lady. A few moments and you shall be ready to 'go gently into that good night.' Give in to it, Mrs. Spooner. Your mortal struggles are at an end. Have another candy, why don't you. A final sweet; a sweet farewell."

My thoughts were swirling out of focus. Had to wait, to stall until the drug played out of my system. "Why, Mr. Lawrence? What did you have against all those young people?"

He looked surprised. "Why, nothing, nothing at all. They were beside the point. I thought you understood that. They were nothing but a road to travel to my final destination."

"No, I don't understand."

"Oh, my, my. Your powers of comprehension are not what one would hope, are they, Mrs. Spooner? Mr. Diamond was far quicker to grasp the total picture. As soon as he pieced together the history of the Parrish family in that awful book, he knew I . . . we . . . were agents of the curse. He knew it fell on us to avenge our family's right and honor. A deadly knowledge, I'm afraid."

"You killed him."

"K-killed? T-to be p-perfectly honest, I w-would have to ch-check on that." He pulled a large ring of keys from

he pocket of his shapeless slacks and crossed to a door
n the corner of the room. Working a complex of locks,
e opened the door to reveal a tiny, pitch-black, airless
ubicle. A large, shadowy presence was laid out on the
loor.

Lawrence reared back and kicked the inert form. "Mr.
Diamond? Mr. Diamond, are you still with us? Time to
et up."

A flash of rage broke through my stupor. "You leave
im alone." On shaky legs, I made my way across the
oom and knelt over him. He was deathly still. I felt his
eck for a pulse. Barely there.

"What have you done to him, you monster?" My
ongue was thick with the poison. "Diamond? Diamond,
lease!"

"Tsk, tsk. I fear it is too late for your portly Mr.
Diamond. Ruined by his own greedy gluttony, I fear."

One chance. I made my unsteady way back to the
lass table and grabbed a fistful of candy. Kneeling be-
ide Diamond again, I held the sweets under his nose
ike smelling salts. He had to come around. Together we
ould overpower this lunatic.

"Diamond? Oh, please."

There was a soft breath of a groan, and I felt a vague
hudder in his massive chest. Lawrence stood watching
vith his arms folded. "My, my. How very touching. A
cene from *Peter Pan* played by our very own Wendy
nd Tinker Bell. Why bother, Mrs. Spooner? He won't
e any help to you at all, I assure you."

"Diamond? Are you all right?" He was beginning to respond. He rolled loglike on his side and hoisted his bulk on an elbow. I peeled the cellophane from a sour ball and held it to his lips.

His cheek began to roll, and he opened his eyes a crack. "That you, Sarah Spooner?"

"You're all right. Thank God you're all right."

" 'Behold m-m-my absent child, lies in his b-b-bed, walks up and d-down with me, P-puts on his p-pretty looks, repeats his words, Remembers m-me of all his g-gracious p-parts, stuffs out his v-vacant g-garments with his form.' " Lawrence clicked his tongue. "H-how d-delighted I am t-to find you w-well, M-mr. D-diamond. Had you succumbed, f-fat m-men everywhere would m-mourn the loss of a t-true v-virtuoso of the f-f-f-fork." He burst into a fit of giggling.

I bit hard on the inside of my cheek and stuck my nails into my fisted hands. Diamond needed time to come around. We both needed time. Little by little, the pain pushed away the heavy dullness. Still, the drug had a tight hold on me. I had to keep him talking.

Diamond finished the candy and opened his mouth for another. He needed strength. Time. "How did there come to be three of you?"

Lawrence rumpled his hair, and his face drooped. "Oh, my, my. That is an interesting tale. We were small boys, no more than eight or nine at the time. Our dear mother passed on in our infancy. We were told it was influenza, but papers we found years later indicated she took her own life. She was plagued with a recurring sadness, Mrs. Spooner. Sadness can be a most virulent disease, you know. In the grip of one such attack she climbed to the top of the clock tower and plummeted to her untimely death.

"Father hired a nanny to see to us. His university commitments kept him too occupied to attend to the needs of three small, motherless boys. He engaged Nanny Brinn through the finest New York agency.

"All went well, as I said, until we were eight or nine. There was a terrible storm that winter; two feet or more of snow fell in a single night. Father joined a crew of men working to dig out the homes of local widows. He caught his death of a cold and was gone in two days."

Lawrence frowned, remembering. "Nanny changed after that. We didn't know it at the time, but she was madly in love with Father. She took her bitterness out on us, inflicting cruel punishments and beatings for imaginary misdeeds. Lying in bed at night, we heard her praying for our lost souls. She was convinced the devil had taken us and we were somehow responsible for our father's death."

He crossed his arms tightly over his chest and rocked himself as he spoke. "The beatings got worse and worse. We were covered with welts and bruises, terrified to do anything that might incur her wrath. Out here alone, we had no one to turn to. She shut us off, held us virtual prisoners of her cruelty." His voice settled in a helpless whimper. "We tried. How we tried to be good boys. But it was never enough. Never.

"Warren began to stammer. She punished him mercilessly. Beating . . . beating . . . until one day we found him—dead."

His face stiffened, and he brushed away the embarrassing traces of his own weakness. "Enough of this. Enough idle chatter. Mrs. Spooner, I'm a busy, busy man. I have no more time to waste with you and your fat friend. Tomorrow, hordes of unsuspecting Cromwell alumni will arrive on campus in time to discover that their precious alma mater is no longer. After I dispose of you I have final preparations to make for that grand event." He squinted at his watch. "Let's get on with it." He strapped a large camera case over one shoulder.

I was too weak to struggle as he grabbed me by the wrist and forced me, half stumbling, toward the door of the projection room. "Won't you join us, Mr. Diamond?"

Diamond tried to force himself upright, but he wavered like a giant tree in a storm and collapsed. "I can't."

"Oh, my, my. Then you shall miss all the amusements. More's the pity." Lawrence slammed shut the door of the tiny cubicle and flipped the several locks. "Sweet dreams, Mr. Diamond. I shall return for our final good-byes shortly."

I heard Diamond's desperate pounding on the door as Lawrence dragged me out of the room. Back in the tunnel, he turned into a steep, narrow stairwell that led up and outside. We were between two of the pristine houses on Parrish Common. The tunnel entrance was hidden behind a cropped privet hedge, camouflaged to look like part of a gazebo.

He wrapped his arm around my waist and pulled me to the end of the common and out onto the main road. A car approached, and I waved my free arm in a wild plea for salvation, but the driver whizzed past, oblivious. Then Lawrence caught my arm with his free hand and held me in an impossible straitjacket until we were across the street and out of sight in a dense pocket of woods. Prickly shrubs tore at my bare legs, but I was beyond pain. My mind ran in desperate little circles, searching for a way out.

"Move, Mrs. Spooner. Hurry along."

"You won't get away with this, Chairman Lawrence. Everyone knows I was suspicious about the deaths. Even Chief Dexter. If something happens to me, he'll know."

"Chief Dexter? I must tell you, Mrs. Spooner, Chief Dexter is well beyond knowing anything anymore. Poor man fell to his death just hours ago. I suppose the pressure of all the suicides was simply too much for him to bear. A final nail in the Cromwell coffin. Fitting, don't you think?"

"But—" I swallowed back the words. There was no way to argue with lunacy. And I needed every shred of my remaining strength to find some way out of the black hole of this living horror.

"Move on, Mrs. Spooner. We are almost there."

Ahead, beyond the border of the woods, I saw a small clearing set with scrub grasses and whimsical clumps of wildflowers. It might have been a perfect setting for a playground or a Little League field. Might have been, except that any child running back to shag an outfield fly would have fallen over the edge and into the rocky bowels of the Sachem Gorge.

-25-

Lawrence forced me across the clearing, toward the ragged edge of the gorge. He laughed and swept the scene with an extravagant gesture.

" 'Oh! H-here w-will I s-set up my everlasting rest, And shake the yoke of inauspicious s-stars from this w-world w-wearied f-flesh. Eyes, l-look your l-last! Arms t-t-take your l-last embrace!' "

I struggled in his grasp. "You won't get away with this. Let me go!"

His grip tightened as he held me with one hand and set up his camera equipment. He laid the large black camera bag down on a bare patch of ground and unzipped the top. Laying open the flap, he lifted out an eight-millimeter movie camera and an ancient black tripod. With the deft certainty of long practice he propped open the tripod and screwed the camera base in position. Then he snapped in a reel of film and fed the lead through the camera's metal teeth. Squinting through the bulbous viewfinder, he adjusted the focus and set the light meter and the time control.

Satisfied, he turned away from the equipment and stared through me to a place of private inspiration. " 'Mount, mount m-my soul! Thy s-seat is up on high, w-whilst m-my g-gross flesh sinks d-downward, here to d-die.' "

I tested his grip, twisting my arm slowly, but he snapped tighter in response and his forehead sank in a drape of wrinkles. " 'The iron t-tongue of m-midnight hath t-told t-twelve. L-lovers, t-to bed, 't-tis almost fairy t-time.' "

With a sudden lurch I tried to pull away, but my muscles were still limp from the drug, and the sum of all the force I could muster yielded nothing but a pathetic little tug at Lawrence's brick-hard stance.

"Oh, my, my, Mrs. Spooner. That will not do. Please try to relax and enjoy your final drama. Your efforts are entirely useless, I assure you. Face the inevitable."

With a flick of the start switch he set the camera running. Checking the focus a final time, he stepped away and pushed me toward the edge of the gorge.

Terror roared in my head, and my breath came in greedy gulps. Four more steps . . . three.

The others paraded through my horror. Young faces wide with the agony of death. Shattered.

Nicky! How could this mindless bastard steal so many innocent lives?

Two steps . . . one. Looking down, I saw the dizzy expanse of the gorge. An angry, whitecapped stream assaulted the sharp boulders at the menacing base. Sheer, jagged rock walls. Certain death.

Nicky . . .

I felt the hand pressed against the small of my back, the ironic pat of comfort.

In a trance of fury I planted my feet as Nicky had shown me a thousand times. Grip and throw . . . grip and throw!

I ducked and caught Lawrence by the ankle. Startled, he wavered off balance, and a small whimper of a laugh escaped him. "Toss the pebble straight out, Mother, dear. Like this."

An electric surge of strength filled me as I pushed Lawrence to the edge and over. His hands groped for purchase, and he held for a crazy instant, his fists full of scrub grasses.

"Hah," he said in a tiny voice.

The grasses pulled away, and he was falling, lurching through the dead air.

I crept from the edge to safe ground and closed my eyes to block the horror. There was a final shriek of desperation.

And it was done.

-26-

For nearly an hour the plane traced long, lazy circles over the Westchester County airport. We flew through a broth of misty sky. Below us, great strands of colored lights were stretched across the blackened world. The passengers had fallen into an uneasy silence.

Finally a bell sounded, warning signs flashed across the bulkhead, and I felt the harsh, downward pull of the landing gear. Diamond cleared his throat beside me, and I turned to find him staring at the packed compartments in his plastic dinner tray.

"I can't figure it out, Sarah Spooner. Doesn't make a damned bit of sense. I just don't feel hungry."

The flight attendant came by and whisked the tray away to its safe berth in the galley. On her earlier runs through the cabin Diamond had refused to relinquish the small mound of mashed potatoes, the cellophane-wrapped carrot cake, the slices of institutional whole wheat bread and butter. "Give me a minute, miss, will you? A person doesn't like to be rushed when it comes to his food."

"Is something wrong, Mr. Diamond?" I asked him after her last go-round, "Are you feeling all right?"

"Yes. At least I think so. Only . . . Well, you're not going to believe this, but I'm just not hungry."

I was tempted to press my hand to his forehead to check his temperature, but I controlled myself. Diamond was going through an important moment, possibly the beginning of a lifesaving change.

He watched his tray disappear behind the galley curtain. There was a hint of melancholy in his expression. "So it goes, Sarah Spooner. What goes around, comes around."

We dipped and circled a final time, and the captain came over the intercom to drawl the news of the impending end to our flight. I felt the crunch of pressure in my head as the attendant bustled up and down the aisles for a final check of our seat belts and tray tables.

As we lurched down on the runway my heart took a mad leap and hung suspended in uncertainty. The message I had left with Ben's secretary was deliberately off-handed. I hadn't even mentioned the flight's exact arrival time. If he didn't come, I told myself, it was probably all for the best. I could use all the time I could get to reorient myself to the normal world before we got together.

I was swept along beside Diamond in the determined tide of passengers. Down the carpeted jetway. Through the long, monotonous corridors to the baggage claim. One of my bags was first out, wobbling along the con-

334 of Judith Kelman

veyor belt like a proud infant executing his first steps. Diamond's bags followed, and we turned to say our tentative, awkward good-byes.

"You saved my life, Sarah Spooner. How can I ever thank you for that?"

"You already have, Mr. Diamond. Besides, you saved mine first in a number of ways. So we're even."

He tipped forward from the waist and placed a tiny kiss on my cheek. "You take care of yourself and that family of yours. Tell them I said they're lucky to have you."

"Thanks. I'll call you, Mr. Diamond. You'll come over for dinner."

He lifted his cases and began to walk away. At the door he turned and caught my eye. "Make it cocktails. Something tells me I'm off dinner for a while."

"Cocktails it is."

My other bag came in the next wave of luggage. Exiting the claim area, I took a vague look around. Liveried chauffeurs stood in a row waving paper placards bearing their passengers' names. Small family groups with anxious faces awaited their missing members. A skycap dozed, his head lolling against the tall, metal push handle of his luggage dolly. Two uniformed cops leaned against the entrance, feigning interest in the departing passengers.

I walked toward the exit fronting the cab stand, balancing the load of my suitcases and the broad stack of documents from the Cromwell police. Lieutenant Mc-

Dowell had left the copies I requested in the deserted lobby of the Barrington Arms: the autopsy report on Winston/Warren/Wallace Lawrence, photocopies of his diary—a meticulous record of the impossible workings of his ravaged mind. Nice of the man, all three of him, to provide such a detailed account of his madness and the crimes that madness inspired. The coroner's inquest was a record five-minute affair, just long enough for the case to be closed and filed away.

"Sarah?"

Ben stood just inside the exit. His hair was rumpled, his smile stiff and uncertain. "Hey, Miss. Looking for a ride?"

"I guess. You have room in your cab for one exhausted old lady?"

"I think I can manage to squeeze you in." He took my bags and locked me in a brief, urgent hug.

The glass airport door swung open as I stepped on the rubber mat. Ben's car was at the curb, idling beside a stern-faced cop.

"Move it out, will you, buddy?"

We giggled like nervous children as we jumped in, slammed the doors, and made our thieves' getaway. Then, as Ben followed the signs and arrows leading out toward the parkway, we fell silent.

I watched him drive, hands fast on the wheel, face tight with concentration. "I didn't ask what you charge to Stamford, driver."

He glanced at me and put his hand over mine. "You can afford it, lady. Don't worry."

Staring out the window, I watched the dim world race by in a dizzy blur. "Everything looks so strange. I feel like I've been on another planet."

"Maybe you have. Maybe we both have."

The city melted away. Houses were spread farther and farther apart and plunked behind hedgerows and picket fences. We crossed over the Connecticut line, and a familiar lump of regret settled in my throat.

The house was dark. He opened the door and flipped on the lights. I stood back from the flood of scents and memories until he took me by the arm and led me inside.

"You want something, Sar? A drink?"

He brought two crystal glasses of chilled white wine and sat beside me on the den sofa. My eyes were drawn to the sadness in his. "Thanks for coming to get me, Ben."

We clinked glasses. "To having you home. . . . What now, Sar? Where do we start?"

"I don't know. Maybe from here. Maybe back from the beginning. I guess we'll hav; to play it by ear for a while."

He set his glass down and put his arm around my shoulder. "Do you want to tell me about it? Did you find what you were looking for?"

"Yes . . . no. Of all of them, it's funny that Nicky's case is the one they can't be positive about. But that doesn't seem so important anymore. I suspect I was looking for the impossible, a way to rewrite the ending of Nicky's life so everyone lived happily ever after. I did find out other things—about myself.''

"Care to tell me?"

I shrugged. "Right now I'd rather talk about anything else. How's Ali? Is she enjoying the visit at the Cape?''

"She called to tell me she got one of those haircuts where one side looks like a putting green and the other side's a cross between a palm tree and a porcupine.''

I made a face. "What did you tell her?''

"I told her I miss her.''

My head settled in its familiar resting spot in the hollow of his shoulder. "Me too.''

"Pat Scofield has been calling all day. He said to tell you Hotlips won a long-term lease at the big house.''

I felt a smile coming on. "That's great, wonderful. Now we'll get that grant for our rape crisis-intervention program.''

"And your mother said to tell you she's glad you've finally come to your senses and decided to come home where you belong. She said she and your sister are going shopping on Saturday and you're welcome to join them.''

"I don't know," I mused. "Saturday doesn't give me much time to get myself in the peak emotional condition

I have to be in to take on Honey and my mother at the same time. I'll have to see.''

"Sar?''

"Yes.''

"We're going to be all right. Aren't we?''

I settled back and felt a dreamy wash of comfort. My eye caught the rows of pictures on the wall: Nicky and Allison playing in childish oblivion; Ben and I posing in neat family scenes with vivid backgrounds and clear focus. My mother and father standing at the beach behind two plump, little girls with pigtails and camera smiles. Lost strangers from another life. Nothing but memories.

"I don't know, Ben. I hope so.''

"Good. I hate sleeping alone. Haven't really slept with you away.''

I felt him relax. He yawned, settled his face against the side of my head, and propped his feet on the coffee table. In seconds his breathing gentled to the easy rhythm of sleep, and he started the light, familiar snoring that had lulled me to sleep for more than twenty years of nights.

I slipped away and eased Ben's head down on the plump sofa cushion. Leaving the room, I dimmed the lights and straightened a crooked picture in the bottom row: a circle of children with wide, toothless grins kneeling around a cake with three candles.

The little jogger on my watch danced to an electronic chorus of ''Yankee Doodle Dandy,'' and lights flashed, reminding me it was a respectable time to get some very welcome rest. At the foot of the stairs I paused to look over the giant pile of mail on the hall shelf and a long list of phone messages.

Tomorrow was going to be a very busy day.

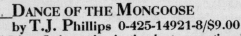